A NOVEL

EVASIVE SPECIES

BILL BYRNES

To pragmatic environmentalists everywhere and especially to the staff and volunteers of the Conservancy of Southwest Florida.

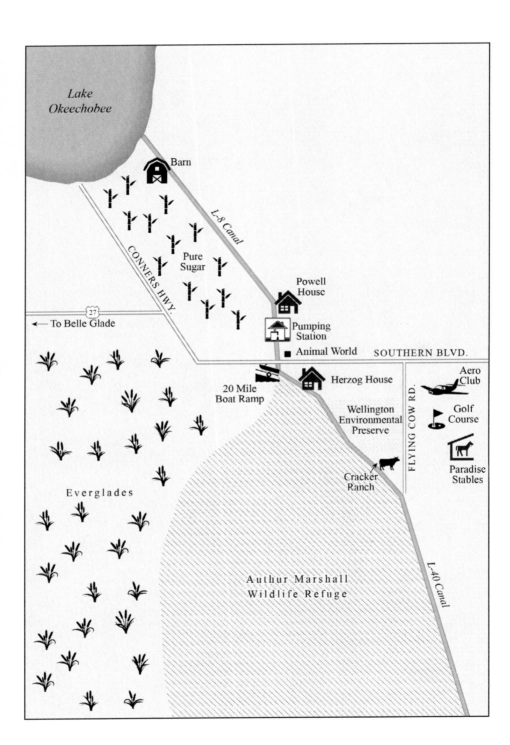

Lake Okeechobee

Barn

L-8 Canal

CONNERS HWY.

Pure Sugar

27
← To Belle Glade

Powell House

Pumping Station

■ Animal World

SOUTHERN BLVD.

20 Mile Boat Ramp

Herzog House

Wellington Environmental Preserve

FLYING COW RD.

Aero Club

Golf Course

Paradise Stables

Cracker Ranch

Everglades

Authur Marshall Wildlife Refuge

L-40 Canal

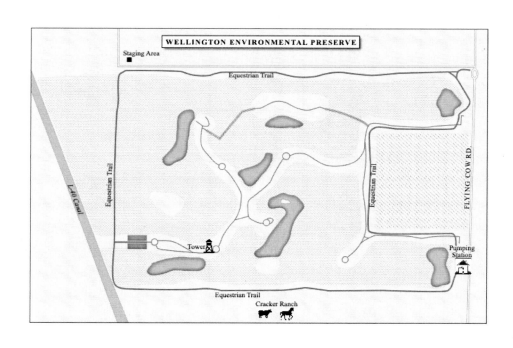

WELLINGTON ENVIRONMENTAL PRESERVE

Staging Area

Equestrian Trail

Equestrian Trail

Equestrian Trail

L-40 Canal

FLYING COW RD.

Tower

Pumping Station

Equestrian Trail

Cracker Ranch

C O N T E N T S

PROLOGUE 1

CHAPTER 1 6

CHAPTER 2 12

CHAPTER 3 17

CHAPTER 4 22

CHAPTER 5 26

CHAPTER 6 32

CHAPTER 7 36

CHAPTER 8 43

CHAPTER 9 52

CHAPTER 10 62

CHAPTER 11 69

CHAPTER 12 75

CHAPTER 13 81

CHAPTER 14 87

CHAPTER 15 95

CHAPTER 16 104

CHAPTER 17 107

CHAPTER 18 116

CHAPTER 19 124

CHAPTER 20 130

CHAPTER 21 135

CHAPTER 22 139

CHAPTER 23 147

CHAPTER 24 153

CHAPTER 25 158

CHAPTER 26 166

CHAPTER 27 173

CHAPTER 28 181

CHAPTER 29 186

CHAPTER 30 192

CHAPTER 31 199

CHAPTER 32 209

CHAPTER 33 215

CHAPTER 34 222

CHAPTER 35 230

CHAPTER 36 238

CHAPTER 37 244

CHAPTER 38 251

EPILOGUE 257

ACKNOWLEDGEMENTS...261

SUGGESTED NONFICTION READING..264

ABOUT THE AUTHOR 266

ALSO BY BILL BYRNES 268

PROLOGUE

The earth was still, but beneath it, an egg wiggled, then shook violently. The snout of the Komodo dragon appeared as it broke through the leathery shell. Tiny black claws came next, rapidly enlarging the opening. Her survival depended upon completing three tasks. The first, she'd just successfully accomplished. Her second was digging through the four feet of sandy soil that lay between her and the surface. In the dirt around her was a clutch of twenty-three eggs. Several were already broken, their inhabitants gone, although not all had made it out of the ground. Some eggs were throbbing as the baby Komodos inside assaulted their shells. A few were still and unbroken. They wouldn't hatch.

Driven by an innate sense, she knew which way to dig. Breaking through the earth, she blinked at her first exposure to sunlight. The newly hatched Komodo dragon was greeted by the tropical heat and humidity of Flores, an east Indonesian island. Her second task was completed.

She was a foot long and weighed only a few ounces. Her skin was black with yellow and white bands. She was on her own, and time was of the essence. The activity at the Komodo nest attracted birds, snakes, and larger Komodo dragons. Her mother had stayed near the nest until the rainy season began and then left—typical behavior of mother Komodos. The hatchlings raced to the surrounding trees to escape the gathering predators. She was one of the lucky ones. Not all the young Komodos made it. Scrambling up the trunk with her sharp claws, she completed her third task.

* * *

She lived the first two years of her life in the trees. She was fast, and her instincts were true. Her skin colors blended with the foliage, providing natural camouflage that improved her chances for survival. As she grew older, her skin would darken and harden into a thick, armor-like hide. She ate insects in the beginning, and then learned to steal eggs from unguarded birds' nests. As she grew bigger and bolder, she added nesting adults to her diet.

Her first close brush with death occurred when a large falcon swooped down on her intent on making her its dinner. The predator came in with the sun at its back, so she didn't see it, but like all Komodo dragons, she had a natural photo sensor in the top of her head. The parietal, or third eye, wasn't an actual eye but a patch of photosensitive skin that registered changes in light and functioned as an early warning system detecting danger from above. The shadow cast by the falcon caused the young Komodo to duck and dart away, saving her life. She learned that she was sometimes predator and sometimes prey.

One day, as she spent more time on the ground, she encountered a recently hatched Komodo, the same size she'd been at birth. She quickly devoured the newborn. Days later, the tantalizing scent of rotting flesh caught her attention. She couldn't see the carcass, but her keen sense of smell told her it was just beyond the cluster of trees she lived in. She cautiously ventured onto an open plain, head swiveling, forked yellow tongue shooting in and out of her mouth, gathering scents. The remains of a deer awaited her. It was the first time she'd eaten carrion, and it was delicious. So much so that she almost became a meal herself. An adult Komodo also had been attracted by the scent and came around to investigate. Spotting the juvenile Komodo, the adult took chase. She caught movement out of the corner of her eye and abandoned the deer. Running for her life, she made it up the closest tree, just ahead of the open jaws of her pursuer.

Safe in the tree but breathing hard, the young Komodo waited until the large Komodo lost interest and disappeared from sight. She waited even longer until its diminishing scent told her the adult was gone. Only then did she descend the tree and approach the carcass again. She was no longer hungry, but a new attraction drew her. The adult Komodo had defecated before leaving. Kodra rolled in the fresh feces, changing her scent from that of prey to something very undesirable, a practice she'd continue doing until she was an adult.

* * *

At four years old, she was five feet long and weighed eighty pounds. She'd survived the time when she was most vulnerable. Now the only predator left that might harm her was a bigger Komodo dragon. She roamed the tropical deciduous forests and savannas of Flores, quickly learning to lie in wait near water for an unsuspecting animal to come and drink. Young deer became her preferred prey. As with all Komodos, she found and ate carrion whenever she could. One day, she took down a large boar, the first time she'd killed an animal larger than herself. But the confidence gained in that kill got her into trouble soon thereafter.

An alpha-male Komodo had taken down a water buffalo. The kill had attracted other Komodos, and they anxiously circled the buffalo while the big male fed. There is a strict hierarchy of feeding among Komodos, with the largest ones eating first. She violated Komodo protocol by moving in to eat before the alpha was done. The male turned on her and attacked, sinking his teeth into her flank. Although he was more than twice her size, she was able to twist out of his grasp and scramble away. Fortunately for her, the male wasn't interested in giving chase. He returned to his kill but not before leaving her with a second set of scars that she'd carry for the rest of her life.

The young Komodo encountered humans on Flores but usually no more than two or three at a time. Sometimes they stopped and watched her, but more often they backed away. Occasionally, the smell of fresh-killed deer or boar drew her to one of the small villages that dotted the island, but the carcasses were too well attended by humans for her to approach. She had greater success with the butchered remains they discarded, and chance meetings with dogs that strayed into her path.

* * *

At the age of eight, she mated for the first time, the male disappearing immediately afterward. She dug a nest, covering a clutch of eighteen eggs. Like her mother, she would stay around her nest until the rainy season began. She mated again the following year and would likely mate many more times over her expected fifty-year life.

Fully grown at eight feet long and weighing two hundred pounds, she had a broad flat snout, a solid muscular body, and short thick legs. Each foot had five toes, and each toe had a three-inch-long curved claw ideal for disemboweling prey.

Her thick hide was reinforced with tiny bone-like scales, osteoderms, giving it great toughness. These scales had saved her life when the big male Komodo had bitten her some years before. Shaped like beads packed tightly together, her hide had a pebbled texture that resembled chain mail armor. Indeed, her skin wrinkled just behind her head, giving her the appearance of a medieval knight sheathed in his coif.

From a distance, the Komodo's hide looked to be shades of greenish brown and slate gray. Closer up, her coloring revealed itself to be more complex. There was a dull red band around the base of her tail and her lower legs were almost black. Her head looked darker than her body, even though her snout had traces of white. On a dirt plain, she looked distinctly gray and brown; in grassy areas, she looked more green. Her irregular coloring and the interplay of sun and shadows on her rough skin enabled her to blend in well with the forests and savannahs of Flores.

She was a fearless hunter and didn't hesitate to take on animals much bigger than she. Even a full-grown water buffalo wasn't safe. She'd lie in wait and strike quickly. She was faster than the fastest human. A good swimmer, she wouldn't hesitate to follow her prey into the water. She could slash her prey with her sickle-shaped claws, wounding or disemboweling it. She could knock it down with her long whip-like tail, so powerful it could break a man's arm. But her most dangerous weapon was her bite. It wasn't her sixty one-inch-long serrated teeth, although they were ideal for cutting through flesh and bone, but the toxins in her mouth. Her saliva carried a witch's brew of bacteria, made more powerful by the decaying food around her teeth. If that weren't enough, two small openings, one on each side of her lower jaw, secreted a venom that prevented blood from clotting, causing extreme pain, and, ultimately, paralysis. Thus armed, she could go for the immediate kill or just wound her prey and wait for her poisons, and her victim's loss of blood, to finish the job. She feared no animal, not even other Komodos, or man. Then the men with the nets came and took her away.

She'd just taken down and eaten a sixty-pound deer. Bloated and sluggish, she only wanted to lay dormant and digest her meal, which could take several days. Her distended stomach made movement difficult in any case. It was then, as she was at her most vulnerable, that the hunters, coming from downwind, encircled her with pole snares and nets.

She saw the danger and, to make herself mobile, vomited up the deer. She was lighter now and about to run, but the hunters quickly entangled her in their nets and a dart from a tranquilizer gun put her down. Subsequent drugs were administered to keep her in a deep sleep. When she awoke, she was ten thousand miles from home.

CHAPTER 1

TJ Forte hurried through the Publix supermarket parking lot. He'd come in response to an urgent call even though it meant he was going to be late for the meeting that was key to his plan.

A group of onlookers parted as he strode through them. He wasn't physically imposing but he carried himself well and moved with determination. Thirty-four years old and just under six feet, he had a tight, ropy body and the deep tan and light brown hair that came from daily exposure to the Florida sun. In front of the crowd, a Palm Beach County sheriff's deputy held up his hand. TJ stopped and flashed his credentials—federal wildlife officer. The deputy eyed TJ's khakis and a polo shirt and grinned. "Working undercover?"

TJ shot him a look. The deputy stepped aside, revealing a thick-bodied snake, dark brown with light-brown blotches, which lay curled on the asphalt. The snake looked up and flicked its tongue. TJ studied the snake for a moment, then exhaled. A python, yes, and a good six feet long but not one of those. They weren't here—yet.

"Is it one of those snakes that's been eating everything in the Everglades?" an onlooker asked.

"No. This is a Ball python," TJ said. "Those are Burmese pythons."

"How'd it get here?"

"Probably someone's pet. Pythons are master escape artists. Or it was released because it got too big. Happens all the time."

He scanned the crowd and saw a white-haired woman who was holding an empty mesh shopping bag. "May I?" he asked. Then he reached down and took a loose hold of the snake about a foot behind its head. The crowd gasped. He used his other hand to support the snake's body. The python curled around his arm. The bystanders gasped again, probably thinking the python was trying to crush him. But he knew the snake was just trying to secure itself. Snakes, like people, didn't like to be left dangling. He calmly shook his arm, and the python slid into the bag. He handed the bag to a nervous deputy and pulled out his phone. To the deputy holding the bag, he said: "Someone from the Palm Beach Animal Sanctuary will arrive soon. She'll take the snake." He turned away without waiting for a response and hustled back to his car. He hoped the man he was anxious to meet would still be there.

* * *

An hour later, TJ sat in a metal chair that was about as comfortable as the seats in the navy jets he used to fly. In front of him was a half-eaten slice of pizza and outside was a turquoise—artesian turquoise, according to the build sheet—1965 Chevrolet Impala two-door hardtop that he'd just restored. He tried to focus on the man seated across from him, but he couldn't get the white Corvette out of his mind.

Owning a 1963 split window Corvette with a L84 fuel-injected engine had been his father's dream and now was his. Only about one thousand had been built, and fewer were in existence today. Pristine cars went for $250,000. After years of searching, he'd found one in Jacksonville. It had a blown engine and needed all its rubber parts replaced, but it was priced accordingly, and TJ could do the work. He could just swing it if he sold the Impala and took out a second mortgage on his home.

The potential Impala buyer had driven down from Daytona Beach, so he was definitely interested. "It's a classic," TJ said. "And it's got AC. Not a lot of Chevies had factory-installed air in '65. Real nice if you live in Florida."

"I don't know," the man said. "I just don't know."

A 737 roared low overhead on its final approach to nearby Palm Beach International Airport. TJ leaned forward, elbows on the chair arms, back straight. He appeared relaxed, but he feared his dream of buying the Corvette was slipping away. His deep brown eyes studied the man seated across from him.

The buyer continued after the jet had passed. "I've been looking for a '65, and it's the right color but . . ." He abruptly stopped when he heard Kenny Loggins singing the opening lines of "Danger Zone."

"My phone," TJ said. He made a face as he looked at the screen. The call was from a Richard Rodriguez, a name he didn't recognize, and a 561 area code, which was Palm Beach County. *Could be another inquiry about the car but probably just somebody selling something,* he thought. He tapped the red decline button.

The buyer continued, "You did all the work on the Chevy yourself?"

"I did. I specialize in cars from the sixties. They have the right combination of style, power, and reliability." What he didn't say was that his father had worked in a Chevrolet transmission plant and implanted his love for cars, particularly GM cars, on him from an early age.

"They have so much unique detail," TJ continued. "Look at the lines on my Impala out there. I hate to let it go, but I love bringing old cars back to life. It's both a business and a hobby. I restore, sell and buy another. If I'm lucky, make a little money along the way." Just like his father had taught him, although if he got the Corvette, he was going to keep it.

"Huh. From your website, I thought you were a professional car dealer."

"No. I work for the US Fish & Wildlife Service. My specialty is invasive species."

"Invasive species? You mean illegal immigrants?" The buyer laughed.

Asshole! Maybe he didn't want to sell his Impala to this guy after all. "Reptiles," TJ replied with a tight smile. He didn't say pythons. He'd learned not to.

"Oh." The buyer appeared befuddled. He was about to speak when Kenny Loggins interrupted again. TJ glanced down: 772 area code, Vero Beach, and this time a name he recognized. He hesitated but only for a moment. He didn't want to lose his buyer, but he had no choice. "Excuse me, I have to take this. It's my boss."

TJ listened for a while and then said: "Yeah. I see. But why me? I'm not a gator guy. Yeah, Rodriguez called already." He listened again, then said, "Oh. Palm Beach sheriff. Of course. I've met him a couple of times. Never worked with him, though. Should've said Sheriff on his caller ID and I'd answered. I'll call him back pronto."

"Problem?" the buyer asked.

"Something's come up at work. I have to go."

A small smile crept across the buyer's face. "I understand. Look, I'll give you 20k for your car right now."

TJ shook his head slowly, even though he knew that if he didn't sell the Chevy today, he probably wouldn't sell it until late fall, when the weather cooled and the snowbirds returned. By then, the Corvette would be gone. "Thirty thousand is a fair price," he said.

"Sorry." The buyer rose to leave. If he thought TJ was going to counter, he was mistaken.

TJ watched the man leave and wondered how he could find another buyer before the Corvette was sold. The sky had darkened while they'd been negotiating, and large raindrops began falling. *Great! No sale and now I'll have to detail the car when I get home.*

He looked at his phone again. Rodriguez had left a message. He ignored it and hit redial. The call was answered on the first ring. "I assume you heard about the little boy, Bobby Powell, who went missing yesterday in Loxahatchee?" Sherriff Rodriguez said.

"It's all over the news, although my boss told me it's now a recovery operation."

"Sadly, it is. We think he may have been attacked by an alligator."

"Heard that, too. Only the news isn't saying *may have*."

"The news deals in sound bites. I'm burdened by the facts. And now some of the talking heads are saying the alligator ate the child, but I'll come back to that one. What we know is Bobby Powell disappeared from his back yard. He was alone for only a minute. Nobody saw or heard anything. There was blood in the yard, and we found more along with one of the boy's shoes at the edge of a canal that runs behind the house." The sheriff paused. "Officer Forte, I'd like to know if what happened to Bobby Powell sounds like an alligator attack to you."

"First, please call me TJ."

"Okay, TJ. And I'm Richard. But sheriff is fine too."

"What's the area like behind the house?" TJ asked.

"Neatly mowed back yard runs two hundred feet plus to a row of mature cypress trees. The trees extend the width of the lawn and beyond. Then about another hundred feet of grass and a grass berm sloping up to the L-8 canal."

"And where did the attack take place?"

"The boy's blood was found in the yard about twenty-five feet inside the tree line."

"Sheriff—"

"One more thing, there was a large amount of saliva on the ground around where the attack took place and more where the boy's shoe was found. So, tell me what you think."

"Initial reaction . . . it doesn't add up. For one thing, the attack happened too far inland. Alligators hunt in the water or near the water's edge. Water is where they feel safest. It's their escape route. For a gator to leave sight of the water, travel through trees and over land . . . They just don't do that."

"But they do move between ponds and the like. You see them crossing roads. We get calls about alligators in yards all the time."

"True, particularly during mating season but that was in the spring. I don't buy it."

The sheriff chuckled. "You'd make a good detective, TJ, but the blood and saliva suggest the animal picked up Bobby Powell and carried him to the canal, knocking off his shoe as it entered the water."

"That's another thing. I don't think alligators are big secretors. Dogs and wild boars are. You might want to consult an expert, maybe a trapper. I'm not a gator guy."

"Okay. I'll follow up on the secretor angle, but it certainly doesn't rule out an alligator attack."

"No, it doesn't, but alligator attacks on humans are extremely rare and a gator killing a human is even rarer. We can go for years without a single fatality. Dogs kill more humans than alligators do."

"For argument's sake," the sheriff said, "let's assume it was a gator. Would it eat him?"

"Nope. Just doesn't happen. Has never happened in Florida. Alligators don't eat people. They've been known to take bites out of people, but they don't eat people. An alligator may have attacked Bobby Powell, may even have carried him off and drowned him, but an alligator didn't eat him. I hate to say this, but I think the poor child is at the bottom of the canal."

"If he is, we'll find him."

"I'm sure you will but I don't see how I can be of any help."

Rodriguez took a breath, then said: "TJ, I wanted to get a feel for you before I told you this but there's a gator out there, and it's killing and eating people."

"Sheriff, I don't mean to be rude, but I just told you why I find that hard to believe."

"Well," Rodriguez said, "maybe you'll start believing when I tell you it's just happened again. And this time there's a witness."

"Okay. Let's meet." An image of the rear of the Corvette as it drove off into the distance went through his mind. But the facts bothered him. If the killer wasn't an alligator, then what was?

CHAPTER 2

THREE DAYS EARLIER

Emilio Sanchez entered the barn. The small windows let in very little of the evening light, but the first wisps of smoke were already drifting in. He studied the sleeping Komodo dragon, then jerked backward when her eyes shot open. They were a myriad of angry colors—coal black pupils, each surrounded by a narrow yellow ring separating it from the swirling bands of her red and yellow irises. Anyone foolish enough to get close might say they resembled the surface of the sun. The lizard's tongue shot from her mouth. A foot long, it twitched while picking up scent molecules. Then it disappeared as quickly as it had appeared. She was a Komodo dragon, highly intelligent, an alpha predator and one of the most dangerous animals on earth, but now she shifted nervously in her cage.

The six-foot-long metal box that held her was not much bigger than her body, and her tail lay outside of it. She was being held in a work barn, deep within a large sugarcane farm in Palm Beach County, Florida, at the base of Lake Okeechobee or Lake O, as the locals called it. Despite the beaches, ritzy Worth Avenue, and the many upscale gated golfing communities, Palm Beach was the largest agricultural county in the state of Florida. The crop that grew on seventy-five percent of its farmland, and whose tall green stalks tourists mistook for corn, or sometimes bamboo, was sugarcane.

The Komodo rose to her full height, extended her neck and swayed, hitting her head on the top of the cage. As the smoke became thicker, she threw herself against the metal bars. The rectangular box jumped each time her powerful body slammed into it.

It was Sanchez's job to make sure that nothing happened to the valuable reptile, but he had no idea how to calm her. He had no way of telling the Komodo, or the other animals in the barn, that the smoke came from a controlled burn. After the recent rains, one of the sugarcane fields had become diseased, and burning the stalks was the easiest way to prevent the blight from spreading. Nearby were snakes and rats, trapped like her. The snakes were rare Sunset ball pythons, a mating pair. They released a foul-smelling musk when the smoke came. The rats frantically ran back and forth in their cages.

The Komodo stopped moving. Mouth open, she panted like a dog. She'd gone a week without food or water, and during the day, the temperature in the barn reached over one hundred degrees. Her native Flores didn't get that hot, and confined to the cage, she couldn't dig a hole or bask in a pool of water to cool herself. She swayed, then collapsed on the floor. She was dying from dehydration.

* * *

She slept until the following afternoon when the wind and Sanchez appeared at the same time, as if the wind had brought him. A gust of air, signaling an approaching thunderstorm, swept through the barn, accompanied by a distant peel of thunder. The Komodo lifted her head and sampled the air. Then seeing the man coming toward her, she shrank back and hissed.

Sanchez, carrying a pail full of pig organs, stopped in front of the lizard's cage. He'd worked on the farm for three years, and for the past two, he'd also taken care of the reptiles for the animal traffickers who'd smuggled the Komodo into the county. He liked feeding rats to the snakes. He dangled them by their tails above the cage as they squirmed in fright. Then he dropped them in and watched their frenzy as the snakes closed in. He'd fed all the animals that'd come through but nothing as big and dangerous as a Komodo dragon. He'd seen her eyes flare, and her long, curved raptor-like claws rake the metal bars of her cage in fury. He wasn't superstitious, but he wondered if she really could breathe fire. He'd never seen an animal anything like her. She was a dragon, and that's what he called her.

The Komodo flicked her tongue in the direction of the pail. Her stomach was empty from having regurgitated the deer she'd eaten back on Flores, although vomiting up the animal had saved her life. Being confined slowed her digestion, and the deer would have rotted in her stomach, poisoning her.

But she needed water more than food. She often dripped thick saliva from her jaws, the juices lubricating her mouth and throat to facilitate swallowing food. Now her mouth was dry. Lowering her head, she took a mouthful of water from the bowl at her feet, just as she'd done since the first day she'd awoken in the cage. Then she raised her head, but, as before, it bumped against the top of the steel box, and the water spilled out of her mouth. Unlike other reptiles, Komodos didn't drink by sucking in water. They had to lift their heads above their bodies and let gravity do its work. Sanchez saw an empty bowl and assumed she'd been drinking, but the Komodo dragon was not.

Sanchez remembered the first time he'd tried to feed the Komodo. She'd struggled against the bars, and the pig organs had slopped on to the floor as he shoved the pan into the cage. He'd come back later to wash away the mess. The lizard had immediately snapped at the water streaming from the hose in his hands. He'd recoiled in fear, thinking she was attacking, not knowing that she was only trying to drink. Recovering, he'd aimed the hose at her face, not to quench her thirst but to punish her.

The next day, he'd returned with more food and a three-foot-long fiberglass rod with two metal prongs at one end. The shock stick, or electric cattle prod, was the animal version of a stun gun. Sanchez put the food in her cage then jabbed her with the stick when she approached it. He'd watched her limbs quiver, then give out. Unable to move, she endured a new agony as Sanchez held the stick against her skin until the charge burned into her thick hide. When she began to stir, he burned her again. He came back with his stick again the following day. He enjoyed watching her writhe and listening to her angry hiss turn into a deep guttural cry. That's when his boss, Doug Kirkland, had come in the barn and saw the burn marks on the Komodo's right shoulder and leg.

"Don't hurt the damn lizard! She's worth more than you are!" Kirkland barked.

Sanchez had heard stories about Kirkland's cruelty and had seen it firsthand. He feared Kirkland even more than he feared the dragon. So after that, he didn't activate the shock stick, he only poked at her burns with it. But the Komodo had learned that the prod brought intense pain. Now her eyes tracked the stick as he waved it in front of her and snapped at it when he thrust it into her cage, but Sanchez was too quick and pulled it away.

Sanchez saw the water bowl was upside down and again waved the shock stick at her. The Komodo immediately backed away, but Sanchez only used the stick to right the bowl. He'd fill it after he fed her. Then he rested the prod on the side of the cage and emptied the bucket of pig organs into the pan.

The metal cage that held her had two doors at one end. The larger opened the entire side for loading and unloading. Within it was a smaller door, big enough for food to be passed through but too small for the lizard to get out. Sanchez released the safety on the feeding door and lifted it. "Enjoy your pig guts."

He was sliding the food tray into the cage when a crash of thunder made him to flinch and look up. In that moment of distraction, the Komodo thrust her head through the opening and sunk her sharp teeth into his arm.

A bolt of pain radiated through Sanchez and a stream of expletives spewed from his mouth. The cage shook as he tried to wrestle his arm out of the lizard's grasp and the shock stick fell to the ground. He flailed for the stick, but it lay just beyond his reach. The Komodo dragon wouldn't let go, and he couldn't free himself. In desperation, he used his free hand to open the loading door and kicked at her.

Their eyes locked. The Komodo's were ablaze with anger; his were wide with panic. Then the Komodo released Sanchez's arm, reared back, and sprang from the open cage. She dashed out of the barn, into the now falling rain, quickly disappearing into the sugarcane. She crossed the neatly planted rows of tall green plants, scuttled up a small incline, then stopped abruptly.

In front of her flowed a canal, fifty yards wide. A short muddy bank sloped down to the water. The lizard looked around as she sampled the air with her tongue. She stepped carefully down to the bank, took a mouthful of water, raised her head high, and swallowed. After drinking her fill, she turned to go back up the bank, but as she shifted her weight, she lost her balance. She flailed, her long sharp claws carving ruts in the mud as she slid sideways into the water. She momentarily went under, then her head broke the surface, and she began to swim.

The Komodo dragon who'd become known as Kodra was free, and she was hungry.

CHAPTER 3

TJ headed to where the vultures were circling. The call had come in as they often do. Someone had seen an animal in distress and gave the location. The caller hadn't given her name, no doubt, because she was where she shouldn't be. His attention focused on the sky, he jerked back when a large black bird flew up in front of him. He looked down and saw the remains of a chicken. Four other vultures turned toward him and one by one causally flew away, not afraid but annoyed because he'd interrupted their next meal. But it wasn't the chicken carcass that interested them, they'd been circling a bobcat.

The bobcat bared its teeth at TJ, but its eyes were pleading. It tugged weakly against a hind leg that was held securely in the grasp of a coil spring, or what is commonly called a bear, trap. TJ noted the animal's rapid shallow breathing and glassy eyes. The leg was clearly broken. He estimated the bobcat had sprung the trap sometime during the night and been lying in the hot sun all day.

The snap of a branch and the crunch of dried grass under foot caused him to turn. The barrel of a rifle was pointed at him. The man with the gun saw TJ's uniform and quickly lowered it.

"This is private property," the man said.

"I know that," TJ replied. "We received a call about an animal in distress. Why'd you set out the trap?" He knew the man was within his rights to trap the bobcat, and Florida was one of the few states where bear traps were still legal.

"Ever since the hurricane passed through last week, that damn animal has been killing my chickens."

TJ looked back at the bobcat. "Cat's too far gone to be saved. The right thing to do is to put it down."

The man shrugged. "Be my guest."

TJ unholstered his Sig Sauer and approached the bobcat. He hesitated for a moment as the familiar scene flashed through his mind. He was back in the Shiawassee Refuge in Michigan with his father. They were on the shore, waiting to push off in their small boat. It was late in the day, and TJ was tired. A mother duck and her brood of ducklings were paddling in front of the boat, and his father was waiting patiently for them to pass. TJ picked up a rock and threw it in their direction to speed them along. His aim was off, and the rock hit the mother duck in the head, killing her. TJ knew that in his haste to leave, he'd also killed the ducklings. They were too young to survive without her. His father looked at him but said nothing. Killing an innocent animal was the worst part of his job. Raising his pistol, he took careful aim and shot the bobcat in the head. The sky was darkening, and TJ knew the afternoon thunderstorm was rolling in. He faced the man and said: "I suggest you bury the remains before the vultures come back for your chickens."

* * *

Kodra wasn't bothered by the rain or being in the canal. She felt her energy return as the water drew off her excess body heat, cooling her. Her powerful tail casually swished back and forth, propelling her, but mostly she rested and let the current carry her.

She didn't know she was in the L-8, one of the many canals that criss-crossed Palm Beach County. It ran southeast for twenty-five miles from Lake O, past the homes of the rich and the not-so-rich, until finally flowing into the Arthur Marshall National Wildlife Refuge. High levees on each side of it ensured that runoff and pollutants from the lake wouldn't contaminate the DuPuis Wildlife and Environmental Area and the Corbett Wildlife Management Area to its east or flood the sugarcane farm on its west. The canal was designed so water could be pumped either into or out of Lake O. The direction depended upon the depth of water in the lake and in the Arthur Marshall.

Hurricane Chris had touched southeast Florida the week before. Although its winds did little damage, the big slow-moving storm dumped much water. South Florida was well prepared for hurricanes. The water, though, continued to be a problem. August already had seen unusually heavy rains, and they continued after Chris had passed. Low-lying areas remained flooded. Lake O rose to dangerously high levels, forcing South Florida Water Management to pump water out of it.

Kodra was propelled south by the swollen canal. The water was only a couple of feet from the top of the earthen banks of the levee but what she saw was an unchanging straight line of water with grass sloping up and away from it on both sides. Periodically, she'd raise her head and sample the air. She smelled the marshes on her left and the sugarcane plants on her right. Further down the canal, the scents gradually changed to humans and small animals as the wetlands and farms gave way to houses and backyards. The humans were a concern, but the scent of prey was exciting.

The rain had passed, and the sun was lower in the sky. With a whip of her tail, she reached the side of the canal and clambered to the top of the slick grassy bank. A group of small white ibis walked along the side of a hard-packed dirt path and were methodically plunging their long curved yellow beaks into the soil, searching for insects. Kodra contemplated the birds, but decided they were too far away to go after. She flicked out her forked tongue. It was long and yellow like the ibis' beaks. Pulling it back, it touched a receptacle in the roof of her mouth. The vomeronasal, or Jacobson's organ, transmitted the information it carried to her brain. She could distinguish scents up to five miles away, determine how recent they were, and the direction they came from, but the scents that came back were too faint to be of interest. She tested the air some more. Dogs. Lots of dogs. She knew dogs. She'd eaten dog before. She set off to investigate.

Heading away from the canal, she descended from the levee to an expanse of lawn. It ended at a large two-story Mediterranean style pink house with white trim. The house held no appeal, but the four bull terriers in the long rectangular dog kennel behind the house did. Recognizable by their distinctive egg-shaped heads, they were good sized dogs, thick and muscular. Their size didn't deter her. She'd taken down much larger animals. And she knew she could scale the fence. Keeping low to the ground, her coloring blended in with the surroundings, she quickly crossed the lawn and approached the pen.

The dogs moved around freely, occasionally pressing their noses against the chain-link fencing that made up the sides of the kennel, happy to be outside. Like most dogs, they could not smell reptiles.

Despite her good hearing, she was intent on the penned dogs, and it wasn't until the last second that she became aware of the rapid movement from behind. She twisted her neck and saw a sixty-pound white male bull terrier charging her. Kodra went low as the terrier leapt to attack, closing her powerful jaws on the dog's left rear leg, and slammed it on his side. As quickly as she had struck, she released her grip. The attack lasted only a moment. Yelping, the bull terrier limped away, trailing blood. He didn't know it, but he was already dead. Upon biting, the two venom glands in Kodra's lower jaw released a toxic protein that mixed with septic bacteria in her mouth and entered the dog's wound, although it wasn't her venom that would kill him. She'd severed an artery in the terrier's leg, and he'd bleed to death in a few short minutes. But Kodra wasn't going to wait. She moved in and took a bite out of the still living dog's hindquarter. The bull terrier squealed and thrashed spasmodically. Lying on one side and unable to right itself, its front legs fought for purchase as the dog tried to drag itself away as Kodra moved in for another bite. Aroused by the male's attack, the dogs in the kennel threw themselves against the near side of the pen and barked frantically.

The commotion brought Bennett D'Costa out of the house, vodka and tonic in one hand, air horn in the other. He looked at the yelping dogs in the pen and pressed the button on top of the can. The shrill sound immediately silenced the pack. They stopped their frenzied movement and looked toward the house.

Kodra froze at the piercing noise. She'd never heard anything like it. She regarded the man holding the object that was the source of the sound and remembered Sanchez and the strange object he held. She forgot about her kill, dashed to the other side of the yard, and disappeared into a grouping of bushes and coconut palms just beyond it.

D'Costa saw a flash of movement out of the corner of his eye before his attention was drawn to his bull terrier who lay lifeless in a pool of blood.

Kodra huddled in the bushes and saw the man run to the dog. He stood over the bull terrier for a few moments, then walked away. She watched and waited, finally taking an anxious step toward her meal when the man reappeared with a wheel barrel. She retreated into the bushes once again and looked on as the man carted the dog away.

The adrenalin of the hunt had worn off, and the sun was low in the sky. During the day, she could see the length of three football fields but, like all Komodo dragons, she had very poor night vision. So despite her hunger, it was time for her to settle down. She would resume hunting in the morning. Kodra moved deeper into the thicket and, using her sharp claws, scooped out a hole just big enough to curl up in. She wrapped her tail around herself and immediately fell into a sleep so deep that a person could walk up and touch her and she wouldn't wake. It was the sleep of an alpha predator.

CHAPTER 4

Kodra stirred under the palm trees where she'd rested for the night. A gentle breeze swayed the palms' large green fronds, alternately bathing her in sunlight and shadow. She felt refreshed and hungry. Walking back to the edge of the bushes, she scanned D'Costa's yard. The dog kennel was empty. She swiveled her head as her long forked tongue tested the air. She saw a pool of water, but it gave off the sharp smell of chlorine and other chemicals, and she detected no prey nearby. On Flores, she'd lie behind a large tree along a game trail or by a watering hole, breeze coming toward her, carrying scents, until an unsuspecting animal passed by. She'd find a similar spot here and wait for her meal to come to her.

Kodra turned back into the bushes. The neat landscaping of D'Costa's property gave way to Florida scrub brush. Branches and leaves she normally wouldn't feel irritated the wounds that Sanchez had inflicted causing them to bleed. She remembered the short grass on the side of the levee and the trail along its crest. She headed back to it.

There were scents of many animals on the path, including deer, her favorite meal. Some were recent, some not so. As she walked, her parietal eye registered a shadow, and she instinctively crouched and prepared to defend herself. Two large egrets flew overhead and landed on the far bank. The shadows passed, and she relaxed and resumed walking. This might be a game trail, but she needed to find a place where she could hide.

She spotted a line of cypress trees, beyond which a grassy plain extended to a pool of water. The water had the same unnatural smell as at D'Costa's, but it was water, and there was a place to hide near it. She descended the levee and settled in to wait at the base of the trees.

Sometime later, new scents drifted to her, the same noxious smells as on the farm mixed with the scent of a human. She peered around a cypress. A man was walking back and forth, each time coming a little closer. The smell of exhaust was coming from the noisy object he was pushing. Kodra watched with interest, trying to determine if the man was a threat or a meal. Man and mower came closer. She rose to her feet, deciding whether to attack or flee when the man stopped and the machine went quiet. George Powell skirted his pool and disappeared into the house. It was time for a beer. He'd finish mowing the lawn later.

The Powells' house was a typical Florida 1950s one-story, three-bedroom, yellow stucco ranch. A screen door led to a stone patio with wooden lawn furniture in need of refinishing. A fenced-in pool abutted one side of the patio. The well-off who lived in manicured gated communities called it a charming "old Florida" house. Powell called it the best he could afford. The screen door opened and slammed shut. Six-year-old Bobby Powell bounded into the yard, his short-haired yellow lab puppy half running and half stumbling behind. Only eight months old, the dog weighed as much as the boy. The boy squealed delightedly in his high-pitched voice, happy to be outside.

Kodra's head snapped up and her body tensed. The boy's cries of joy were similar to the sounds made by an animal in distress. A flick of her tongue and she picked up the scents of the boy and the dog. She moved to her right, now only partially hidden by the cypress tree, but blending in with the green grass and brown tree trunk. She spotted the lab and tracked the dog coming toward her.

The lab ran toward the cypress trees where the Powells had taught him to do his business. The lab neither saw nor smelled Kodra. Bobby skirted the pool and meandered some distance behind, following the dog.

Kodra's eyes grew bigger as the dog approached. She burst into the open yard. The saliva that would facilitate her prey sliding into her stomach dripped from her mouth, leaving a trail on the ground. Her stomach enlarged in anticipation of receiving a meal. She sprinted past the startled lab who skidded to a stop.

Young Bobby froze. His jaw dropped. He'd never seen an animal like this before. His parents had warned him about alligators, but this wasn't an alligator. He stared as Kodra ran past his dog and bore down on him. His eyes grew wide with fear as he stood transfixed. He watched her stop; as she rose up on her hind legs, he saw her white scaly belly and felt the heat of her putrid breath.

* * *

Emilio Sanchez winced as he peeled the compression bandage off of his two-day-old wound. Why did his arm hurt so much? Blood had soaked the gauze under the bandage. The lacerations were edged in black and the angry red inflammation surrounding the bite continued to spread. He gently touched the skin around the wound. It was still hot.

The hum of machinery and the voices of workers tending the sugarcane drifted into the barn as Sanchez sat not far from Kodra's empty cage, pondering what to do. Barely over five-foot tall and stocky, he had an energy and an infectious laugh that belied his size. A self-starter, after he'd migrated from Honduras, he'd taught himself English by watching TV. At night, he watched gardening shows. During the day, he learned all he could from the other workers at the farm. His dream was to start his own landscaping company. For that, he needed money, and Kirkland paid him well for taking care of the reptiles. Besides, you didn't say no to a man like Kirkland, but now he cursed himself for his greed. He regretted tormenting the dragon, not because she'd bitten him, but because the incident had driven home the realization that he was becoming a cruel man like his boss.

Sanchez was sweating and cold at the same time. His fever spiked, and his arms and legs quivered despite his efforts to hold them still. He feared his body was shutting down. He rolled clean gauze around the wound with his good hand, then used his teeth to pull it tight as he reached for the strip of tape he'd cut. Having rewrapped his wound, he shook open a bottle of Tylenol and swallowed four tablets. He knew where Kirkland kept his stash of oxycontin and longed to take some but Kirkland had told him Tylenol was better for fevers. That was after Kirkland had beaten him for letting the dragon escape. Sanchez suspected Kirkland wanted to keep the oxy for himself. It was becoming harder to get. After his rage subsided, Kirkland had washed Sanchez's wound with hydrogen peroxide. It hurt like hell, but the bottle of cheap vodka Kirkland gave him to drink made it bearable. He took the oxy anyway, after Kirkland left. Then he'd smoked some weed and fell into a restless sleep. He dreamed he was pushing the pan of slop into Kodra's cage and she bit him, just like it'd happened. Only this time, she didn't let go. She pulled him into her cage by his arm. Her red-glowing eyes never breaking contact with his, and he knew the fate that awaited him.

CHAPTER 5

Belly almost touching the ground, Kodra lumbered back to her spot behind a cypress tree to digest her meal when a shrill scream caused her to stop and turn to the Powell house. Bobby's mother, hands at her face, stared down at the ground. The lab puppy sat in front of her looking up expectantly. Kodra watched with curiosity as the man she'd seen before burst out of the house, beer in hand. He ran to the woman. She pointed. The man dropped his beer and touched the grass. Rising, he rubbed his thumb across his fingers, then wiped his hand on his shirt. He said something to his wife and rushed around the side of the house, the lab dashing after him. Both humans were shouting. Kodra had never seen such behavior.

Powell reappeared from the other side of the house. He yelled to his wife as he passed her and ran toward the row of cypress trees. Kodra rose, alert to the approaching danger, but Powell sprinted through the line of trees and never saw her. He summitted the levee and ran up and down the dirt path that paralleled the canal. Kodra looked back and forth from the man to the woman in the yard. Eventually, she became bored and plodded further down the row of cypress to get away from the ruckus. The humans' screams gave way to more methodical calls as she settled in to digest her meal.

She didn't rest for long. Her eyes popped open at the sing-song wail of a siren. It was followed by multiple sirens with different pitches, their highs and lows clashing with one another. The sirens were getting louder and coming in her direction. Kodra shot her tongue and recognized the scent of the man and the woman and smelled their stress. There were other scents too. They'd been joined by more humans, neighbors who'd heard their frantic cries and came to help. She watched anxiously, the commotion making her uncomfortable. The first siren went silent as a white Palm Beach County sheriff's SUV pulled up to the side of the house. The humans ran to the vehicle. The other sirens grew louder and louder, and then they stopped as Palm Beach County Fire Rescue units arrived.

Kodra watched with interest. She'd only seen this many humans once before when she'd stalked a pig in a village on Flores, although she'd never seen green and blue humans—the uniform colors of the sheriff's department and fire and rescue. The humans formed into three lines. Two lines had their backs to each other and stretched the width of the yard. One line started walking north, the other south. They moved at a deliberate pace, shouting loudly as they went, stopping to examine clumps of tall grass and bushes. The third line had their backs to the house and began moving across the lawn, toward the tree line. They were coming her way.

Reluctantly, she rose and retreated from the advancing lines toward the levee behind her. Her heavy belly dragged as she left the safety of the trees. She climbed to the top of the levee. Breathing hard from the effort, she looked around. The humans had just passed the cypress trees, moving slowly in her direction. She was visible on top of the levee, but she sensed the humans hadn't spotted her. She looked across the levee and saw a forest of green sugarcane plants. She took in the surrounding scents. There were no humans among the stalks. She contemplated the canal and instinctively knew she couldn't swim north. The current was too strong, and her body was bloated with the child. She looked south. A short distance downstream was a large concrete and metal structure that blocked the canal. It was a combination dam and pumping station that enabled South Water Florida Management to move water up or down the canal.

Two men appeared on the levee near the dam. The humans were surrounding her. Her only avenue of escape was the canal. She half-ran, half-slid down the berm to the water's edge. The stress and exertion triggered her vomit reflex, and she spewed out the contents of her stomach. Bobby's body tumbled headfirst into the canal and disappeared with a splash. Her teeth had knocked off one of the boy's shoes as his feet emerged from her mouth and covered in saliva it lay glistening on the ground

Recovering quickly, she plunged into the canal and, ignoring Bobby's slowly sinking body, swam to the far side. She mounted the bank and looked back. People were standing on the bank where she'd just been. She didn't know that they wouldn't cross the canal or that their attention was elsewhere. A first responder had found Bobby's shoe, and the rescuers were now focused on the pumping station, knowing that if Bobby had entered the water, the current would have carried him toward it.

Kodra threaded her way through the sugarcane moving parallel to the canal and past the pumping station. There she stopped to rest. The heat and humidity of the day, along with her ordeal, had raised her body temperature uncomfortably high. She considered moving inland to find a cooler place, but her unpleasant memories of the sugarcane farm were too strong. Testing the air, she satisfied herself there were no humans close by. She walked down the bank and slid into the canal, the water once again cooling her, and continued her travel south.

Although she'd lost her meal, the movement of the search and rescue teams looking for Bobby Powell had sent her on a journey around the pumping station. Had she entered the canal near the cypress tree, the current would have carried her into its gates and pumps and a gruesome end. Kodra had avoided death for a second time.

* * *

An old bull alligator, twelve feet long, was floating motionless in the canal a little above the Powells' property. Only its eyes and the tip of its snout showed above the water. The alligator remained still, tracking Kodra when she'd appeared on the bank of the levee. With her distended stomach, Kodra was even larger than usual, and the gator regarded her with caution. Despite his size, the alligator was lazy. Long ago, he'd found an ample source of food around the pumping station. He'd survived a couple of close calls with the gates and pumps in his younger days. Now he could tell when the gates were open or closed, when the pumps were on, and in which direction the water flowed.

He'd learned, as had other alligators throughout Florida, that the waters around dams and pumping stations were ideal places to catch fish, turtles, and other wildlife. With the gates closed, the canal was dammed, and there was no place for a prospective meal to escape as the alligator closed in. Even better, when the gates were open and the pumps were on, fish and other animals were sucked through, emerging stunned or dead, making for effortless feeding. He even knew which side of the damn to wait on, depending on the direction in which the water was being pumped.

The alligator smelled the carrion as soon as Kodra disgorged Bobby. With a few swishes of his powerful tail, he moved toward the body. On his way, he passed Kodra, who was swimming in the opposite direction. Neither reptile paid any attention to the other. Each was focused on its immediate objective.

Bobby drifted down and gently bumped along the earthen side of the canal as the current propelled him toward the pumping station. The alligator dove and caught up to him. He eyed Bobby and took an exploratory bite out of his side, turning the water a misty red. Then he gently took the child's body in his mouth and swam to a chamber in the bank of the canal. Known as an alligator hole, or simply, a hide hole, some time ago, he'd scooped out earth just below the water line to make a cavity. He'd done the same thing on the other side of the dam. Sticks and other debris gradually became caught in it, making it a natural trap. He opened his mouth and released the child. Using his snout, he pushed Bobby's body into the hollow until it caught on a tree branch. He nudged the boy's body twice more, testing to make sure it was secure.

The alligator had no immediate plans to eat Bobby. As the boy's body decayed, it would attract fish, turtles, and all sorts of animals wanting to feed on him. As they ate him, the old bull gator would eat them.

* * *

TJ wiped the sweat from his brow. The hunt had gone well. Three Burmese pythons caught and killed over the course of eight hours. It was unusual to find that many pythons in one area after mating season, but the rains had driven them to dry ground. He and four of his rangers were in the Everglades below the Arthur Marshall Refuge. Keeping Burmese pythons out of the refuge was both a professional and personal mission for TJ.

The pythons had arrived en masse thirty years ago when Hurricane Andrew struck Miami. An animal importer had a greenhouse full of Burmese pythons. The building disappeared in the storm, and the snakes were literally scattered to the winds. Now there were at least one hundred thousand roaming free in South Florida.

A remarkably efficient hunting machine, Burmese pythons consumed everything in their path. It pained TJ to think that ninety percent of all mammals had disappeared from Everglades National Park since the pythons arrived. Now the birds were disappearing. With no food left on the ground, pythons were climbing trees and eating eggs out of nests.

Florida had been slow to recognize the problem and even slower to respond. They hired python elimination specialists, and paid trappers eight dollars an hour, eventually upping it to fifteen. Few trappers wanted the work, and the snakes were hard to find. Pythons were tan with brown blotches, ringed by black, coloring that blended in perfectly with the wetlands of South Florida. A person could walk right by one and never see it.

Animal rights activists also created obstacles to eliminating the snakes. They were concerned that the pythons weren't being killed humanely. Chopping off the snake's head with a machete was deemed cruel because the snake's body twitched after the head was severed. Activists insisted that the snakes be shot in the head with a gun. Trappers pointed out a python's head was a small and moving target. Animal righters were unimpressed.

The Burmese python population grew as females gave birth to as many as one hundred young at a time. They could live for twenty years and grow to twenty feet, weighing two hundred pounds. As their numbers increased, so did their territory in their relentless search for food.

"I found another!" a ranger cried. "Must be an eighteen-footer, and it's on the move!"

TJ turned to see the ranger run after the snake. The python was surprisingly fast as it slithered into a wet marsh, intending to escape in the water. The ranger caught up to the snake, grabbed it by the tail, and began pulling it back. The python whipped its body into a U-shape and struck the ranger's hand. The momentum of the attack knocked the ranger off his feet, and he landed hard on his butt. The python quickly coiled itself around the man.

TJ and the other rangers raced over. One grabbed the snakes' tail and another grabbed its trunk. The python's head was as big as a garden spade, and it had the ranger's hand firmly in its mouth. TJ didn't hesitate. He grabbed the python's upper jaw in his left hand and the lower jaw in his right and pulled. The python resisted, but its jaws gradually opened. TJ continued pulling, and the jaws suddenly spread wide, making a crunching like the sound of someone walking on gravel. The python went limp, and TJ dropped the snake's head.

"Thank you," the relieved ranger said.

"You know, TJ, that's not an approved way to kill a python," another said with a smile.

TJ looked at the snake and thought about how quickly it had overcome the ranger. *It's only a matter of time until a python is going to kill a person,* he thought.

CHAPTER 6

Doug Kirkland walked into the barn and saw Sanchez sitting on a box hunched over, shivering. He was as tall and thin as Sanchez was short and squat. He always left the top two buttons of his work shirt open. The five-inch-tall cross tattooed on his chest, just below his neck, was plainly visible. He had a crude blue spiderweb tattoo on his left elbow, a reminder of the time he'd spend in prison. From a distance, the web looked like scales.

"Two days and not a trace. I'm going to launch the drone again as soon as it recharges," Kirkland said.

"It's a big farm," Sanchez replied. "Could be anywhere. Maybe it's not even here."

Florida Pure Sugar Incorporated was the legal name of the farm. Locals just called it Pure Sugar. Well over one hundred square miles in size, it was one of the largest sugarcane farms in the state, extending from the bottom of Lake Okeechobee to Southern Boulevard, a major thoroughfare that bisected central Palm Beach County. Its eastern border was the L-8 canal; it extended west almost to the city of Belle Glade.

"I did some research last night," Kirkland said. "Komodos don't travel very far if they have food and water. Lots of both here."

"What about the dairy farm just west of us? It might go after the cows."

"For your sake, you better hope it doesn't and that we find it. That's a $250,000 animal on the loose. And I can tell you, Big Al's not happy with you."

In addition to being the principal foreman, Kirkland ran the illegal reptile import business for Big Al Mumford, the son-in-law of the farm's owners. The pair had gotten into the business by accident when a driver for one of the farm's suppliers asked if he could leave some boxes with them for a few days. The money was good, and Mumford was never one to pass up a buck. He said yes and was surprised when the trucker arrived the next day with crates full of turtles. He queried the trucker, and then did some research on his own. He was amazed to learn that smuggling animals into the US was a multibillion-dollar business and that reptiles made up the largest class of illegally imported animals. He was even more astonished to learn how much a single reptile sold for on the black market. And, unlike the illicit drug trade, there were very few law enforcement officers tasked with finding animal smugglers. That was all he and Kirkland needed to know. They liked dealing in reptiles. The animals didn't make noise and, with the exception of the Komodo dragon, were small. Feeding them wasn't a problem. The snakes ate rats, squirrels, and rabbits, all of which Kirkland could catch on the farm. No one questioned the traps he'd set out, ostensibly to keep the farm pests under control.

With a background in stolen cars and chop shops, Kirkland worked his way through the underworld and set up his network. His work paid off when their first import, an angulated tortoise from Madagascar, was sold for seventy-five thousand dollars. With states, particularly Florida, banning more and more exotic animals, their business was thriving.

* * *

Kodra let the water carry her. She was tired from having regurgitated the boy and fleeing the humans. Periodically raising her head and testing the air, she became intrigued when traces of strange animal scents reached her. Climbing to the top of the levee, she found herself on a large expanse of flat barren land. The hot sun beat down unmercifully and reflected off the white earth, forcing her to squint. The scents were strong and were joined by roaring and whooshing noises. She walked slowly in a circle, sampling the air and looked around. Inputs flooded her brain. She didn't distinguish whether they came from sight or smell. It was the information that mattered. Her tail kicked up a fine white dust as she moved.

A neatly planted expanse of palm and pine trees stood on the east side of the canal. Just beyond the trees was Animal World, a small wildlife park best known as a place for grandparents to take their bored grandchildren. It had a petting zoo and housed the usual fare of domestic and African herbivores, including zebras and giraffes, and a few dangerous animals.

She smelled the many warm-blooded animals, but they were not familiar. The scents of many humans were mixed with the animals, and she sensed she should avoid that area, so she turned her attention to the source of the strange noises. Just past the flat white earth, unfamiliar objects flashed by. The larger the object, the greater the noise. Oil and exhaust, odors like those at the farm only much stronger, accompanied the rumbling and buzzing. She watched cars and tractor-trailers racing along Southern Boulevard.

Beyond the strange moving objects was the smell of wetlands and more familiar prey. Energized, Kodra returned to the canal and swam with the current, passing under Southern Boulevard. As she did, the L-8 canal became the L-40. Of course, arbitrary human labels and boundaries meant nothing to her. She was now in the Village of Wellington, known for its fancy houses and equally fancy horse stables, where the rich and famous gathered every winter for jumping, dressage, and polo events.

She climbed up the canal's western bank where a broad expanse of marshland stretched out all around her. She was on the edge of the Arthur R. Marshall Loxahatchee National Wildlife Refuge, a two hundred and twenty-one square mile wetland managed by the US Fish & Wildlife Service. It had a shape something between a tear and an oval. Beyond it were wetlands that went by a variety of different names but were all part of what was once simply called the Everglades.

The refuge was home to over two hundred types of birds including eagles, herons, and the endangered Snail Kite. Twenty different types of mammals including deer, bobcats, river otters, and rabbits lived there as did numerous reptiles and amphibians. Forty species of butterflies, with colorful wings, flew in the preserve. Most of the Arthur Marshall was off limits to visitors. Boating, hunting, and fishing were allowed only in the lower third of the refuge and only at certain times of the year.

The marsh directly in front of Kodra was a dry prairie, solid enough to walk on during the winter arid season but flooded during the rainy season. Because of the recent storms, it was under four feet of water. It was dotted with specks of dry land, islands too numerous to count. Small islets, called hammocks, were thick with low growing plants and scrub pines. Larger tree mounds that were home to oak, hackberry, and pine rose above the water.

She turned facing the breeze and sampled the air. Beyond the canal, there were dogs, cats, horses, humans, and other animals. There also were the now familiar artificial scents of houses.

She liked the dry land and abundance of prey. Tired but hungry, she looked for a group of trees near the houses where she could safely rest but saw only tall skinny palms and small clusters of shrubs and plants. There weren't any good hiding places. The fresh, natural smells of the refuge with its hammocks and tree islands beckoned to her. She would sleep there and return tomorrow to hunt.

CHAPTER 7

It had started out as a normal workday for TJ. He was looking forward to taking a couple of hours off around lunch and hopefully selling his Impala. Sheriff Rodriguez had donned his green uniform and drove off to the Powells' house to check on the recovery mission for little Bobby. They were up before the sun.

At the sugar cane farm, Sanchez woke to sunlight and an empty barn. He debated which was worse, the infection from Kodra's bite or incurring Kirkland's wrath when he insisted he had to go to the hospital. Kirkland was somewhere out in the fields with his drone, a high-end model purchased by the farm for viewing the rows of sugarcane and saving the time and expense of having someone physically walk the fields. He was enthralled with the drone, using it as his personal toy. For fun, he buzzed the workers, much to their annoyance, but what could they say? He was their boss. Today, though, there was no buzzing; he was searching for Kodra.

Sanchez picked up the two-way radio on the workbench next to him and called Kirkland. He knew they were on an open channel, so he just asked the foreman to meet him in the barn. Kirkland wasn't pleased to interrupt his search but reluctantly agreed. He arrived at the barn on his ATV, with the white drone strapped in a basket on the back. He carried the drone into the barn and gently set it on a table. Turning, he glared at Sanchez: "What's this about?"

Sanchez swallowed. "It's getting worse. I've gotta go to the ER. I'd drive myself, but I'm afraid I'll pass out."

Kirkland pulled out a cigarette and lit it. "No way. They'll ask too many questions, and you're not smart enough to give the right answers."

Sanchez held out his swollen arm. The red infection extended beyond the bandage. "Look at this! If you don't take me now I'm calling 911." Sanchez knew he risked another beating or worse for the threat, but he was desperate.

Kirkland's face darkened and he stared at Sanchez before finally saying: "Okay. But we'll go to MediRedi. And we'll go over your story on the way."

They took one of the farm trucks. Kirkland waved to the guard as they exited Pure Sugar and turned west toward Belle Glade, home of MediRedi, a walk-in urgent care clinic. Entering the town, they passed a sign, saying, *Welcome to Belle Glade, Her Soil is Her Future.* Locals, they knew, called it Muck City because of the area's thick wet soil. The soil was ideal for growing sugarcane but even better for breeding insects. Belle Glade, a city of twenty thousand, existed because of sugarcane and the three crops the farmers could plant and harvest annually. Planting was still done by hand, Sanchez knew all too well, and required the most workers. Burns also were labor intensive. Harvesting was largely done by machines. The thick, fibrous cane stalks were then transported to local mills. Planting, burning, and harvesting were 24/7 operations, with the farm hands often sleeping in the fields. The luckier ones worked in town at the Sugar Growers Cooperative sugar mill, chopping and crushing the stalks, turning them in to raw sugar.

Despite the surrounding sugarcane farms, Belle Glade's unemployment rate was forty percent, and only five percent of its high school graduates went on to college. In the 1980s, it had the highest per capita rate of AIDS in the country. Later, its notoriety came from having the second highest per capital rate of violent crimes in the US. Everyone used drugs: narcotics and opiates. A city of immigrants and seasonal workers, how many were undocumented was anyone's guess. Kirkland knew some of his crew were illegals, but he didn't care.

MediRedi's hours mirrored the sugarcane cycle. It was open fourteen hours a day during growing times and twenty-fours a day during planting, burning, and harvesting. The clinic had an arrangement with the farm. If an injury or illness was work-related, the clinic would bill the farm directly. No need to file a worker's comp claim and have state inspectors come around. The sugarcane growers liked that. The clinic never asked their patients for documentation or reported their drug use. The workers liked that.

* * *

Sanchez and Kirkland sat in a small examination room. A nurse charted Sanchez's history and took his vitals. They looked up expectantly when gray-haired Dr. Michael Dudnick, in a white lab coat and a stethoscope around his neck, breezed in. Kirkland had heard on the radio about Dudnick's background when he'd joined MediRedi. Twenty-years as an army doc and tours of duty in Iraq and Afghanistan had well prepared him for the gunshot, knife, and other wounds and injuries that occurred all too frequently in Belle Glade.

Dr. Dudnick asked what had happened and listened to Sanchez's story as he undid the compression bandage. Kirkland sat silently, watching them both. The doctor slowly rotated Sanchez's arm, gingerly inspecting it. "Well, that's a nasty bite. You're lucky a vein wasn't cut. A gator, you say. Three days ago?"

"Since they opened the flood gates on Lake O, the farm's been overrun with them," Kirkland answered for Sanchez.

"I'm not surprised," Dudnick said. "Here's what we're going to do. A nurse is going to draw blood and give you a tetanus shot." The nurse would draw an extra vial of blood, a habit Dr. Dudnick had developed in the Middle East. The techs looked for the obvious that had to be treated. He looked for the hidden, the microbes and unusual infectious diseases that were often missed. "I'd also like you to give a urine specimen."

Kirkland and Sanchez stirred nervously. Dr. Dudnick saw their reaction and added: "Don't worry, I'm only looking for the source of the infection."

The two men relaxed.

Although what he said was true, Dudnick knew that anything else in Sanchez's system would show up. "We'll run both quickly. While we're waiting for the results I'll debride the wound."

Kirkland and Sanchez looked at him blankly. "I'm going to anesthetize your arm, wash the bite, and cut away the black skin around it."

Sanchez nodded reluctantly.

As Dr. Dudnick finished attending to the wound, the nurse returned and handed him the test results. He studied the paper. Traces of opioids and marijuana. *No surprise there.* An elevated white cell count indicating an infection. *No surprise there either.* Prothrombin and INR results were high. They suggested Sanchez's blood wasn't clotting properly, and that was troubling. Dr. Dudnick gave an imperceptible shake of his head. The drugs and weed were messing with the results.

"You say you washed the wound with hydrogen peroxide?"

Sanchez nodded.

"Well, that might explain the continued bleeding. Hydrogen peroxide is good for scrapes and small cuts, but not for animal bites. In deeper wounds, it can interfere with your blood clotting."

But something nagged at Dr. Dudnick. He wasn't sure hydrogen peroxide was the cause of the problem. "Have you been taking anything besides Tylenol?"

Kirkland answered. "I gave him some Cephalexin."

"A prescription antibiotic. You got that from a doctor?"

"We use it around the farm," Kirkland said.

Dr. Dudnick didn't hide his exasperation. "Taking drugs that are lying around isn't a good thing." *Nor is taking opioids for that matter.* "A gator bite is a serious matter. Their mouths are petri dishes of virulent bacteria." He gave Sanchez a stern look. "You should have come in right away rather than trying to treat this yourself. I'm going to give you an IV. It's a three-dose treatment. You'll have to come back tomorrow and the day after for the next two. And let me know right away if your condition changes."

As they left, Kirkland said to Sanchez: "You'll be fine by tomorrow. No need to come back."

"But what if I'm not?"

"Gut it out. It's your fault you got bitten. No more doctors. Nothing to attract attention."

* * *

Kodra was the last to rise, waiting for full light before moving. She assessed her surroundings. There were spots of land, but they were too small for game trails or to support many animals, and there was too much water around them for her liking. Better to head back to the houses she saw yesterday, where there were strong scents of prey.

She entered the water and swam the short distance to the levee. Then she swam the canal and clambered up its side, perching herself just below its ridge. She peered over the top, surveying the strip of neatly manicured lawns and houses that reminded her of where she'd found the boy. She anxiously sampled the air, searching for food.

As she watched, activity increased in the neighborhood. Doors opened and closed, people briefly appeared, cars drove off, dogs barked. There was the strong scent of horses nearby but nowhere to be seen. Kodra patrolled back and forth on the top of the berm, moving parallel to the houses. Her skin tones rendered her almost invisible in the tall green grass. She picked a spot and settled down once more. Hours passed, and the sun grew hot. Her eyes grew heavy and closed, but the occasional appearance of her yellow tongue showed she was resting, not sleeping.

Loud high-pitched squeals caused her eyes to shoot open, her red irises flaring as she zeroed in on the activity. She saw two humans standing next to a pool of artificial smelling water. Their scents confirmed it. Here was food, but it wasn't moving in her direction. She'd have to cross an open plain to get to it and would be exposed. She'd have preferred to use cover and stealth as she approached her target, but there were no trees, no hiding places, between her and her meal. And she was hungry. Kodra ran down the berm and across the lawn.

Judy Herzog, a petit woman, and her seven-year-old daughter, Anne, were wearing matching blue bathing suits and flip-flops. Anne also had on a float ring that looked like a smiling yellow duck with an orange beak around her waist. She sat down on the edge of the pool and delightedly kicked the water, all the while unknowingly making sounds that attracted Kodra.

The grass gave way to hot stone pavers underfoot as Kodra moved from the yard to the patio. She flicked her tongue. The woman smelled like the small human she'd eaten two days ago. The girl had a distasteful odor, given off by the vinyl swim ring she wore. But driven by hunger, Kodra had made a mistake. She'd come straight on, and the swimming pool separated her from her prey. If she ran around the pool, it might give the humans time to spot her and escape. Not slowing, she made her decision and leapt into the pool. To her surprise, she landed on a sun shelf, only six inches deep. She splashed through the water toward her target.

The sound caught Judy's and Anne's attention, and their expressions changed from joy to bewilderment at the sight of the large greenish brown lizard charging them. Kodra sprang out of the pool, trailing water on the pavers. She leapt at the woman, wrapped her jaws around Judy's torso, and drove Judy to the ground. The sound of air being forced out of Judy's lungs and her skull cracking on the patio stones occurred at the same time.

Kodra raised her head, lifting Judy, and shook her like a rag doll, bouncing the woman's head off the ground. Judy's blood, mixed with Kodra's saliva, flew in all directions splattering the sliding glass patio doors and the pavers. Jagged lines of red floated atop the pool. Anne and her duck ring were sprayed with a slashing streak of crimson from her left knee to her right shoulder. Kodra opened her mouth and dropped Judy, watching to see if her prey moved. The woman did not. Blood and saliva dripped from Kodra's jaws as she turned and looked at the wide-eyed, open-mouthed girl. She stepped toward Anne, her claws clicking on the patio. A stream of urine ran down the girl's leg and puddled at her feet.

Abruptly, Kodra turned, her tail brushing the girl as she did. She looked around and flicked her tongue. Nothing threatening nearby. Although she usually ate her prey where she killed it, Kodra remembered how quickly many humans had appeared the day before. She decided to carry off her meal. She briefly considered some shrubbery on the adjacent lawn but it was too close and too small to provide protection. Lowering her head, she picked up the woman's limp body in her mouth. She crossed the lawn, crested the levee, and stopped just below the ridge of the bank sloping down to the canal, near where she'd lain in wait earlier in the day. A trail of blood on the patio and the grass marked her path.

Satisfied that she could now safely eat her meal, Kodra took Judy's head and shoulders into her mouth, raised her head to align it with her throat and stomach and worked her jaws. Slowly, Judy's body disappeared into Kodra as she continued working her mouth and swallowing. A final gulp and Judy was gone. Blood and saliva marked the feeding site.

Stomach bulging, Kodra swam the canal, mounted the far side of the levee, and returned to her nest in the refuge. This was a strenuous activity in her engorged state, and once she reached the safety of her burrow, she fell into a deep and contented sleep. She was only vaguely aware of the distant wailing of sirens as the skies darkened and heavy rain fell, the same rain that at that very moment was spoiling the finish on TJ's Impala in the parking lot outside the pizzeria. She groggily awoke, registered the rain, and fell back to sleep. She'd learned humans were prey just like any other animal. Some were dangerous, like the man with the stick in the barn and some, like this woman, were not. And now she knew where to find them.

CHAPTER 8

TJ's potential buyer stuck him with the bill for the pizza. He paid it and dashed through the parking lot as the rain pelted him. Sliding onto the Impala's big bench seat, he tossed his iPhone down next to him, and pressed an AirPod into one ear. He twisted the small silver ignition key and cranked the starter. There was no mindless foot on the brake and pushing a button like nowadays. You had to think to start this baby. The Chevy rumbled to life, and he swung the car out of the parking lot. His destination was Wellington, the site of the second attack, where he'd meet Sheriff Rodriguez. The windshield wipers slapped away the rain as he drove.

On his way, TJ accessed Siri on his iPhone and instructed it to read him news about the disappearances of Bobby Powell and Judy Herzog. He noted the progression of the Powell story. It started out as a missing child and possible drowning. When the press learned there was blood and one of his shoes was found near the canal, the stories quickly changed to a likely alligator attack. There were no witnesses, so it was all speculation.

Bobby Powell's disappearance was pushed aside by the news about Judy Herzog. The story had just broken but quickly morphed into a mother being carried off in the jaws of an alligator. Dramatic, but Sheriff Rodriguez had said there was a witness this time. The most recent stories speculated, although some presented it as fact, that the two deaths were linked. The same alligator had attacked both. TJ thought it unlikely, as the attacks had occurred miles part, but he couldn't come up with a better explanation. The more sensational accounts said there was a man-eating gator on the loose.

The rain stopped and the sun immediately appeared as he wound his way west through Wellington. Not the quickest route to the Herzog house, but he wanted to get a feel for the area, particularly the wetlands and waterways. He stopped to look where two canals met at a gated community, and a guard came out of a gatehouse, eyeing him. A little farther on, he passed a stable. Then he turned on to Flying Cow Ranch Road. *Flying Cow? Maybe the people here have so much money their cows really do fly.* He smiled at the thought even though he knew the road's name had nothing to do with cows. In the 1950s, Charles Oliver Wellington, a wealthy New York investor, had purchased vast tracks of what was then swampland. Flying came from the grass airstrip, now the Wellington Aero Club, he'd built to facilitate his arrival and departure. Cow didn't refer to the animal but was Charles Oliver Wellington's initials. Ranch was a stretch, but, after all, they did keep horses.

TJ passed a cluster of homes surrounding the Wellington Aero Club, where every garage housed at least one plane. Commuting to work had a different meaning for these people, he thought. He turned his Impala into a neighborhood of large homes that backed up to the L-40 canal. It once had been wetlands and home to wildlife and horse trails that ran through the Wellington Environmental Preserve just to its south, but in Florida when developers and nature collided, nature lost. Perhaps not surprisingly, the development had been approved soon after Governor Johnson had taken office. TJ shook his head. *Politics.* Sometimes he wondered why he even tried.

Another call came in from his boss. It seemed the agency's mission had changed from consultation to formal involvement. US Fish & Wildlife would assist the Palm Beach County Sheriff's Office—FWS and PBSO, respectively, in agency jargon—and search the Arthur Marshall Refuge. TJ would lead the FWS effort, manage the rangers tasked with the search, be the agency's spokesperson, and assist the PBSO outside the refuge. "Why not State Fish and Wildlife?" he asked.

His superior responded that the governor had requested the feds because they had greater resources. *Not my usual assignment*, he thought, but he didn't argue. Annapolis grads knew when to lead and when to follow orders.

On his way, TJ called a friend over at state. She told him that the chairman of Florida Fish & Wildlife was the other party's likely next candidate for governor which was why they'd been told to stand down. "Politics may cost someone their life," he said.

TJ didn't need his GPS to find the Herzogs' house. The street in front of it was filled with official vehicles. Palm Beach County deputies were keeping the curious away. TV vans with large antennas sticking up were parked nearby. He showed his credentials and asked for the sheriff. A deputy waved him into the driveway. A second deputy directed him to the back of the house. Sheriff Rodriguez was off to one side, talking on his phone.

The sheriff had short-cut gray hair and a slightly darker, neatly trimmed mustache. TJ thought Rodriguez had gained weight since he'd last seen him, but on a closer look, he realized the sheriff's girth came from the body armor he wore under his uniform. Rodriguez appeared tired, *his years are catching up with him*, TJ thought, although the sheriff's eyes were constantly moving, taking in everything around him as he spoke.

The sheriff broke off the call and sighed. "Guy calls for the third time complaining that we aren't doing anything to find the animal that killed his dog. The fact that two people are missing doesn't seem to register. Oh well." Then he extended his hand and said: "Thanks for coming."

"Walk with me," the sheriff said. They crossed the yard and came to the berm leading up to the canal. As they walked up the hill, the sheriff slipped on the slick grass, leaving a muddy streak on his pant leg. He recovered without saying a word and continued to the top.

On the bank, TJ surveyed the area. The L-40 canal ran parallel to the homes on the street. He knew it was about one hundred and seventy-five feet wide. A dive team was already working the water. He looked beyond to the refuge. Men, some wearing hip waders, were slogging through the marsh along the edge of the levee. Further out was a boat with Palm Beach County Sheriff department markings on its side. PBSO was already searching the Arthur Marshall. *Fine by me*, TJ thought. The Arthur Marshall Refuge was US

Fish & Wildlife territory, but when it came to missing persons, jurisdictions melted away. The lead law enforcement agency could go wherever it wanted.

He tuned back at the house. It was a two-story contemporary design that he estimated to be over five thousand square feet. He looked for security cameras and points of ingress and egress.

The sheriff directed his attention to a line of yellow flags stretching from the Herzogs' pool to near where they were standing. "Blood trail. There was more, but the rain washed it away."

TJ looked at the markers, and then at the sheriff. "Something doesn't seem right. It's just like I told you about the Powell boy. Alligators don't behave this way. If the woman had been standing right next to the canal, maybe, but gators don't run across lawns, snatch their victims, and run back to wherever they came from."

"Well, unless you've got a better theory, that's what this one did."

"Sheriff, you said there was a witness. Can I talk to him or her?"

"Her. Judy's daughter Anne."

"She saw the whole thing?"

"Apparently."

"What happened?"

The sheriff recounted the events. "That's according to Mitchell Herzog, Judy's husband. He heard a commotion and came out. His wife had disappeared. Anne was standing beside the pool, white with fear. Herzog knew something bad had happened. He called out for his wife. There was no answer. Then he saw the trail of blood and ran to here. No sign of his wife. He ran back to his daughter and wrapped a towel around her. Herzog asked her what happened. The girl said a large alligator jumped out of the pool, took Judy in its mouth, and carried her off."

A concerned look swept TJ's face. "What a horrible thing for the girl to see. How is she?"

"Physically okay, but, as you can imagine, she's traumatized. Their doctor gave her a sedative, and Mr. Herzog is with her and his son in the house. Nobody's going to speak with the girl for a while."

"I didn't see any security cameras?"

Sheriff Rodriguez shook his head. "There are none."

TJ threw up his arms. "That would be too easy." He paused, and then continued, "How can the FWS be of assistance, Sheriff?"

"I want you to find the alligator that did this."

"We'll help in every way we can; I'll put boats in the refuge." He inclined his head toward the marsh. "Looks like you already have men there."

"I hope you don't mind that I put one in to take a look."

"Not at all, but I'll mobilize our people, and we'll take over from here. Also, I suggest you hire some professional trappers. If this was a gator attack, the animal could be in any of the canals, lakes and ponds around here. They'll know the best places to look."

The sheriff put his hand on TJ's shoulder. "And, there's something else. Two attacks in two days. The press is saying we've got a man-eating alligator on the loose."

"Yeah, I've heard, but the attacks were miles apart."

"We calculate the distance to be about seven miles from the Powells to the Herzogs, if the animal swam the canal." The sheriff continued, "I'm told this will be the lead story on the national news tonight. We don't want people panicking and doing crazy things. And the governor . . ." He let out a sigh. "Let's just say she's worried about tourism, too. I need someone credible, someone who's been in front of a camera before."

"I did a show on public TV, but that was recorded. I've never—"

Rodriguez motioned with his hand for TJ to stop. "Your agency speaks highly of you and"—he made a sweeping gesture—"for all we know, the gator could be in the refuge. I have every confidence that you'll come up with a plan to find the gator and reassure everyone they're safe in the meantime. And you have to do this by nine a.m. tomorrow morning."

"Why nine a.m.?"

"Because we have a press conference scheduled for then. Governor Johnson is flying in from Miami, and, trust me, you don't want to disappoint her."

TJ looked west out over the Arthur Marshall Refuge, using his hand to shade his eyes. The bright sun was low in the sky. He couldn't see Kodra, who'd been roused from her nap by a helicopter flying overhead and was resting on a spit of land, digesting Judy Herzog. She couldn't see him either, but his scent carried across the water.

* * *

Kirkland walked into Mumford's office. "You wanted to see me?"

Mumford was sitting behind his desk, dressed in his typical Hawaiian shirt and stretch pants. His massive six foot three inch, two hundred fifty pound body was spilling out of his chair. He looked up at Kirkland then back to the television he'd been watching. On the screen was a newswoman, microphone in hand, in front of a house. "Close the door," he said without looking up. With the door closed, he spoke again. "I know where the Komodo is, and she's not on the farm." He motioned to the TV. "Woman was carried off today, supposedly by an alligator. The house's in Wellington, backs on the L-40. Little boy disappears yesterday, maybe drowns in the L-8 or, so the news says. Different name, same canal. Maybe he was eaten. Maybe there's a man-eating alligator on the loose."

"You think it's the Komodo?"

"What else could it be? It ain't no alligator. Obviously, after the Komodo bit Sanchez, she got into the canal and headed south. And now she's killed two people. Before I was just out some money. Now it's jailtime unless we find her first."

Kirkland thought for a moment. "I could take the drone there and look for her."

"No. There's too much activity. Someone would wonder what you're doing. It's too big an area anyway."

"So how do we find her?"

"We create a diversion. Get people looking for another animal while we look for the Komodo."

"How are we going to do that?

"Meet me back here at midnight. Bring Sanchez with you and the truck with the winch," Mumford said.

* * *

TJ turned into his neighborhood. A boy of perhaps ten or eleven, a soiled Miami Marlins baseball cap on his head, was dangling two large iguanas by their tails. One iguana, with a distinctive reddish front leg and foot, craned its neck looking around. *No doubt wondering how he got himself in that position. TJ smiled to himself.* The boy and he exchanged small waves. At first the boy had run away whenever he saw TJ. TJ figured it was his uniform that scared the boy, but the boy quickly determined that TJ wasn't after him. *Was the boy offering the iguanas for food or a pet? Probably didn't make a difference to him. Poor kid, just trying to make a buck.*

On a whim, TJ stopped and put the Impala in reverse. He powered down the window. "What's your name?"

"Miguel, señor."

"Tell me, Miguel, do people actually buy those things?"

The boy smiled "Si, señor." In only slightly accented English he continued, "They eat them. My mama uses them in huevos rancheros, sometimes she wraps the meat in a tortilla."

Please don't tell me they taste just like chicken, TJ thought with some dismay. "How much for them?" he asked.

The boy broke out a big smile. "Ten dollars each, señor."

TJ suspected the price was negotiable, but he wasn't interested in bargaining with the boy. He figured the kid's family could use the money. "Have you got something to carry them in?"

The boy nodded enthusiastically.

TJ pulled a twenty out of his wallet.

The boy pulled a burlap bag from around his belt and dumped the two iguanas into it.

When TJ got home, he opened the bag and released the iguanas. They were an invasive species, and by releasing them, he knew he was breaking the law he'd sworn to uphold, but he'd killed enough animals over the past few days, and two more iguanas wouldn't make any difference to Florida's ecosystem.

An idea struck him as he watched the iguanas disappear into the bushes. He called Sheriff Rodriguez. "I've been thinking," TJ began. "Sam Brown, lives on Lake Trafford, is a croc and gator expert. She's very highly regarded. I had her on my TV series when we did a show on the American crocodile."

"She?"

"Yeah. Sam's short for Samantha."

"Let's add her to the team if she's willing."

Sheriff Rodriguez liked the idea. Lake Trafford, east of Naples, was only a three-hour drive away. Sam could be in Palm Beach County in the morning. He took her number from TJ, a landline he noted with some amusement, and called her. His call went straight to voicemail, and the recorded message came as a surprise. Sam, it turned out, was in the Mary River wetlands floodplain in the northern territory of Australia. She was working on a project with the University of Queensland, studying saltwater crocodiles, and wouldn't be back for six months. Evidently, she wasn't worried about burglars, the sheriff thought. He left a message for Sam on the faint hope she checked her voice mail and pondered his next move.

Sheriff Rodriguez wasn't a man who easily gave up. He'd learned that from his parents who had twice attempted to escape from Cuba before finally making it in a small boat across the perilous Straits of Florida to Miami. A quick online query told the sheriff that Queensland, Australia, was thirteen hours ahead. A call to the Queensland Police Service was in order.

The local police found a graduate assistant who knew how to contact the team in the field. The budding herpetologist gave the sheriff a satellite phone number to call. Sheriff Rodriguez was mildly surprised when the phone was answered on his first attempt. Sam Brown was located, and, with a remarkably clear connection, Rodriguez was speaking with her in a matter of minutes.

"I'm very sorry about what happened to the two people but I don't know how I can help," she said. "I'm on a research trip in the northwest territories and won't be back in the States for a long time."

"Do you have any suggestions?"

"Why don't you contact the herpetology department at the University of Florida in Gainesville," she replied.

"Thank you," Rodriguez said.

The call ended pleasantly enough, and both parties thought that was the end of it. Neither could have imagined that Sam Brown would be on her way to Florida in twenty-four hours.

CHAPTER 9

Mumford opened the service gate at Animal World. Kirkland drove the farm's flatbed with the winch into the delivery area. Sanchez, pale and sweaty, sat next to him in the truck.

"You sure we won't be caught?" Kirkland asked.

"We won't," Mumford replied. "Guy on the cameras is probably asleep. I'll take care of the video when we're done." He pointed to the crocodile exhibit. "Drive to the back. Sanchez, get the meat."

Mumford unlocked a door behind a faux waterfall. "This is where it gets tricky."

They peered through a window. Yellow eyes were looking back. Some were swimming toward them.

"I don't know how they know we're here, but they know," Mumford said, holding a tranquillizer gun. "Quickly now." He opened the door to the croc pool. "Throw the meat out," he said to Sanchez as the crocs swam toward them.

Sanchez threw it out, and Mumford slammed the door shut. The crocs attacked the meat and soon afterward grew quiet. Mumford looked through the window. "Meat's laced with carfentanil. That'll keep them clam for a while." He looked through the window again. "Show time."

Kirkland and Sanchez each grabbed a pole with a hook on the end that resembled a shepherd's staff. Mumford pointed to a fourteen-foot croc that was sitting on the edge of the pool nearest them. "You know what to do." He opened the door to the pool and the door leading outside.

Kirkland and Sanchez stepped into pool area. A crocodile swam half-heartedly toward them. They ignored it and prodded the big croc. It sluggishly opened and closed its jaws but responded to their jabs and made its way out of the exhibit. Kirkland and Sanchez prodded it some more, and it wandered toward the delivery area.

"Stand back. Let it roam," Mumford said.

After a while, he walked up to the crocodile and shot it with a tranquilizer dart. The croc collapsed. "Get the truck and winch it up," he said to Kirkland. "But get some scales first."

Kirkland pulled out his knife and scraped some skin off the crocodile's belly.

"Why not just kill it?" Sanchez asked.

"How would we dispose of the body? And if somebody found it and figured out it didn't die of natural causes, there'd be a whole additional investigation."

They drove across Southern Boulevard to a marsh situated between the northeastern part of the Arthur Marshall Refuge and Flying Cow Road. It was a sixty-five-hundred-acre man-made preserve filled with aquatic plants. Formally known as a stormwater treatment area, it naturally filtered excess nutrients from the water before it flowed into the Everglades.

Kirkland and Sanchez wrestled the crocodile off the back of the truck. With a splash, it tumbled into the water and sank from sight

"Is it dead?" Sanchez asked.

"Don't know," Mumford answered.

* * *

TJ dreamed of a young boy and a woman crying for help as they disappeared into the dark waters of the canal. Awakened by his dream, his mind churned.

Two fatal alligator attacks on back-to-back days? Nothing like that had ever happened before in Florida. Unable to sleep, he got up and made some coffee.

He dressed in his uniform, a tan dress shirt with a gold Federal Wildlife Officer's badge on the right front pocket, the FWS patch on the left shoulder, dark brown trousers, and brown dress shoes. His preferred dress was more casual, a polo shirt with the FWS patch embroidered on it, but he was the FWS spokesperson and image was important.

TJ left his house and entered the large metal garage in the side yard he'd built after buying the house. The garage had room for six vehicles and was filled with many automotive tools, including lathes, compressors, and a hydraulic lift, he needed to rebuild cars.

His ride of choice for the drive up to Palm Beach was a 1964 Ford Thunderbird convertible, medium metallic blue—Brittany blue according to the build sheet—with a vinyl-blue interior and dark-blue top. His father wouldn't have approved of him driving a Ford, but TJ loved the styling, the sweep of the dash, and the airplane-like controls of *the flight deck instrument panel.*

He backed the car out of his driveway, careful not to put too much sideways pressure on the steering column as he turned the wheel. The car was equipped with a Swing-Away steering wheel, an option that moved the steering column and wheel to the right, allowing the driver to more easily get in and out of the car. It was designed to prevent the column from moving when the car was in motion. Unfortunately, the locking mechanism on the sixty-plus year-old T-Bird was worn, and if pushed too hard, the wheel and column would pop out of place and the car couldn't be steered. He chastised himself for not repairing it, but the T-Bird needed its exercise regardless. He'd be careful. He had a good feel for the mechanism's breaking point. As he pulled away, he looked to his left. The iguana with the reddish leg that he'd released the previous night was looking back at him.

He lived about an hour south of Palm Beach and an hour north of Miami. He was convenient to all the major highways in South Florida, and as the regional FWS expert on invasive species, he traveled a lot. Home prices were reasonable where he lived because if he were any farther west, his house would be in the Everglades.

The Everglades comprised 1.5 million acres, reduced from its natural three million by agriculture and development. The parks, preserves, refuges, and water treatment and storage areas within the remaining Everglades went by a variety of different names and were overseen by a myriad of different federal and state agencies, many with overlapping authority. The Seminole and Miccosukee Indian tribes also held rights to parts of the land. The plethora of overseers made coordinated management of the Everglades an ongoing challenge. Squabbles ensued over water levels and quality and how to address both issues. Developers played one agency off against the other.

Even the Federal government didn't have a unified approach to managing the Everglades. Jurisdiction was divided between the Fish & Wildlife Service and the National Park Service. Most people, he knew, were unaware of the difference between the FWS and the NPS, but it'd made all the difference to him when he'd decided which agency to join five years ago. FWS's mission was to protect wildlife and its environment. No camping and only limited visitor access were allowed on the lands they managed. On the other hand, the National Park Service was established to facilitate public enjoyment on the land it oversaw, which included such bucket-list destinations as the Grand Canyon and the Everglades National Park. The Park Service, somewhat derisively, referred to their sister organization as the protector of local fishing holes, while they protected culturally significant monuments. TJ would respond by saying the FWS protected animals from people, whereas the National Park Service protected people from animals.

The sun beat down on the T-Bird, and its aged air conditioner struggled to keep up, but he didn't mind. It was a pleasant change from the rain of the past few weeks. The big 390-cubic-inch engine hummed along effortlessly. He kept both hands firmly on the wheel because the car floated at high speed.

The Palm Beach County's sheriff's office was located, appropriately, on Gun Club Road, just off of Southern Boulevard. Sheriff Rodriguez and a short rotund man were having an animated conversation in one corner. TJ noted their rigid postures and sensed the tension in the air.

A striking African American woman, tall, thin, and dressed in a gray power suit, stood off to the side, talking on her cell phone. He knew the governor of Florida, Gail Johnson, by reputation. The first woman and the first African American to be elected governor of Florida. Still not fifty, her political aspirations were widely rumored to extend beyond the state.

The sheriff broke off his conversation, greeted TJ, and walked him over to the governor.

"TJ, I'd like you meet Governor Johnson."

The governor curtly nodded and continued with her phone conversation.

Next, Rodriguez introduced Bennett D'Costa. TJ looked down at the short man. He was greeted with a limp handshake and a cold look.

"Your damn gator killed my dog, then it killed those people. That was a champion show dog."

"I'm sorry about your dog," TJ said, "but how do you know it was killed by an alligator, and how do you know it's the same one we're looking for?"

"What else could it be? I live on the same canal as the people who were eaten."

TJ winced. "Did you see an alligator attack your dog?"

"No."

"Did anyone see it?"

"No."

"What about security cameras?"

D'Costa seemed to shrink slightly. "They aren't working."

Governor Johnson finished her call and turned her attention to TJ and Sheriff Rodriguez. "Gentlemen, I just got off the phone with officials from Disney World, which just happens to be the largest employer in our state. Bookings are being cancelled, even though Orlando is one hundred and fifty miles north of here. As you doubtless know, tourism generates over fifty billion dollars in revenue and ten percent of the jobs in our state. If they stay away, the economic impact on Florida will be disastrous."

She continued, "Just so you're clear, I want you to be upbeat and positive. We've had two tragic accidents in this state, and that's two too many. Tell the press how you're going to find this alligator and that everyone is safe."

"I understand," TJ said, "but finding one alligator is like finding a needle in a haystack. It might never be found."

D'Costa addressed the governor: "You see, I told you it was a mistake to have him involved."

"Why?" TJ asked.

"I did my research on you. You're an alarmist. You tell young children they're going to get eaten by pythons," D'Costa said.

"Don't be ridiculous," TJ fired back.

Sheriff Rodriguez and Governor Johnson turned to TJ.

"I did a Saturday morning children's TV show on local public television. I talked about animals in the Everglades—" TJ said.

"And, one morning you told the kids about giant pythons taking over the Everglades and to be careful because a python could eat a child," D'Costa charged.

"That's not exactly—"

D'Costa interrupted again, "Your show was cancelled right after that."

Sheriff Rodriguez held up his hands. "Okay. That's not important." He fixed his eyes on TJ. "Unless you think a python's involved."

"No, I don't."

"Then let's get back to business," the sheriff said. "We have the forensics report on Bobby Powell's shoe. Bobby was blood-typed at birth, and the blood on the shoe is a match. And the saliva on it is reptilian."

"That confirms it," Governor Johnson said. "Now we know we have a man-eating alligator on the loose."

Killer, yes. Man-eater, probably not, TJ thought, but he'd keep it to himself.

The governor and D'Costa left for the news conference.

"Guy's a piece of work," TJ said after they'd gone. "Two people dead, and all he cares about is his dog. Who is he?"

"Bennett D'Costa. A legend in his own mind. Attorney for the finest strip clubs, massage parlors, and other such establishments in Palm Beach County. Throws his weight around, and I mean that figuratively as well as literally, in political circles. He's the guy who's been calling me about his dog. When I didn't drop everything to run out to his house, he called the governor . . . and his research on you . . . no doubt it was done by his paralegal."

"Too bad his surveillance equipment wasn't working; we might've gotten lucky . . . But that'd be too easy . . ."

The sheriff chuckled. "You have a thing about cameras don't you." Then he continued, "I asked him the same question before you arrived. It wasn't working because he's in a dispute with his security company."

* * *

The sheriff's department auditorium was filled with press and concerned residents. Governor Johnson stood at the podium with the Powells and Mitchell Herzog just behind her. He noticed D'Costa whispering something to Herzog, then disappearing backstage.

"Our hearts go out to the families of Bobby Powell and Judy Herzog," the governor began. "I have assured them that we will find their missing loved ones. And we will find and kill the alligator that was responsible for their deaths. These were tragic but isolated instances, and I want our residents and visitors to know that you have nothing to fear."

TJ was impressed by Johnson's self-assuredness and the absolute certainty with which she spoke. Her brief remarks concluded, the governor moved aside, and stood next to Herzog.

Next, Sheriff Rodriguez stepped to the microphones and described what was known about the two disappearances. The audience stirred when he revealed reptile saliva had been found on Bobby Powell's shoe. "Our search for the missing persons is ongoing. We will find them. And, we're utilizing walkers, scent hounds, boats, divers, and trappers to find the alligator."

"Now I would like to introduce Supervisory Officer TJ Forte of the US Fish & Wildlife Service," the sheriff continued. "He's in charge of search efforts in the Arthur Marshall Refuge and is liaising with our department. He's here to discuss alligator behavior."

TJ tried not to look directly into the bright light of the television news pool camera and to ignore the photo camera flashes. On the podium in front of him were the notes he'd made last night. "There are more than a million alligators in the state of Florida, but they don't eat humans," he began. "Only about ten humans a year are bitten by alligators in Florida. Almost all are the fault of the person bitten for approaching or feeding the animal. Fatalities are even rarer, only about one every three years. A person is fifteen times more likely to be killed by a lightning strike than an alligator. Bees kill more people in Florida every year than do alligators."

He paused for a breath. "Alligators avoid people and typically flee when approached. They stay in or near the water for two reasons. First, their diet consists of mainly fish, turtles, and small animals they come across in or near the water. Second, it's their means of escape if threatened."

He felt Governor Johnson's eyes boring into him. He knew he was raising doubts as to an alligator having killed the boy and woman, but he wasn't going to bend the facts to placate her.

"Alligators have been more active than usual due to the rains and high water, but if you're careful around water, there's nothing to worry about. Report any suspicious alligator sightings, especially any alligator near a home, or one that doesn't flee from humans."

With TJ's remarks completed, Governor Johnson opened the briefing for questions. The reporters pounced. "Officer Forte, were Bobby Powell and Judy Herzog eaten by an alligator?" one reporter shouted.

"Not in the sense that they were devoured. An alligator may have bitten off some flesh, but, as I said, alligators don't eat people."

"Even if they weren't eaten, it must be a horrible way to die," the reporter persisted. "We've all seen the videos of alligators rolling around with victims in their mouth."

TJ squirmed. "What you're referring to is called the death roll. Most of the videos are of crocodiles in Africa or Australia. They're much more prone to do that. They spin around rapidly in the water, drowning their prey." What he didn't go on to say was that the death roll was a way to pulverize the victim's body, making it easier for the killer to tear off chunks of flesh.

"How will you know for sure Bobby and Judy weren't eaten until you either find the bodies or the gator?" another reporter asked.

"Obviously, we won't, but alligators drown their prey, so there's every reason to believe we'll recover the bodies." He quickly pointed to another reporter.

"Were there two alligators?" a second reporter asked.

"It's possible," he said.

Behind him, TJ heard Governor Johnson groan.

"How will you know if any alligator you catch is the killer?" a TV reporter asked.

"The only way we'll know for sure is to gut the animal and examine its stomach for human remains." Trying to bring the session to a positive and less grisly close, TJ said he was confident the victims' remains would be found, but he said nothing about finding the alligator.

Governor Johnson picked up on TJ's omission. She stepped in front of him and assured the audience that the gator would be quickly found and killed. Then she ended the press conference. When they were off stage, Johnson shot TJ a withering look. "Didn't you hear what I said before we began? Be upbeat, positive. And what did you say? One gator, maybe two. Don't know if we'll ever find it?"

"It's not magic," TJ said in defense. "It's not like when someone calls about a gator in the pond behind their house. Practically speaking, all alligators look alike, and we aren't even sure where this one is." He was tempted to say one or ones, but he didn't want to further provoke the governor.

"You did a helluva job reassuring everyone we had this under control." Johnson didn't hide her sarcasm. "The press is going to have a field day." She turned to confront Sheriff Rodriguez. "You better find those bodies and that damn gator fast." Then she gave TJ a baleful glance. "And he never speaks to the press again."

CHAPTER 10

"Not a good ending," TJ said after they'd returned to Sheriff Rodriquez's office.

"Don't let it get to you. Problem is politicians don't have to tell the truth," the sheriff responded. "We do."

"Thanks. I'll remember that if I ever run for office."

"What's your next step?"

"I'd like to see the Powells' property."

"Okay. I'll take you."

TJ and the sheriff left the PBSO building by a side door to escape the reporters milling about. They needn't have worried. It was raining, and no press were in sight as they exited. Evidently, staying dry was more important to the media than follow-up questions. They drove off in the sheriff's SUV, tires splashing through puddles as they went.

They drove west on Southern Boulevard into Loxahatchee, and then turned north on Seminole-Pratt Whitney Road. It was one of those odd Florida roads that went from being a major four-lane divided thoroughfare to a two-lane highway and, then a dirt road in under three miles. TJ and the sheriff turned into a residential area before the road narrowed. On the way, the rain stopped as quickly as it had begun, and the bright sun immediately reappeared.

They arrived at the Powells' home. Water was steaming off the driveway. It was hotter and more humid than before the rain. Such was the nature of subtropic South Florida in August. TJ walked around the house, while the sheriff spoke with the Powells. They'd been through enough; he'd leave them alone. He was looking at dark stained grass staked off with bright yellow crime scene tape when Rodriguez joined him.

"What we know is Bobby was playing with his dog in the yard," the sheriff began. "His father was mowing the lawn and went into the house to get a beer. His mother came out immediately after. The dog was still here, unharmed, but Bobby was gone. They started looking for him, and Mrs. Powell called 911. Neighbors heard their screams and joined in the search."

"Anyone see or hear anything?"

"No and it's a quiet neighborhood. No registered sex offenders or the like, so we ruled out kidnapping. Come on, I'll show you where the shoe was found."

They headed to the levee, and Sheriff Rodriguez pointed out dried drops of blood on the grass. They walked past a row of cypress trees. Beyond the tress, the still wet grass was uncut and darkened TJ's khakis up to his knees.

Suddenly Rodriguez let out a yell and jumped back. TJ tensed, a puzzled look on his face. Then he spotted movement on the ground and grinned as a three-foot-long black snake slithered past. "I don't think he's the culprit."

Rodriguez ignored the comment.

At the top of the berm was a hard dirt path that ran parallel to the canal, just like the one behind the Herzogs' house. TJ was struck by the fact that both the Powells' and Herzogs' houses backed on a berm that was a good eight-feet tall. An excellent vantage point for a hunter. There the similarities ended. The Powells had a modest one-story house that could fit inside the Herzogs' house with plenty of room to spare. Yet both were joined by a common tragedy and one that the Herzogs' money couldn't change.

At the edge of the canal was another marked off area. "This is where the boy's shoe was found. The rain's washed away the saliva." He then pointed down the canal. "That's a bidirectional pumping station. It's running south because of the discharge from Lake O. The suction could have pulled the boy in or through."

"Not a pleasant thought," TJ said. He looked down the canal. There was an aluminum boat in front of it with a black-suited diver holding on to the side. The diver said something to the men in the boat, put his regulator in his mouth, and disappeared under the water.

"I didn't want to say this at the news conference, but there was a problem closing the gates," Rodriguez said. "Tree trunk got lodged in one. South Florida Water Management just got them closed this morning. But with the discharge from Lake O, they have to be reopened within twenty-four hours, or the canal will overflow, so we've got to search quickly. We've also got divers working south of the station."

Sheriff Rodriguez was about to continue when his mobile rang. He took the call. A concerned look came over his face as he listened. "Tell him we'll meet him there in five minutes." The call finished; he said to TJ, "Come on. We're going to Animal World," and started down the hill.

"Animal World? Why?"

"One of their crocs is missing."

* * *

Back in the sheriff's SUV, TJ entered Animal World into a map app on his phone. "Less than three miles," he said. "The canal runs close by, and it's about halfway between the Powells' and the Herzogs.'"

"You thinking what I'm thinking?" Rodriguez replied.

"Yeah. What do you know about the place?"

"Run by Al Mumford, goes by Big Al. You'll see why. He married the daughter of the owners of Pure Sugar. Smartest thing he ever did. Took over running it when they got too old. World class jerk, if you ask me. The land was no good for growing sugar cane, so some years ago, he put an animal park on it. Small time. Okay operation. Some issues with the regulators over the years. I recall that they once had to close down for a few days. Don't remember why, though."

Arriving at Animal World, they passed under a large archway, surrounded by lush tropical plants, with a brightly colored sign welcoming visitors. There were surprisingly few cars in the parking lot despite Florida schools being on summer break for only a few more days. "Parents are keeping their kids at home," TJ speculated. Sheriff Rodriguez didn't comment as he pulled up to the entrance pavilion and stopped in a no parking zone. *Must be nice to park anywhere you want*, TJ thought.

Mumford was waiting for them in a six-passenger golf cart. "Let's go to the crocodile exhibit, and I'll show you how it escaped. I'll be happy to answer any questions on the way."

As they weaved through the park, TJ noted they were headed in the direction of the canal. Mumford pulled to a stop in front of the crocodile pen. It consisted of a large pool of water, with a tall artificial rock wall and waterfall behind it. The men got out and a pair of cruel greenish-yellow eyes with a black vertical slit silently broke the water's surface. They were quickly joined by others. A dozen crocodiles with cold reptilian stares tracked the men.

TJ nodded toward one of the crocs. "Nile or Australian?"

"Nile," Mumford replied. "How'd you know?"

"The way they're tracking us is way too aggressive for an American croc."

"TJ, please stop talking in code," Sheriff Rodriguez said.

TJ smiled. "Of course, Sheriff. Let's start with the difference between an alligator and a crocodile. Alligators have rounded snouts and will run from humans unless surprised or protecting their nest. Crocodiles have longer narrower snouts. They're also a little lighter in color but the snouts are the tell. As for the American croc, they're relatively few in number and found farther south of here. They're pretty laid back. Nile crocodiles will eat you as soon as look at you."

"And now one is missing," Rodriguez said. "When and how?"

"We've reviewed the surveillance tapes," Mumford said. "It was three days ago."

"Finally a security camera that works," TJ said.

Mumford gave him a puzzled look.

"Private joke," Rodriguez said. "We'll want a copy."

"You don't count them every day?" TJ asked.

"We're always watching the animals, but no," Mumford replied. "They move around, hide in their dens, and, in the case of the crocs, spend a lot of time underwater. The animals don't give us problems. It's the humans that misbehave, try to get into exhibits, and the like. You'd be surprised at how many people think it would be fun to spend the night here. We count the crocs when we feed them and when we lower the water level to clean the pool."

Sheriff Rodriguez nodded thoughtfully.

"As to how, please follow me," Mumford said. He led them behind the enclosure, then through a door. They were standing between a nine-foot-tall reinforced chain-link fence and an artificial rock wall that formed the back of the exhibit.

"He jumped the fence," TJ said.

"You're right," Mumford said.

"How'd you know?" Sheriff Rodriguez asked surprised.

TJ pointed to the top of the fence. The twisted wire prongs were bent in one place. "The discoloration is dried blood, and it looks like your croc left a couple of belly scales behind."

"Right, again," Mumford confirmed. Then he directed their attention to another door, with a small window, that led directly into the croc pen and pool area. He pointed through the window at a small ledge high up on the front of the rock wall. "We think the croc jumped up there, came down the back of the wall behind the exhibit, and climbed the fence."

"Oh, come on, how is that possible?" Sheriff Rodriguez asked.

"Crocs and gators can use their tail to propel their entire body vertically out of the water," TJ said. "How big was the one that escaped?"

"Fourteen feet," Mumford said.

TJ whistled. "That's a big boy."

"You mean to tell me a crocodile can jump fourteen feet straight up?" Rodriguez asked in dismay.

"Out of the water, yes," Mumford replied. "We thought the ledge was too small and too high for a croc to get to but, apparently, we were wrong."

"You had an Olympic-class jumper," TJ said.

"What about the fence?" Sheriff Rodriguez asked. "How'd he climb that?"

"Crocs are excellent climbers," TJ said. "They can climb trees. The links in the fence were perfect toe holds for him."

"Why would he do it?" Rodriguez asked.

"Don't know," Mumford replied. "All the animals have been a little crazy since the hurricane. Maybe there was a fight, maybe he smelled something, or maybe he just jumped and found himself on the ledge and one thing led to another."

"And you're sure he did this by himself. He wasn't helped or stolen?" asked Rodriguez.

"Nope. Our cameras captured him wandering around the park, eventually disappearing through the trees between the park and the canal.

"Great. Just when I thought the day couldn't get worse, now we have a man-eating crocodile on the loose," the sheriff said.

On the drive back to the sheriff's office, both men were on their phones. TJ called the Arthur Marshall headquarters station to close the refuge and deploy his officers. He enlisted park rangers to supplement them and sent everyone out in boats into the marsh and the L-40 canal.

Sheriff Rodriguez knew Governor Johnson would be angry at him for not calling her first, but it was more important that he warn his deputies and the civilian searchers. There was a man-eating crocodile out there somewhere. It would attack and kill without hesitation. Any search team not accompanied by an armed deputy was told to stand down.

"Most trappers don't carry guns," TJ reminded the sheriff. "They consider it a badge of honor to capture alligators with ropes and hooks."

"My orders apply to them too."

Predictably, Governor Johnson wasn't happy with Sheriff Rodriguez when he called her. She said she was coming back to West Palm. They'd hold their second press conference of the day and get out in front of this. She reminded him that TJ was not welcome. The call with Johnson ended, and the sheriff sighed. "Have we found our killer?" he asked TJ.

"Maybe. The timeline fits and the canal runs past the two houses and Animal World. You know I had doubts about the alligator hypothesis. It's much easier to believe a Nile crocodile killed the boy and the woman. At the same time, the distance bothers me. The croc would have to swim three miles against the current and get past the pumping station. Then he'd have to get past the pumping station again and travel another six or seven miles south to the Herzogs'. That's a lot of swimming."

"Well, we know this guy's very active," Sheriff Rodriguez said.

TJ responded without conviction, "I guess."

"Please don't tell me you think we're looking for a crocodile *and* an alligator," Rodriguez said.

"I hope not."

CHAPTER 11

Sanchez peeled back the bandage and studied his wound. It hurt and wept blood when pressed, unchanged from twenty-four hours ago. Why wasn't the antibiotic working? He wiped his face with a damp towel. He knew he wasn't sweating from the heat. He was just as weak as the day before and still unable to work for more than short periods of time.

Doug Kirkland wasn't an easy man under the best of circumstances. Now the foreman was doubly angry at him: for letting the Komodo escape and being unable to work. Even worse, Kirkland knew he had forged papers and had threatened to turn him in. That would mean a one-way trip back to Honduras and the vicious gang members he'd fled three years ago. Still, he doubted Kirkland would call the authorities because Sanchez knew all about his reptile smuggling business. But he couldn't be sure how Kirkland would react. He'd once seen him beat a farm hand almost senseless over nothing. Sanchez sighed deeply. He knew Kirkland didn't want him going back to the doctor, but something was very wrong with him. He was getting worse, not better. He made his decision, took a set of keys off a peg, and drove a farm truck to MediRedi.

At the clinic a nurse took Sanchez's vitals. Shortly thereafter, Dr. Dudnick entered the examination room, studying the chart he held in his hands. "Back for your second IV?" He paused when he saw Sanchez's pale and clammy appearance. He consulted the chart again. Temperature 101 degrees. "Still have a fever, I see. Blood pressure low, pulse high. Hmm."

Dr. Dudnick unwrapped the bandage and manipulated the wound. Sanchez winched at the pressure. "Hurts?"

"Yes. A lot."

"Your wound appears septic, and you aren't responding to the antibiotic. We need to get you to the Lakeview ER right away."

Sanchez squirmed and thought for a moment. "There's a guy waiting for me outside," he lied. "He can take me to the hospital. But since I'm already here, will you give me the second IV?"

Dr. Dudnick agreed on the condition that Sanchez would go to the ER right afterward. Along with the antibiotic, he gave Sanchez a liter of normal saline to keep him hydrated and to raise his blood pressure.

Sanchez left, hoping Kirkland hadn't missed him and wondering what he was going to do next.

* * *

The second press conference of the day began at 5 p.m. The crowd was bigger than in the morning and spilled into the hallway of the PBSO headquarters building. Monitors had been hastily set up outside the auditorium to accommodate the overflow.

Governor Johnson had helicoptered back up from Miami. She had a home and satellite office there and preferred it to spending August in Tallahassee. She'd grudgingly relented, at the urging of her staff, to allow TJ to speak again. After all, he'd been introduced in the morning as the FWS wildlife expert, and it would raise questions if he weren't there to talk about the crocodile. Now TJ, Sheriff Rodriguez, and the governor stood on the stage, facing the crowd.

Sheriff Rodriguez stepped up to the podium, adjusted the microphones, made introductions, summarized the day's events, then explained when and how the crocodile had escaped from Animal World. The audience gasped as he described the fourteen foot, fourteen-hundred-pound predator. "The crocodile that escaped from Animal World could have been responsible for the death of one or both individuals," he said. "Officer Forte will have more to say about that. But I want to caution everyone that despite speculation in the media, there's no proof that the Animal World crocodile attacked or ate either person. All other animals are accounted for, and the park has pledged all possible assistance to help us find the crocodile."

Then it was TJ's turn. He began by describing the difference in appearance between a crocodile and an alligator. He went on to say: "Nile crocodiles, like the one that escaped from Animal World, are highly aggressive toward humans and can easily kill a person. Local residents need to be extra vigilant and stay away from ponds, lakes, and canals until this dangerous animal is found."

Animal World, he pointed out, was on the same canal system as the Powell and Herzog houses. "The Powells' house is about three miles north," he explained. "And the Herzogs' house is about the same distance south. A crocodile could easily swim those distances." But, like the sheriff, he cautioned the audience not to rush to any conclusions. There were still questions to be answered. "Why would the animal swim north against the current and then turn around and swim south? How did the crocodile twice get safely past the pumping station on the canal just below the Powells' house?"

TJ felt an obligation for full disclosure. The Powells and the Herzogs deserved that, but he knew he had to make his next point very carefully. Governor Johnson wasn't going to be happy. He took a breath and pressed on. "Alligators, crocodiles, and reptiles in general, don't eat twice in two days. This suggests either the individuals weren't attacked for food, or there were two different animals involved. Also puzzling is the fact that crocodiles, just like alligators, hunt in or near water. Why did the animal or animals leave the water and travel some distance over land to attack the two victims?"

Governor Johnson stirred uncomfortably behind him.

Sheriff Rodriguez then opened the meeting up for questions. The first was for him. He answered: "We asked the same question, and yes, all their animals have microchips implanted in them."

"Then can you track the crocodile?" the reporter continued.

"No. Microchips don't have a power source and can't transmit. They aren't GPSs. They respond to a scanner that's held close to the animal. When the crocodile is found, we can confirm it's Animals World's, but, no, we can't track it."

The next question was for TJ. "Officer Forte, can a crocodile from Africa survive in the Everglades?"

"Certainly. The Everglades is a very hospitable environment for a Nile crocodile. In fact, they're already here." TJ heard Gail Johnson's groan and saw the audience stir. "Let me explain," he said. "The US Fish & Wildlife Department and the Florida Fish and Wildlife Conservation Commission have captured Nile crocodiles on a few occasions. Thus far, they've all been genetically related. This suggests they came from a common source and either escaped or were released. There have been no recent sightings, but we assume there are others out there."

"How's that possible?" the reporter asked.

TJ knew his answer would provoke the governor, but he felt compelled to make people aware. "South Florida is an ideal home for many exotic species. We have a hospitable climate and lots of places to hide and find food in our wetlands. You've all seen iguanas and many of you have seen tegus. Twenty years ago, no one imagined Burmese pythons could establish a breeding population in South Florida, but now we estimate there are over one hundred thousand of them. Just recently a sixteen-foot female, with almost eighty fertilized eggs in her, was caught."

The governor stepped up to the podium. "I think we're all familiar with your views on pythons, Officer Forte. You've scared us enough, so let's move on."

"Could an American crocodile be responsible for the attack?" another reporter asked.

Governor Johnson reluctantly ceded the podium back to TJ but glared at him from off camera.

"There are only about two thousand American crocodiles in Florida," he explained. "They're mostly found in the Miami area, mostly near the coast because they like brackish salty water. They aren't like Nile crocodiles. They have a calm temperament, and they haven't been known to attack humans, although I don't recommend going near one."

"How likely is it that you'll catch the crocodile?" a third reporter shouted.

"If he stayed in the area around the Herzogs, it's quite possible we will. African crocodiles are too aggressive to hide. Someone, hopefully a law enforcement agent, will spook him, and he'll attack. However, if he's gone into the Everglades, we might never find him."

"And as long as he's out there, no one's safe," the reporter said. "He will keep killing." It was a statement, not a question.

"There's no need to panic, just take sensible precautions."

The governor started toward the podium again but froze when a reporter from one of the TV stations yelled out: "Do you think the Bobby Powell and Judy Herzog were eaten alive?"

TJ frowned. "Let's not sensationalize this."

"But it's possible?"

"Yes, it is."

Governor Johnson stepped in, "That's enough questions for now." She faced TJ. "Despite Officer Forte's overactive imagination, the logical conclusion is that there is only one animal involved, and it's the escaped Animal World crocodile. This crocodile will be found and killed. I want to again assure everyone that our waterways, tourist attractions, and your homes are completely safe."

Guffaws and catcalls erupted from the audience. Stone-faced, Governor Johnson stepped back from the podium.

The briefing was over; the speakers left the stage. Governor Johnson confronted TJ and Sheriff Rodriguez in the hallway behind the auditorium. "This is a nightmare." Turning to TJ, she said: "Forte, how stupid can you be? You've got a crocodile on the loose. A little boy and woman are missing, certainly dead and probably eaten. And what do you say? *Why did the crocodile swim upstream? Why?* Who knows why? *Why did it escape?* Who knows? Who cares? I've already told you twice today that your job was to calm people down, assure them that you'd find it. And what do you do? Suggest there may be two man-eaters out there, and they may never be found. They may strike again. So much for reassuring the public. You made all of us look like fools. I shouldn't have listened to my staff. I knew it was a mistake to let you speak. Every hotel and restaurant owner in the state is going to be calling me. And, what do you know about crocodiles? Nothing." She looked at the sheriff. "I want you to do something."

Rodriguez remained silent for a moment and then said, "There is a croc expert."

"Who? Where?" the governor demanded.

"Samantha Brown. She lives in Lake Trafford, but she's in Australia right now and not coming back anytime soon."

"Oh, yes she is!" Governor Johnson said and then turned to TJ. "You're fired. Off the investigation."

As the governor stormed off, TJ held his temper and didn't tell her that she couldn't fire a federal officer, although he knew she could make trouble for him. Better to let things cool down, he thought, than to contradict her.

When the governor was out of earshot, Rodriguez apologized for not giving TJ the credit for the Sam Brown idea. "If she knew it was your idea, she probably wouldn't have agreed to it."

"I think you're right about that." They agreed to speak in the morning.

TJ left the building and crossed the parking lot. He saw the governor's helicopter on the nearby helipad as he settled into his T-Bird. He was about to close the door when the handle was ripped out of his hand and the door yanked wide open.

Governor Johnson leaned in. "You let me down Forte," she hissed. "And I won't forget it."

Before TJ could respond, she stepped back and slammed the car door shut so hard that the steering column jumped out of position.

CHAPTER 12

Up before the sun, TJ had a plan and smiled to himself. *A little adversity didn't stop an ex-navy pilot.* He put his dishes in the dishwasher, grabbed the trash, then his gear, and headed out the door. He looked over at the garage and saw the red-legged iguana looking back at him. On a whim, he opened the trash bag, took out the remains of a salad, and put it on the ground.

In the garage was his eleven-year-old, big-block 5.3-liter V-8 Chevy Trailblazer, the only practical vehicle he owned. He tossed a duffel bag in the back seat. Experience had taught him to bring a change of clothes when he was going on the water. His duty belt and holster holding his Sig Sauer pistol were next to him. He liked Sigs because they worked when wet, and things got wet in the Everglades. He was trained in its use by both the navy and FWS, but he rarely saw the need to carry a weapon. Today was an exception.

He listened to the radio as he drove. The talk was all about the escaped Animal World crocodile and that it had probably eaten both Bobby Powell and Judy Herzog. There was speculation as to when and where it would strike next. The locals were worried enough. TJ didn't like the press stirring them up any more than they already were but, he had to admit, he was wondering the same thing.

Arriving at a warehouse at the Arthur Marshall Refuge, he checked his texts. There was one from the Corvette owner asking if he was still interested. He texted back that he was. *Wonder when I'll find the time to sell any of my cars.* Then he called Sheriff Rodriguez. The sheriff chuckled. "Wasn't sure I'd be hearing from you this morning. Before she left last night, the governor said something about calling Washington."

"Well, she did and I got an earful last night. But federal agencies don't like being told what to do, even by governors. And the Arthur Marshall Refuge is in the jurisdiction of US Fish & Wildlife, so I'm still on the case. But don't expect to see Governor Johnson and me in the same room anytime soon."

Sheriff Rodriguez chuckled again. "How're you holding up?"

"This may be worse than plebe summer at the Academy, at least I knew when that was going to end."

"We've got help this morning. Broward's sheriff's department is working the lower part of the canal. The Highway Patrol is assisting with traffic. By the way, the state has closed Animal World until further notice."

"Probably a good idea. What about state fish and wildlife?"

"Not a word."

"I guess politics still prevails."

"Apparently so. On another subject, my IT guys tell me the YouTube videos from the press conference yesterday have gotten one million hits thus far. You don't want to know what the comments say."

"I can only imagine. Any good news?"

The sheriff hesitated. "News, yes. Good, not so. We've gotten over a hundred calls this morning from people saying they've seen the croc. Parents everywhere below Lake O won't let their children outside. Hotel reservations are being cancelled not just here but throughout the state. According to Johnson, Florida hasn't seen that many cancellations since COVID-19."

"You can't blame people for being careful."

"Tell that to the governor."

The call completed; TJ hitched a trailer with an airboat on it to his Trailblazer. The boat had a flat bottom and a flat front angled upward, resembling a World War II landing craft. It had one bench seat, running from side to side, with the driver's seat centered behind it. The driver sat five feet off the floor of the boat, which provided for excellent visibility. The trade-off was a high center of gravity, and an inexperienced operator could easily capsize the boat. The GM V-8 marine engine that powered it was below the driver, and the airplane propeller, surrounded by a safety cage, that pushed it forward was directly behind the motor. The airboat was steered by an airplane-type stick connected to two rudders mounted behind the propeller. Designed to skim over the water and grasses of the Everglades, the airboat could even travel over dry land, but it was a bumpy ride.

TJ towed the boat up the highway. Its rudders acted as sails, and he wrestled the Trailblazer left and right to compensate. Kenny Loggins repeatedly sang Danger Zone, beckoning him to answer, until he'd put his cell on vibrate. He had his hands full managing the trailer in the morning traffic. There were too many people texting and drinking coffee. The woman behind him appeared more worried about applying her makeup than running into the airboat. His phone had starting ringing as soon as he'd left the sheriff's office last night. How did so many people get his phone number? There were calls from the press that he knew better than to return. A friend called telling him that a cable channel was having a TJ Forte marathon, showing all the episodes from his short-lived television series. Every third and fourth being the episode about crocodiles in Florida and his final show about pythons in the Everglades.

With a sigh of relief, TJ exited onto Southern Boulevard, passed Flying Cow Road, crossed over the canal, and arrived at the Twenty Mile Boat Ramp. He was at the top of the Arthur Marshall. Sweat trickled down his back and the armpits of his shirt darkened as he winched the airboat into the water and secured it. Despite the heat, he wore a big floppy hat, long-sleeve shirt, lightweight work pants, and boots. The hat and shirt were better sun block than any cream or lotion. The long pants and boots were protection from snakes.

With the Trailblazer parked and locked, TJ climbed in the airboat, untied the rope, and gave a push. The boat slid easily and began turning in a lazy arc. He gave a sigh of relief. He was on the water, where he should be, leading his team and looking for the crocodile.

He radioed instructions to his teams in the refuge and received word back that all was quiet. He put on a pair of noise-suppressing headphones and turned the key. The big engine roared to life. He engaged the propeller, and the boat took off. His destination was the marsh behind the Herzogs' house.

The airboat skimmed over the waters of the flooded wet prairie. TJ navigated around the hammocks and tree mounds, staying in the sloughs, the clear channels, as he headed south. He passed a large bed of tall cattails, an invasive plant that was crowding out the natural vegetation. Occasionally, he had to go over sawgrass that buffeted the flat-bottomed airboat, causing it to tilt and skid sideways. If it slid too far to one side, it would spin around and flip. He worked the throttle and tiller. It was a challenge even for an experienced operator like him.

TJ felt good being on the water. He was at home in the refuge. He knew its sloughs were deceptive, their depth changing from a few inches to many feet with no warning, and that the grasses that grew in the waters, providing safety for small fish, could easily tangle and drown a person.

Being in the refuge reminded TJ of time he'd spent with his father. Saginaw, Michigan, one hundred miles north of Detroit, was a great place for a boy to grow up. His fondest memories were of the times he and his father took their motorboat up the Saginaw River and into the Saginaw Bay on Lake Huron. It was on these trips that TJ came to love and respect the water. Sometimes he and his father would take the river south. They'd cross into the Shiawassee National Wildlife Refuge and silently drift up to great flocks of Canadian geese and hear the splash of a turtle as it disappeared from view. Years later, he discovered that the Shiawassee marsh was remarkably similar to the Everglades and, like Great Blue Herons, many of the same species of birds and animals inhabited both places.

Life in the Rust Belt was difficult back then. Chevrolet was losing a little more market share each year, parts production had moved overseas, and employment opportunities were shrinking. He was conflicted because he wanted to help, but he knew he had to leave.

Acceptance at the Naval Academy satisfied his dual desires to serve and to be on the water. He went to Annapolis with the goal of captaining a destroyer. He'd never been on an airplane, even the ten-hour trip from

Saginaw to Annapolis was by car. Then, one day, a navy pilot took TJ up in a trainer, and he was hooked.

After his five years in the navy, he entered the University of Florida's program in Wetland Sciences. Upon graduation, he knew he didn't want to return to the Rust Belt. There were too many bad memories, and the vibrant community in which he'd grown up was now empty buildings and rundown houses. So when the US Fish & Wildlife Service recruited him, he requested a posting in the south. His skills for observation and pursuit honed as a pilot made him ideally suited for finding and removing invasive species from the Everglades.

TJ continued on, zigzagging to keep in clear water as much as possible. He waved to a pair of rangers in an FWS bass boat as he passed by. The second story of the Herzogs' house soon came into view over the levee. He cut the engine, letting the boat drift, removed his headphones, and looked around.

The current gently carried TJ's airboat deeper into the refuge. He looked to his right. There was an FWS boat in the next slough over and two more in the sloughs beyond. They drifted south in a parallel line. He looked left and saw officers on the top of the levee. Two men, holding rifles, walked in unison with the boats. *Like beaters trying to flush a tiger,* he thought. This was his plan. They might see the long, pointed snout of the crocodile, or it might attack as they approached. Of course, it might be basking on a hammock or tree mound and ignore them as they passed by. Or it could be somewhere else. He knew it was a longshot, but no one had come up with a better plan.

The roof lines of the Herzogs' neighborhood gave way to treetops as TJ passed the Wellington Environmental Preserve. The staccato tapping of a woodpecker caught his attention, but he couldn't spot the bird. He glided past herons and egrets, wading in the water at the edge of the many small islands rising up out of the marsh.

A shiver of excitement bolted through him when he saw the first pair of eyes and nostrils seeming to float on top of the water. But the snout was too short, and too round. He passed a second alligator, and then a third. His hat provided ample coverage from the beating sun, but sweat trickled down his back. He took a swig of water, then tossed the empty plastic bottle into the well of the boat and reached down for a new bottle on the seat in front of him. As he did, he spied movement in the water. A snake, its body undulating in the shape of an S as it swam. The sun's reflection on the water and its wet skin made it hard to tell its color. *Small head, not a Water Moccasin,* he thought. *Not a python, either. Not yet.*

His cell phone, still on mute, vibrated. TJ dug it out of his shirt pocket and looked at it. A text. It was a picture of Bobby Powell's shoe, with a tooth mark and a clear dried substance visible on it. TJ assumed it was taken by a sheriff's department photographer, but no picture like it had been released to the press. Below the picture was a message: *Urgent. We need to talk.* The heading above the picture said: *No Name.*

An exchange of texts ensued. The two agreed to meet at the Twenty Mile Bend Boat Ramp in fifteen minutes. TJ put his headphones back on, turned the boat around, and gunned the engine. He arrived at the boat launch and saw a small thin man, manilla envelope in hand, waiting for him.

"Officer Thomas Jefferson Forte?" the man asked.

"Yes, what can I do for you?"

The man handed the envelope to TJ. When he took it, the man said, "Officer Forte, you have been served with a subpoena to appear at a deposition in the case of D'Costa vs. Animal World."

TJ opened his mouth but was speechless. He quickly recovered. "How did you get my number and where did you get the picture of the shoe?"

"I'm sorry, but you'll have to ask my client, Mr. D'Costa." Then the man headed back to his car.

TJ walked to his Trailblazer, threw the envelope on the front seat, and slammed the door. Walking back to his airboat, he was about to step onboard when Sheriff Rodriquez called.

"I was thinking of calling you," TJ said. "I just got served by our new best friend, D'Costa."

"Yeah, I did, too. But that's not why I'm calling. Bobby Powell's body has been found. I'm at the Powells'. It's not something you want to see, but you should see it."

"I'm on my way."

CHAPTER 13

Doug Kirkland was worried. The boy and the woman had disappeared after the Komodo dragon escaped. He'd tracked her to the edge of the canal. Some quick research told him that Komodos were good swimmers. He knew the Komodo had eaten the two humans. He'd rather she'd drowned in the canal.

Things didn't get any better when Al Mumford walked into the barn and glared at him. "The state health department called my office. They've been trying to reach Sanchez. Said he wasn't returning their calls. Want to talk to him about his gator bite. Seems a MediRedi doc reported it yesterday."

"Damn him! He must have gone back for the IV. I told him not to," Kirkland responded.

"We can't let him talk to anyone. He knows about the Komodo."

"He may suspect," Mumford said.

"And the croc. What about the tape the sheriff wanted?"

"I sent his office a flash drive with a video of the croc outside his pen, wandering around the park and getting out. The security system overwrites the hard drive every three days so what I gave them is the only record. There's nothing that shows us releasing it."

"Still, we can't risk it," Kirkland said. "Sanchez has to disappear."

* * *

Highway patrol cars, having taken over for the PBSO, blocked the street in front of the Powells' house and kept the reporters at bay. Two press helicopters, circling like vultures, vied for air space. *Must have picked up the news on the police radio band,* TJ thought as he pulled up. An ambulance sat in the Powells' driveway and deputies milled about. The house was quiet.

Sheriff Rodriguez met him and the two men walked to the ambulance. "As I told you, this isn't going to be pleasant, and it has to be quick. Bodies taken from the water start decomposing quickly when they're exposed to air, and we need to get him to the medical examiner and autopsied ASAP."

The sheriff opened the doors, and they entered the back of the ambulance. Two first responders, each on one side of the stretcher, moved forward to accommodate TJ and the sheriff. Up front, the driver sat looking straight ahead. On the stretcher lay a black rubber body bag. Rodriguez unzipped it, revealing Bobby Powell's body. TJ inhaled sharply at the sight and his stomach churned. Even the sheriff, who'd seen accident victims and death many times, momentarily looked away. The boy's body was wrinkled and porcelain white. Eyeless sockets stared back at them. His face and body were pockmarked. The fish had been at him. Numerous bites had taken small pieces of flesh. Part of his left side had been ripped away, exposing three ribs. The two men stared in silence.

"Seen enough?" Rodriguez asked.

TJ felt like a voyeur looking at the little boy's body. "The bite marks." He pointed. "On the shoulders, thighs, and above the ankles. The shape of the bites indicates that the animal bit down on him headfirst. He may have tried to swallow the boy whole. Then there's this fourth set. Perpendicular to the others, across his stomach, and the teeth appear to be bigger."

"Probably just the result of being in the water, but we'll let the ME tell us." The sheriff zipped up the bag and looked at one of the first responders. "Okay. Take him away."

They exited the ambulance and watched it, lights flashing, pull away. "Poor kid," TJ said.

"Let's go talk to the guys who found the body," Rodriguez said.

They walked in silence across the backyard, past the cypress trees and up the slope to the canal. Two men were sitting on the path at the top of the levee. Nearby, a silver boat with a green Palm Beach County sheriff's star painted on the side was staked to the shore. The men rose as TJ and the sheriff approached. One, wearing the black bottom of a wetsuit had a neatly trimmed beard and was bare chested. The matching black jacket lay on the ground. The other was dressed in the green deputy sheriff's uniform and held a rifle.

"Tell us how you found him," the sheriff said.

"Water's murky," the bearded diver replied. "There's more debris than usual, but I finally spotted the boy's body wedged in a tangle of tree limbs in a hollow about two feet below the surface. He was pushed too far into the branches to have been wedged there by the current. Something had intentionally lodged him there. I freed him and brought the body up."

"I take it there were no gators loitering about?" TJ asked.

"No."

"Something a gator would do," TJ continued. "Stash the body and come back to feed on it later. A croc might do the same thing, I don't know."

Sheriff Rodriguez and the two deputies nodded in agreement. "We found the body," Rodriguez said. "Now we have to find the killer,"

"Or killers," TJ said. "Did the croc escape from Animal World, swim up the canal, get past the pumping station, kill the boy, lodge his body, then change his mind, get past the pumps again, and swim south? I think we may be looking for two killers."

"Remember, one of the gates was lodged open," Rodriguez said. "The croc could have gotten through it. Maybe a little banged up, but we know he's a big fellow and could take a few licks. A Nile crocodile killing both people is more plausible to me than a gator and a croc."

"Maybe," TJ said unconvinced. "So why did the croc stash Bobby's body if he wasn't going to hang around?"

"As you said, maybe he changed his mind. Maybe the current swept him through the pumping station. Maybe he wanted to get back to Animal World. Who knows? Crocs aren't the smartest animals."

"I'm not giving up on any theory yet, Sheriff."

Rodriguez sighed. "You're not making this easy, are you, TJ?" The sheriff thought for a while. "Okay let's see if we can find anything else here." To his deputies he said, "Back in the water, boys."

"Be careful," TJ said to the diver. "If the animal that put the boy's body into the gator hole is still here, he's not going to be happy to see you mucking around his food source."

Sheriff Rodriguez thanked the men for their hard work and bravery, and then he and TJ retraced their steps. On their way, the sheriff said: "Sam Brown's on her way here. Should be coming in tonight."

"From Australia? I thought you said she was gone for six months?"

"Apparently the governor worked her magic."

As they neared their vehicles, TJ turned back to the house and saw Bobby Powell's parents looking out the picture window. They stood motionless, hugging each other, staring vacantly toward where the ambulance had been parked. The pain the couple was feeling was palpable. He had to look away.

* * *

It was twilight by the time TJ got back to his airboat. He was armed with a powerful flashlight. Alligators and crocodiles had excellent nighttime vision and liked to hunt when it was dark out. This presented an opportunity for him and his rangers because the source of their sight—an enlarged retina and guanine crystals behind it—made them easy to spot. Their eyes glowed bright red when a light was shined on them.

TJ headed back down the Arthur Marshall Refuge running parallel to the canal. The air was hot and thick, and he repeatedly slapped at his neck. The insects were out in force. He caught up with the picket line of FWS boats.

Motors off, the boats silently drifted south. There were two officers in each boat. One wore night-vision googles, the other used a tactical flashlight, being careful to keep its intense beam away from the officer wearing the goggles. The officers' eyes swept the sloughs, hammocks, and tree islands as they went.

At three a.m., TJ called off the search. Many pairs of red eyes had appeared in the water and along the shore, but they all had the rounded snouts of alligators. None of the animals had attacked the boats, and the FWS wasn't about to kill every alligator it came across and slash open its belly to check for human remains. He returned to the PBSO and crashed on one of their couches.

* * *

West of TJ and his rangers, another boat drifted silently in the dark. Virgil Polk had grown up hunting and fishing in the Everglades. Tonight he was hunting for alligators. The price for their meat and hides had risen, as it always did outside of hunting season. He knew the FWS would be on the water looking for the crocodile, and he'd glimpsed their boats more than once. He crouched low in his boat, even though he was well away from them and drifted silently; his small outboard motor swung up with its propeller out of the water.

Polk's hunting weapon of choice was a length of rope with a two-inch piece of broom handle tied to one end. The block of wood would be baited and tossed into the water. When a gator went for the bait, the wooden peg would become trapped in its throat. The gator would be caught and unable to dive, the peg blocking the palatal valve at the top of its throat that prevented water from entering its lungs when it was underwater. Polk would then pull the gator to the boat and kill it. The preferred method was to shoot it in the head with a gun or a bang stick, the lethal cousin of the shot stick, but shells made noise, and noise attracted attention. Polk was both where he shouldn't be and hunting when he shouldn't be. He'd use his sturdy eight-inch hunting knife to sever the gator's spinal cord at the base of the skull. The animal would make a lot of noise thrashing around after it'd been caught and as it was pulled to the boat, but those were sounds natural to the Everglades; a gunshot was not.

In theory, the gator was quickly dispatched, but things didn't always go according to plan. Lines broke, or gators dove and lines became tangled, drowning the animal. Pegs pulled on too hard ripped out palatal valves or became lodged in the alligator's throat, causing painful and prolonged deaths. If the hook and line held, the next challenge was killing the animal. An angry jaw-snapping, thrashing alligator, bigger and stronger than the person trying to subdue it, wasn't very cooperative. Even for someone like Polk who'd done this many times before, kills with a knife were often neither quick nor clean.

Polk spotted a pair of red eyes swimming toward him. He wrapped some meat around the wood peg, tossed it in the water, and played the line. He paid no attention when his boat bumped into a hammock. The impact was slight, but Kodra jerked awake. She raised her head and could only make out indistinct shapes. She shot her tongue out and knew one was a human. The shapes came toward her, retreated, then came toward her again as the boat bumped the shore and Polk pulled in the rope and tossed it out again. She rose to meet the threat. Her full stomach slowed her, but she mounted the boat and bit Polk in the side, knocking him into the water.

Polk surfaced and looked up at his boat. A type of animal he'd never seen before looked down at him. He was about to swim away when he saw the pair of eyes swimming toward him. Holding his side, he clamored to shore just as the alligator snapped at his heels. He grabbed a limb and pulled himself higher on the hammock. Glancing back, he saw the gator follow. It was only a juvenile, but it was emboldened by the scent of blood. Then the gator changed its mind and slid back into the marsh.

Relieved, Polk turned only to discover why the young gator had departed. Kodra had left the boat and was standing on top of the hammock. He dropped back to the beach. His boat bobbed against the shore just a few feet away. As he moved toward it, Kodra descended the hammock and blocked him. He feigned left and Kodra shifted her weight in the same direction. He took a step to the right, and she did the same. Then she charged, driving her head into his stomach. Polk flew into the marsh, landing with a splash. Floating on his good side, he used one arm and leg to swim away, leaving a misty red trial in the water.

CHAPTER 14

"This isn't good," Sheriff Rodriguez said, slowly shaking his head, staring at the two Sausage McMuffin wrappers on his desk. "My wife says I should stop eating these things. She might be seeing me for breakfast every day if we don't find the crocodile." He paused and looked at TJ. "Don't say: *or maybe the crocodile and the alligator.*"

TJ nursed his black coffee and said nothing.

They were waiting for the medical examiner to call with the results of Bobby Powell's autopsy. It'd had been delayed because Governor Johnson had insisted a state ME be flown in from Orlando to lead it.

While they waited, TJ asked: "What do you know about the D'Costa lawsuit? I was so mad at the deceitful way I was served yesterday that I haven't looked at it."

The sheriff chuckled. "Yeah, servers can be a sleazy bunch. The suit alleges that the Animal World crocodile killed his dog and claims damages. Hard to prove, since there are no witnesses."

"What does he expect to get out of it?"

"He claims he invested over $150,000 in that bull terrier—its name was Pernicious Prosecutor, by the way—and it was going to win the Westminster Dog Show. Then there's lost prize money and stud fees of at least another one fifty or so he says. Lastly, he's asking one million dollars for emotional distress."

"And, I guess, a lot of free publicity riding on the coattails of the croc."

"Probably."

"Big waste of time when I should've been out in the refuge."

"Yeah. I've worked in law enforcement my whole life. What I always wanted to do. But I spend half my time dealing with lawyers and politicians."

At 7 a.m., the medical examiner called. The results came as no surprise to the two men. Three rows of teeth marks, each shaped like an inverted U, on the boy's upper chest, thighs, and just above his ankles. A fourth bite, almost perpendicular to the others, but not as deep, crossed his stomach, and abdomen. Despite TJ's request, the ME couldn't say for sure if the teeth marks on Bobby Powell's torso matched the other three bites. The bite on his side had been too worked over by the fish to be compared to the others. There was no water in Bobby's lungs. He was dead before he went into the canal.

"So, where does this leave us?" Rodriguez asked.

"The whole bite thing bothers me," TJ responded. "The three bites are what you'd see if the boy was swallowed whole headfirst, but obviously he wasn't because we recovered his body. Then there's the different bite across his mid stomach."

"Maybe different. You heard the ME. The stomach bite was post-mortem. It could be different because Bobby was dragged by the predator or due to the time the body spent in the water. And the fish went to town on all his wounds."

"Okay. We aren't going to settle that now. Let's focus on finding the crocodile."

As they brainstormed, Sheriff Rodriguez received a text from Governor Johnson. Sam Brown had arrived back in Florida. The governor was holding a press conference in one hour to introduce Brown as a crocodile expert and the state's search advisor. TJ was not invited. The conference would be held on the lawn of the Herzogs' house, not at the sheriff's office.

"Nice of her to give you ample notice," TJ said.

Rodriguez just frowned. He declined to attend, texting back that the department's spokesperson would appear in his place.

They went back to figuring out how they were going to catch the animal or animals. There was no high-tech way to do it. Hunters and trappers just searched until they found the alligator they were looking for. Usually alligators that were a nuisance or had attacked a person were in small bodies of water around houses or areas where there was human activity. The search area was finite, and there were few, if any, other gators around.

"We could put out baited traps along the canal north and south of the Herzogs' house. It's where the last attack occurred, so it's the most logical place to start," TJ said.

"I'm not sure that'll fly with the residents."

"We'd use no-kill traps, just big boxes with one-way doors. No bear claws or the like. And we'd watch them. So, no risk of a curious child or dog getting injured."

"And the bait? The smell of meat rotting in the hot sun will attract all kinds of predators and from some distance away."

"Okay," TJ mused. "We'll put traps on hold for a while." He thought some more. "How about if I call the chairman of the Seminoles. They know the area better than anyone. Perhaps they could add something about finding an alligator or, in this case, a crocodile."

TJ had a good relationship with the Seminole Indians and their relatives, the Muskogees. Both tribes respected his love for the Everglades and shared his concern for the environmental dangers it faced.

"Can't hurt," Rodriguez said, "but it's time for the press conference. Let's hear what our esteemed governor has to say this morning." He switched on the TV.

Governor Johnson squinted into the cameras, a strong breeze musing her dark hair. She was standing beside the pool at the spot where Judy Herzog had been attacked and carried off and was flanked by Martin Herzog and the Powells. Behind them was an expanse of lawn, the levee leading to the canal and, in the distance, the Arthur Marshall Refuge. The TV camera panned the group, and TJ spotted Bennet D'Costa standing off to one side and pointed at him on the screen.

Johnson opened the press conference and then introduced Samantha Brown. TJ found Sam striking. Only a couple of inches shorter than him, she had long straight coal-black hair and piercing steel blue eyes. Both were made even more vivid by her light skin. He wondered how she could be out in the sun so much and not be much darker. She wore a small silver ring in her nose.

Sam was born and raised in San Diego, TJ knew, having researched her before he'd asked her to speak on his TV show. He filled in the sheriff. College was at UC Berkeley and then on to Stanford where she received her PhD in biology. Her research earned her an offer to join the Stanford faculty, and she was a full professor by the time she turned thirty. She published a highly regarded paper theorizing why American crocodiles were less aggressive than the other thirteen species of crocodiles.

Four years later, she resigned her position at Stanford and moved to Lake Trafford in Immokalee, Florida, about an hour east of Naples. Lake Trafford's principal residents were alligators, three thousand of them at last count, which explained why Sam was one of the few people who lived on the lake. The lake was renowned for its bass fishing, but anglers were warned to keep their hands inside their boat and definitely not fall into the water. The American crocodiles she liked to study were a short drive away. She published a scholarly paper on how and why they differed from Nile and Australian crocodiles. Then Sam moved on again. She now had a highly successful series of children's books about an alligator name Allie who talked about life in the Everglades and shopping in Naples. She also consulted with zoos and National Geographic.

Sam looked squarely into the cameras and said what happened to Bobby Powell and Judy Herzog was horrible, but attacks on humans were rare. "The Animal World crocodile is an African Nile crocodile," she said. "They are very aggressive, much more so than American crocodiles and alligators, and they do eat people. I suspect this animal is responsible for Judy Herzog's disappearance." She then described the differences between crocodiles and alligators.

"It's impossible to say if or when the Nile crocodile will be found," she continued, "but because of its aggressive nature, there's a good chance it will show itself if it hasn't already gone into the Everglades."

During the Q & A, Sam skirted the question of whether the crocodile had also killed Bobby Powell or if a second animal was involved. In response to another question, she replied that crocodiles can live up to seventy years. If it wasn't found, it could be around for a long time.

As Sam continued taking questions, Sheriff Rodriguez looked at TJ. "She said the same things you said. Maybe a little more diplomatically though."

"And you wouldn't know she's a multimillionaire," TJ said.

"No, you wouldn't," the sheriff said surprised.

"It's all on google. Developed some gene sequencing thing to identify subspecies of animals, which previously hadn't been distinguishable, while at Stanford. Lo and behold, it had an application for humans. Amgen bought it for a pretty penny."

"So she leaves Stanford and moves to lake nowhere. Something doesn't add up."

After Sam finished, Governor Johnson said the parents had a statement they wished to read. D'Costa stepped to the microphone. "Good morning, I am Bennet D'Costa, attorney for the Herzog family." Then with anger in his voice, he lashed out. "It's tragic that US Fish & Wildlife Officer Forte and Sheriff Rodriguez have been unable to find the Animal World crocodile or come up with a credible plan to do so. We greatly appreciate Governor Johnson taking the lead and bringing in an expert to run the search. This crocodile must be caught and killed before it kills again."

An annoyed look crossed TJ's face. "Always one with the kind words. Didn't mention the Powells. Guess they didn't hire him."

Then came the surprise. "To facilitate catching the crocodile," D'Costa continued, "I am pleased to announce that the Herzog family is offering a $100,000 reward to anyone who finds Judy and another $100,000 for killing the Animal World crocodile."

TJ and Sheriff Rodriguez both leaned forward in their chairs. "This is bad. Very bad," Rodriguez said.

* * *

Kodra's eyes—red and yellow surrounding coal black pupils—opened. She raised her head and looked left and right. Her tongue simultaneously shot out in each direction, and then retreated and touched the Jacobson's organ in the top of her mouth. She was sitting up in a shallow hole she'd dug next to a skinny satin leaf tree. She checked for scents and looked around. There was nothing that interested or concerned her. No sign of the man she'd attacked last night. She slipped off the little island into the slough, the water only a few inches deep and walked to an adjacent hammock. She moved freely now. The remains of the Judy Herzog were small in her belly, and the chemically treated water in the Herzog's pool had killed the bacteria in the wounds Sanchez had inflicted, helping them to heal. Soon she would have to eat again, but now she felt a new urge, the urge to nest.

She raked the hammock's surface with her sharp claws removing a thin layer of topsoil and revealing the wet marl below. Instinct told her that a nest wouldn't stay dry. So she descended the far bank and entered a different slough. Stepping onto tall sawgrass, she immediately sank, her legs and feet becoming tangled in the plants. The sharp edges did not injure her thick hide, but the grasses wrapped around her legs. She struggled to free herself, only to become further entangled, the grasses pulling her down. Surrendering, she disappeared below the surface. Then, summoning all her strength, she thrust herself forward. Breaking free of the grasses, she surfaced and swam on to the next spit of land.

In front of her was a tree mound, the largest piece of land she'd seen in the refuge. Kodra cautiously mounted the bank, then set about exploring. The wind carried to her the scents of deer, rabbits, raccoons, and many noisy birds. Along the way she vomited up the indigestible remains of Judy Herzog.

She found a copse of pine trees and scrub brush and determined it was a suitable place to lay in wait for an unsuspecting animal to appear. An indigo snake slithered by, but she showed no interest. For the rest of the day, she waited, but the scents remained distant. A meal the size of Judy Herzog would normally last a couple of weeks, but that was when she wasn't on the move, swimming, struggling through entwined plants, and digging. Kodra was hungry.

* * *

Doug Kirkland watched the press conference and didn't like what he heard. The crocodile woman was fine. Mumford's idea of releasing the croc great. Kept everyone looking for it. The talk about an alligator possibly killing the Powell boy was good too. But Herzog's big reward made him nervous. The money would bring every bozo in the state of Florida and probably Louisiana, Mississippi, and Alabama as well, to his doorstep. He'd have to stop importing exotics for a while. Worse, the Komodo dragon might be found. Then all hell would break loose.

He turned his attention to Sanchez. Kirkland had wanted him out of sight, so he'd sent him into the fields, but Sanchez wasn't getting any better. Kirkland got on his radio and summoned Wilgreen Darisse to meet him in the barn. Darisse was one of the many Haitians who worked at Pure Sugar and the third participant in the animal trafficking business.

Darisse was rail thin, well over six-feet tall, and wore his hair in short twisted curls. Despite being in his early twenties, he had a slight stoop. It was unclear if the stoop came from having to look down because everyone he spoke to was shorter than him or because the hard farm work was already taking its toll. His family had arrived in the United States in the 1980s, along with many other Haitians who were escaping the oppressive dictator, Jean Claude Duvalier. Their destination of choice was South Florida, and there were more Haitians in Palm Beach County than immigrants from any other country. Those who spoke English became shopkeepers. Most spoke only Haitian Creole, and their careers varied from farm laborer to unemployed. Darisse had completed some high school before he followed his parents into the fields. Although not formally educated, he was trilingual, speaking Creole at home, Spanish in the cane fields, one or the other in town, and English less frequently. Like Sanchez, he assisted Kirkland with his animals. Kirkland had made it clear to Darisse he'd join the forty percent unemployed in Belle Glade if he didn't.

As he waited for Darisse to arrive, Kirkland made two decisions. One was to join the hunt for the crocodile and the other was what to do about Sanchez.

CHAPTER 15

After the press conference, TJ called Marcel Holata, chairman of the Seminole tribe, as Sheriff Rodriguez looked on.

"Chairman?" Rodriguez said after the call ended.

"Why not?" TJ replied. "They own casinos, a petroleum company, a rock mining business, and citrus farms. Chief is a bit old fashioned."

Rodriguez shrugged his shoulders. "Makes sense. What'd he say?"

"The Seminoles are happy to help. They have their own police force, as you know, and tribe members will volunteer to join the search. But he didn't have any ideas that we haven't already thought of, and he's not optimistic about finding a specific alligator or a crocodile in the Everglades. He said he should know, since holata means alligator in Seminole. He suggested I talk to his brother, Billy. Good guy. I know him. Everyone knows Billy. He's an exotic animal dealer in Miami and one of the biggest reptile merchants in the state. But he has this thing about talking on the phone. Thinks all phones are bugged."

Rodriguez chuckled. "Who knows. He may be right."

"So I'll have to take a little drive if I want to see him."

TJ left the sheriff's office and drove back to his airboat and resumed his search in the Arthur Marshall. On his way, he thought about how he was going to prepare his officers and rangers for tomorrow. Herzog's reward would draw every fortune hunter and bounty seeker in the south, both the qualified and the unqualified. No doubt with guns and alcohol thrown in. It was going to be a dangerous day.

A midday downpour drove the boats off the water, soaking TJ before he got the airboat back to shore. He sat in his truck, checking his messages and thoroughly annoyed with himself for not having his rain gear with him. He had another text from the Corvette seller. *Have higher offer, but it's yours if you want it at our agreed to price. Let me know ASAP.* TJ sighed and texted back that the seller should take the new offer.

The weather was supposed to clear, but more rain and thunderstorms were expected later in the day. He was fine with the forecast. Bad weather would keep people away from the search areas. He headed to his office and dry clothes. By the time he arrived, the rain had stopped.

He'd just cleaned up when Kenny Loggins started singing *Revvin' up your engine, Listen to her howlin' roar.* He had a call.

"Sam Brown is here in my office. Would you like to join us?" Sheriff Rodriguez asked.

"I'm on my way," he said immediately.

* * *

Sam put down a file—Bobby Powell's autopsy report—and got up to greet TJ as he entered Sheriff Rodriguez's office.

They shook hands. "Nice to see you again Sam," TJ said.

"Same here, although we only seem to meet when there's a gator involved."

"Oh," Sheriff Rodriguez said.

"TJ invited me to be a guest on his TV show. It was right after a fisherman had been attacked by an alligator on Lake Trafford," Sam added. "People were panicking. Turns out, the man had been feeding his catch to the gator to see it jump out of the water and the gator came to associate him with food. Serves him right."

TJ smiled. "You did a good job explaining what happened then, and you did a good job at the press conference this morning. I look froward to working with you."

"Thank you. Sheriff Rodriguez told me it was your idea to bring me on aboard. I appreciate that but I don't want there to be any misunderstanding between us. I'm in charge now, and I report to the governor."

TJ was taken back. He'd expected a congenial working relationship but he kept that thought to himself. *No sense getting off on the wrong foot.*

"The governor's a big fan of yours," Sam added with a smirk.

"Likewise."

"I have a job to do and I will do it. You know the Arthur Marshall Refuge and the surrounding area better than anyone. I hope you're willing to help me."

"Of course."

"Wonderful. Sheriff Rodriguez and I are going to the Powell house. I want to start at the beginning, look around, and work my way south. Care to join us?"

"Let's go," TJ said.

* * *

Only one TV remote broadcast van remained at the Powell house. *Hoping to scoop another morbid detail, no doubt,* TJ thought as they got out and walked through the back yard.

Sam's first reaction upon cresting the levee was: "Wow, that's a lot of sugarcane!" On the far side of the canal, an unbroken line of tall green leafy sugarcane plants, as deep and thick as a forest, stretched as far north as the eye could see. The cane ended a little before the pumping station.

"Florida Pure Sugar Incorporated growing the narcotic of Florida," TJ said.

"Why do you say that?" Sam asked.

"The most valuable cash crop in the state of Florida, but the farms are poisoning the Everglades."

"I thought they'd controlled the runoffs."

"Sure, they've gotten better, and they've built massive containment ponds and gotten better in using fertilizers and insecticides. But they continue to release too many phosphates and nitrates in the water. They're still killing the Everglades, they're just doing it more slowly. And the irony is, the only reason we grow cane in Florida is because it's subsidized by the Federal government. Take away the subsidies, you take away the problem. There is some poetic justice though. When they burn the old stalks, the winds carry the soot into the expensive areas of Palm Beach County. The locals call it black snow. You can smell it and see it on the cars. What all those rich people don't seem to realize is that it's also getting into their lungs."

Their attention was drawn to a sheriff's deputy yelling at two men in a bass boat that they were in a crime scene area and to go back up the canal. The boat had motored to within a few yards of where a PBSO dive team was working.

"They're already coming," Rodriguez said. "Even the rain isn't stopping them. Herzog's reward is bringing out every yahoo and fortune seeker in the region."

TJ looked into the boat. A rifle lay across two of the seats. He felt certain that everyone out there would be armed, even if he couldn't see the weapon. He motioned with his chin toward the boat. "What about the guns?"

"Probably have a license," Sheriff Rodriguez said. "We don't have the manpower to check every boat. I'm hoping it rains for a week straight. Chase 'em away. Or maybe the sun will tire them out."

"Alligator hunting season doesn't start until August 15th, and that's next week," Sam said. "Can't you make them stop?"

"They'll just deny they're hunting gators. Unless they have one, there's no way we can prove intent," the sheriff replied. "Next week, though . . . I don't even want to think about it."

Alligator hunting season, euphemistically called the Alligator Harvest Program, was TJ's least favorite time of year. Hunting was allowed in the lower Arthur Marshall. Since alligators hunted at night, they were hunted at night. That made for long days and even longer nights for the FWS. Boats strayed, intentionally or not, outside the hunting zone. The risk of guns, alcohol, and drugs was ever present.

TJ didn't see the sport in shooting or spearing a dumb animal and knew from observation that many animals suffered. The maximum permissible kill was two, so there wasn't money in it for hunters even if they sold the hide and meat. Of course, not every hunter stopped at two. The money was made by the large alligator farms, which accounted for ninety percent of all alligator products sourced in Florida.

He looked around as Sam studied the area. Across the way, the leaves on tall green sugarcane plants moved ever so slightly with the breeze. A man with a bang stick walked along the top of the berm on the farm side. Head down, he ignored the group gathered on the Powell side. Down the canal, past the pumping station, was a boat with men in it. *More fortune seekers?* TJ wondered. He looked back at the boat with the rifle across the seats slowly motoring up stream as the deputy on the top of the levee walked beside it, encouraging it along.

"Okay, let's go back," Sam said.

The trio walked down the levee toward the Powell house. The berm sloped down to an unkept field, the row of cypress trees and the Powell lawn beyond. "It doesn't make sense," Sam said. "Crocodilians are semi-aquatic."

"Crocodilians?" the sheriff asked. "Are we looking for another animal now?"

"Sorry," Sam replied. "Alligators and crocodiles are part of the crocodilian family. They hunt in the water or near the water. Water is their escape route; that's why they always stay close to it. The canal is a good hundred yards from the Powell backyard. A crocodilian would only go that far on land if it was crossing from one body of water to another."

"That's what I told the sheriff," TJ said.

Rodriguez shot him a look.

"There are many animals, besides alligators, in the Everglades that could kill a child," Sam continued. "Bear, cougar, boar, maybe even a coyote. All the rains are driving them out of their dens, driving away their prey. And, if the animal were rabid, all the more likelihood."

"We found reptile DNA on Bobby Powell's shoe, so we know one of your crocodilians was involved," Sheriff Rodriguez said.

"Yes, I know that," Sam said. "But I think there were two, possibly three animals involved."

The sheriff gave TJ another look.

"The theory that the Animal World crocodile swam north, and then south is far-fetched," Sam continued, "I believe an animal attacked Bobby, biting him three times. Then, a gator or a bigger gator took the body from the first animal. I say this because the bite diameter shown on the autopsy was larger on the boy's stomach. This is an opportunistic animal and is most likely still nearby because the canal is the only large body of water, unless there's one on the farm behind the cane. And gators like to hang out around pumping stations. The gates block and stun aquatic animals, making them easy prey. Given where Bobby's body was found, I'm glad to see you've got a dive team working north of the damn."

"That's the first encouraging thing I've heard in a while," the sheriff said.

"With respect to Judy Herzog's attack, I believe it was the escaped crocodile. The timeline fits and the Herzog's house is south of Animal World and on the same canal. A crocodile would eat her, but there's probably an arm or a leg out there somewhere waiting to be found."

"Let's keep that pleasant thought to ourselves," Rodriguez responded.

"But there's another possibility," Sam said. Both men looked at her expectantly. "Water has been released from Lake O a number of times since the rains began. That's a big flow into canals that were already full. It's possible there was only one attacking animal, and it was flushed down from the Lake O area."

There was a sharp bang before TJ or Sheriff Rodriguez could respond. All three turned toward the farm.

"That was a 357 muffled by direct contact with the skin. Bang stick," the sheriff said.

The three hurried back up the berm to the top of the levee. There was no sign of the offender, but Sam, arm outstretched, pointed. "Look." A four-foot alligator floated in the water along the far bank. The current was carrying it downstream. "Way too small. Who shot it? What was he thinking?"

"Probably wasn't," Sheriff Rodriguez replied. "Caught up in the heat of the moment."

"Someone carrying a weapon is going to use it," TJ said.

"Can't you go after him?" Sam asked.

"We'd never find him in the cane field," Rodriguez said.

As they watched the dead alligator drift toward the pumping station, four ATVs emerged, one after the other, almost in military formation, from the sugarcane plants and stopped at the top of the levee. Three of the drivers carried assault style rifles. The sheriff recognized the fourth man and inclined his head toward TJ and Sam. "That's Doug Kirkland, the principal farm foremen. He's bad news. Stole cars for a chop shop in Miami. Beat up a couple of people real bad along the way."

TJ looked across the canal. Two hundred feet away, a deeply tanned man with silver streaks at the edges of his back hair looked back. Late forties, TJ thought. He noticed Kirkland's arm muscles. *Guy keeps in shape.* "Not classic cars, I hope," he said.

"Notice he's the only one not carrying a gun. Can't. He's a convicted felon. But there's a rifle in the scabbard holster on the ATV next to him, and the driver is holding a rifle. Wonder who the extra rifle belongs to?"

Sheriff Rodriguez moved along the top of the berm until he was opposite Kirkland.

Kirkland dismounted. There was another man sitting behind him, head down. Two other riders grabbed the man, who offered no resistance, and threw him into the water. The man surfaced a moment later and started swimming toward the opposite side of the canal. The current pulled him south toward the pumping station, and the sheriff yelled for his deputies to get the man. One of the sheriff's deputies tossed a rope to the swimmer and pulled him onto the bank.

The men on the farm bank and TJ, Sam, and the sheriff watched. Once the swimmer was safely on shore, the sheriff yelled to the man standing on the bank opposite him. "Kirkland!"

Kirkland nodded but said nothing.

"I see your men are armed," the sheriff continued.

"We've got licenses, and we're on Pure Sugar property."

"And the man in the water?"

"Trespasser. Said he was hunting gators. Thought we'd help him."

"Not that way. We'll question him. But you take notice: we don't want any trouble here."

"There won't be so long as none of these idiots come on our land."

"Well, keep an eye on 'em, but if one slips through, throw him into the canal, too, just not near the pumping station."

As Kirkland and his men laughed, Rodriguez addressed TJ and Sam under his breath. "I know that's not the proper legal response, but a wet hunter is better than a dead hunter." He sighed and slowly shook his head. "That's enough excitement for one day, but the sun's supposed to shine tomorrow. All hell is going to break loose then."

Leaving the Powells', Sam asked to go to her hotel, The Waters Edge Inn & Suites, to check-in. TJ said he'd drive her and offered to take her to dinner, but she declined, saying she was jet-lagged from her flight back from Australia and needed to get some rest. They pulled up to a slightly worn three-story motel that, despite its name, was a good five miles from the ocean and not in sight of any water. After dropping Sam off, TJ headed home and to work on his cars. A couple of hours diversion would clear his mind. Maybe he'd get a new idea on how to find the crocodile.

* * *

TJ filled the plastic water bowel and put some leftovers in another bowl. He'd taken to leaving both outside his back door. The red-legged iguana appeared and headed to the bowls, passing so close that TJ could almost reach out and touch him.

Task completed, he continued on to his garage. The staccato rat-tat-tat of rain beating down on the metal roof announced the arrival of the second storm of the day. TJ ignored it and eyed his newest purchase, a Sierra fawn gold metallic 1967 Camaro coupe, with matching gold vinyl interior. The Camaro was a good deal at $12,000. A six-cylinder engine and three-speed manual transmission with a column-mounted shifter, known as a three on the tree, accounted for the low price. TJ's plan was to drop in a 327-cubic-inch V8 and a floor-mounted shifter mated to a four-speed manual and sell the car for triple what he'd invested in it. He looked forward to listing it on his website.

As he mentally sketched out his plan for the Camaro, his cell rang. It was the would-be Impala buyer. TJ took the call and listened distractedly as the man asked the same questions he'd asked when they'd met over pizza. It struck him that he was listening to the man's stream of consciousness as he debated purchasing the car.

As the man droned on, TJ's thoughts returned to the dead child and woman. Had they known what was happening to them? They must have felt the pain of the bites. What a horrible way to die. Finding the animal or animals responsible and finding Judy Herzog's body would bring some closure for the families. He was determined to do both. The problem was, he had no idea how to do it except to keep searching, which was like looking for the proverbial needle in a haystack. He politely rebuffed the man's price offer and ended the call. He looked at the Camaro and realized his heart wasn't in working on it tonight. With a sigh, he switched off the lights and left the garage. Tomorrow was going to be one helluva day.

CHAPTER 16

TJ was on his way to the Twenty Mile Boat Ramp early the next morning. There was no telling how many hunters and trappers, and the just plain curious, Herzog's $200,000 reward would draw to the Arthur Marshall Refuge, but he figured it'd be a lot.

The refuge was ringed by fifty miles of levees and canals. Biking, hiking, and walking were encouraged on paths that ran along the top of the levees, and boating was permitted in the canals. Boats were not allowed in the two hundred and twenty-one square mile refuge except for small power boats in the bottom third of the refuge. But the Arthur Marshall was just too big to police.

TJ planned to take his airboat—and his was the only airboat allowed in the refuge—to the area behind the Herzog's house. No matter how anyone got into the refuge, that would be their destination. He had rangers in boats on the marsh and canal. Sheriff Rodriguez's officers patrolled the levee and had cordoned off the Herzog's neighborhood, allowing only residents to enter. It was going to be a busy day. Then Sheriff Rodriguez called. "Good news, for once," the sheriff said. "The Powell gator has been found." TJ changed his destination.

Arriving at the Powell home, he walked up on the levee and joined Sam and the sheriff, who were speaking with two men and a woman. He recognized the bearded diver and his partner from the previous day. He'd seen the woman on the news a few times in the past, but he'd never met her. Susan

Hancock was a grandmother and former elementary school teacher. She looked to be in her early fifties but was a good ten years older. She'd retired after twenty years with the Palm Beach County school system and begun her second career as an alligator trapper.

TJ knew the gated communities in the county paid well to have trappers remove gators that were either too big or not afraid of humans. Hancock said she placed the big gators in the witness protection program, which meant she released them deep in the Everglades. She didn't say what she did with the aggressive ones, although their ending wasn't as happy because gators had a way of returning. Some were known to have traveled as far as seventy-five miles back to where they were caught. The big ones were probably too old to do so, but she didn't take any chances with the aggressive ones.

Sheriff Rodriguez made the introductions and graciously credited TJ with the idea of bringing in a professional trapper.

The bearded diver said it was Hancock who'd come up with the plan that caught the gator. The gator hadn't eaten the boy, so, like TJ, Hancock figured it'd stashed his body as a lure to attract other animals that it would feed on. She instructed the diver to bait the hide hole with dead fish. They didn't have to wait long. Whether the gator was coming to investigate the fish or thought the diver was stealing its kill, it arrived promptly. The diver felt a sharp tug. He looked back and saw the largest gator he'd ever seen, a twelve-footer, shaking his flipper. He shook his leg, and the fin broke off in the gator's mouth. He pulled out his knife and shot for the surface.

As his head broke above the water, he heard three gunshots in rapid succession. His partner in the boat had seen the diver coming up and the gator fast behind him. Now, with a big grin, the diver proudly displayed his half-bitten flipper.

"Quite the story," TJ said. "But where's the gator?"

"Already on his way to the veterinarian hospital not far from our offices," Sheriff Rodriguez said. "The vets will open it up and see what's inside, but with luck we've found Bobby Powell's killer."

* * *

The scent of carrion was in the air. Kodra left the tree mound and swam back to the hammock where she'd previously nested. The source of the scent, Virgil Polk's bloated body, floated just offshore. Kodra approached, intent on the easy meal when the air was driven from her lungs. A ten-foot alligator's jaws closed like a vice on her back and chest and pulled her under water. The gator spun rapidly. Kodra flailed her legs but to no effect. She twisted her neck and snapped her jaws, but they fell short of the gator. She trashed her tail. On land, it was a formidable weapon but the water slowed it, and it only gently slapped against her oppressor. She saw a kaleidoscope of sky, water, and land.

Kodra did not know it, but she was in a death roll. The alligator was going to drown her, then tear off parts of her to eat. Kodra could hold her breath for ten minutes under water and her osteoderm-covered hide was thicker than other animals the gator preyed upon, but she was dizzy and growing weak.

As she thrashed, one of her foot's three-inch-long claws caught on a tree root protruding from the edge of the bank. Her leg became a lever, and the gator's rolling flipped them both onto the shore. The gator's mouth opened from the force of the landing, and Kodra sprang free. She turned and, eyes blazing, faced the alligator, their snouts only inches apart. She was on solid ground and ready to fight. The alligator looked at her for only a moment, then scuttling backward, slid into the water. It swam away, taking Polk's body with it. Kodra knew better than to chase the gator in the water, but that knowledge did nothing to assuage her growing hunger.

CHAPTER 17

"I'd like to see the Herzogs' next," Sam said. "TJ, I understand it backs onto the Arthur Marshall. Perhaps you could show me both."

TJ agreed, and Sheriff Rodriguez went back to his office to await the gator autopsy results and to update Governor Johnson. On their way, TJ and Sam drove past the entrance to the Twenty Mile Bend boat launch. Highway Patrol cars blocked the entrance. A line of pickups with boats on trailers extended into Southern Boulevard, obstructing the right lane. They glimpsed a man angrily gesturing as he stood nose-to-nose with a trooper.

"This is going to get out of hand," TJ said.

Arriving at the Herzogs', TJ saw an all-black Bentley convertible with the license plate BD 1 in the driveway. He checked in with his rangers and the PBSO deputy in charge. There were just too many curiosity seekers and bounty hunters to keep off the street and out of the refuge. A quick call to the sheriff, and the decision was made not to arrest anyone unless they caused trouble.

From the top of the levee, Sam scrutinized the terrain in the same thorough manner that she'd studied the area around the Powells' home. "Row of houses on one side," she began. "Undeveloped on the other. The same canal in between."

TJ stood silently next to her, not wanting to interrupt her concentration. He looked up and down the canal. Officers walked along the top of the berms on both sides of the canal. Two more were wading in the Arthur Marshall at the edge of the levee. A PBSO dive boat worked the canal.

His forehead furled as he scanned the refuge beyond. Eight, maybe more, boats, a mixture of bass boats and inflatables, dotted the refuge. Some belonged, some were breaking the law. And TJ was sure there were more he couldn't see. "Lots of uninvited guests, but it looks like our guys have it under control."

"Two hundred thousand dollars is a powerful lure," Sam said, and then looked up as a buzzing sound grew louder and attracted their attention. A small drone zipped past overhead. "Yours?"

"Nope. And civilian drones are illegal over the refuge. Have to ask the sheriff if it's—" He was interrupted by his cell. "Well, speak of the devil." TJ put the phone on speaker and Sam leaned in.

"Traces of human flesh were found in the gator's stomach," Rodriguez said. "More was found between its teeth. It's a tissue match with Bobby Powell."

"That was quick."

"Well, the governor's good for something. It looks like we've found Bobby Powell's killer. One down, one to go," Rodriguez said. "I think it's pretty certain that the Animal World crocodile ate Judy Herzog. I have to hand it to you two. You were both right about there being two animals involved. Now all we have to do is find the other one."

TJ didn't mention that he was still troubled by the different types of bite marks found on the boy.

Sam looked at TJ. "The poor families. I can't imagine what they're going through."

"Sam wants to know about the families," TJ said into the phone.

"The Powells are gone, thankfully," the sheriff replied. "Got family up in Georgia. Had a private memorial service for Bobby, which I was able to keep out of the news. Then they just packed up and left. Not coming back unless there's a good reason."

"I think the Herzogs are home," TJ said. "There's a Bentley in the driveway which I'm betting belongs to Bennet D'Costa, and someone has been watching us out the window since we arrived."

"They're there, all right," Sheriff Rodriguez replied. "D'Costa's raising hell with the governor. I thought finding the Powell gator would at least have made her happy, but I was wrong. Seems to have only made both of them madder." The sheriff sighed.

"Can't imagine why Herzog wants his son and daughter to see all this," Sam said.

"Well, that's progress," Sam said after the call ended. "Mind if we sit while we think this through? It's the middle of the night where I was a couple of days ago."

"Of course," TJ replied. He looked down and slowly circled.

"What on earth are you doing? You're acting like a dog."

"Checking for fire ant nests. You don't want to sit on one."

"Oh."

They sat on the berm, each taking a drink of water from their water bottles. "Tell me about Australia. Never been," TJ said.

Sam described the Mary River area. "The coastal floodplain is made up of marshes, swamps, and small areas of high ground. The water rises and flows during the wet season, and then dries up when the rains stop, leaving wet prairies."

"Sounds a little like the Everglades."

"It is, although the seasons are reversed, so this is the dry season in Australia. The Mary River plain is the breeding grounds for many endangered species. It's also the home to some ten thousand saltwater crocodiles."

"Remind me not to go swimming there," TJ said, with the glimmer of an ironic smile.

"Good thought."

"And what did you do for fun?"

Sam laughed. "That's my biggest regret. The governor called me back here before the annual Darwin Beer Can Regatta. Darwin's the nearest city, and it's on the ocean. Participants build full-sized boats out of beer cans and sail them in the bay."

"Must have to drink a lot of beer."

Sam laughed. "Now it's my turn. What's TJ short for?"

"Thomas Jefferson, ma'am. Named after the third president of these United States. My mother taught high school history and was a big fan of Jefferson, but my father always called me TJ."

"Did your mother call you TJ, too?"

"She died when I was born, so I'll never know what she would have called me."

"Oh. I'm terribly sorry."

They settled into an uncomfortable silence looking out into the refuge when an airboat sped by, sending up a plume of water as it swerved around a hammock. "Isn't that illegal?" Sam asked.

TJ laughed. "Why don't you go out there and tell them?" Then he got on his radio.

"You're the fighter jock, why don't you go out and tell them?

When TJ didn't respond, Sam continued. "How are all these boats getting into the refuge when the boat launch we passed is closed?"

"There's another boat ramp off of Indian Mound Road, about four miles south of here and a couple more beyond that. I'm not sure how many the Highway Patrol has blocked. Someone could sneak in through the Wellington Environmental Preserve or a backyard. We can't chase every boat and look for the croc at the same time. We'll tell them to leave, but if they're minding their own business, today they get a pass."

Sam nodded.

"Why Australian crocodiles?"

"Why not, I suppose. The University of Queensland invited me to join their research project, all expenses paid. Saltwater crocs are pretty interesting. The Aussies call them Salties. All crocs are salt tolerant, but this species can live in the ocean. They're big mothers. The average male is twenty feet long, and they're great swimmers. They can swim in bursts up to eighteen miles an hour."

"They'd give Michael Phelps a run for his money."

"He wouldn't stand a chance. They're three times faster than any Olympic swimmer."

"How do they compare to a Nile croc?"

"Niles and Salties are the most aggressive of the thirteen species of crocodiles. You don't want to run across either. They hunt and kill humans." Sam grew quiet and looked out over the refuge. "Do you think they'll find anything?"

TJ took another swig of water from his water bottle. "Not today. What can you see from a speeding airboat or a drone? And the amateurs out there?" He made a sweeping motion toward the marsh. "They don't know what they're looking for."

"A crocodile with a sign on it saying I ate Judy Herzog," Sam said.

TJ snorted. "That'd be too easy. Ready to go?"

They'd just gotten to their feet when a yell caused their heads to snap in unison toward a nearby hammock. A bass boat was beached on it, and two men were jumping up and down, excitedly pointing. TJ flagged one of the boats working the canal. It ferried them across the levee. From there, another boat took them to the hammock. Sam jumped off in front of TJ and ran toward the two men. They were taking pictures with their cell phones, their fingers manically working the keys.

She came to an abrupt halt and was staring down when TJ caught up to her. On the ground was a mass of brown hair, tangled with a number of teeth, some attached to a jawbone. There were pieces of clothing now a molted blue, and two small blue flip-flops, all covered in a thick mucus. They recoiled from the smell.

"Breathe through your mouth," TJ said.

"I know that." She leaned in. "Gastric pellet," she said in a professorial tone.

"What?" TJ asked.

"Gastric pellet or what some call a vomit sac. The animal throws up what it can't digest."

TJ continued to look, but the life had gone out of his eyes. "Poor woman . . ."

"Odd," Sam said. "Crocodiles and alligators can digest just about anything. They only regurgitate when they've just eaten and something frightens them enough that they have to flee."

"That's not what's here," TJ observed. "It looks like the croc threw up what it couldn't digest. Maybe it was the rubber shoes."

"Maybe . . . but I've never seen an alligator do this." Sam pulled out her phone, leaned in, and began snapping pictures of the vomit sac.

TJ yelled instructions to the rangers who'd ferried them over. After he was finished, he turned to Sam. "Would a crocodile be any different?"

"I doubt it. Something's not right."

"It looks fresh."

"Yes, I'd say within the past twenty-four hours."

"So now we know for sure that Judy Herzog was eaten, and the predator, I assume the Animal World crocodile, is still around here."

TJ's cell rang. "You must be psychic. I was just about to call you," he said.

"Not psychic," Sheriff Rodriguez replied. "I'm watching you on YouTube,"

"Huh?" TJ glanced over at Sam. He was surprised to see her looking at her phone. He was even more surprised to see a picture of himself holding his phone. Sam nodded with her chin. TJ's eyes followed. He saw one of the men who'd discovered the gastric pellet had crept in behind them and was pointing his phone at him. TJ lunged at the man, ripped the phone out of his hands, and threw it into the water. It disappeared with a splash. Sam's screen went blank.

"I take it you just ended the video," the sheriff said.

"Yeah, and I'll probably be named in another lawsuit as a result."

"Nobody's perfect." The sheriff chuckled. I assume those are human remains and blue flip-flops that match the description of the ones Judy Herzog was wearing."

"Yeah. I'm afraid so."

"Put your sidekick on."

TJ handed his phone to Sam.

"Yes, Sheriff?"

"What do you make of this?"

"I think we've found Judy Herzog, but what we found troubles me. It's not typical crocodile behavior."

"Another skeptic?" the sheriff moaned. "TJ was bad enough. Now you, too?"

"It probably was the Animal World croc. I'm going to make some calls to be sure."

Sheriff Rodriguez said he was going to helicopter in, and the chopper would then ferry the gastric pellet and its contents back to the medical examiner's office. Sam ended the call and handed the phone back to TJ.

"The poor Herzogs," she said. "I'm sure they'll see the video, if they haven't already. What a horrible way to see the remains of your wife and mother."

"And I thought there were enough glory seekers out here today," TJ said. "That video is sure to bring out more tomorrow, between the reward and those drawn by the macabre . . ." His voice trailed off, and he turned his attention to the two men who'd found the vomit sac. The second man had his cell phone aimed at him and Sam. He briefly thought about going after that phone, too, then thought better of it.

* * *

A helicopter arrived soon afterward and landed on the street in front of the Herzogs' house. Sheriff Rodriguez and PBSO crime scene techs emerged and were ferried over to the tree mound. As the sheriff went over the men's story with them, the techs removed Judy Herzog's remains.

TJ and Sam were off to one side, watching. The sheriff joined them when he'd finished with the men. "Mad as hell. Wanted me to arrest you for assault and stealing his phone. I reminded him that you could arrest him for illegally entering the refuge."

"Well, we'll see what comes of that," TJ said. "Did you learn anything from them?"

"No. They just stumbled upon the gastric pellet. I did hear from the governor on my way over, though. She saw the YouTube video. Wants to organize all the boaters and use them to supplement our teams."

"That's a sure way *not* to find the crocodile."

"That's what I told her, but she wants the refuge searched 24/7 until the croc is found and to use, as she said, *all available means.*"

"Did you remind her it's federal land. She has no jurisdiction?"

"No. Thought it better to just let her talk, but let's go easy on the boaters for the time being." With that, sheriff joined his techs in the PBSO helicopter and flew off.

The men who found Judy Herozg's remains got back into their boat. TJ watched them leave but was surprised when they motored directly across the refuge to the levee behind the Herzogs'. TJ suspected he knew why. "C'mon," he said to Sam.

* * *

The men who found the remains walked up to the Herzogs' sliding glass door and knocked. They waited, and then knocked a second time, more loudly. Bennett D'Costa appeared and opened the door just wide enough to hear. A conversation ensued, becoming animated and ended with D'Costa angrily shoving the sliding door closed and slowly disappearing from view as the motorized shade behind the sliding glass doors went down. A local TV news cameraman happened to be nearby and caught the confrontation.

TJ and Sam followed the exchange from a discreet distance. "What do you think just happened?" Sam asked.

"If I were a betting man, I'd say that those two guys just asked for the $100,000 reward for finding Judy Herzog and were told to get lost."

"Oh."

"I hope the news crew caught that little exchange. It might discourage some croc hunters from coming out tomorrow."

"That'd be good."

TJ looked up at sky. Dark storm clouds were moving in. "It's getting late. I doubt anything more's going to happen here today. How a working dinner? We can figure out what to do next."

"Sounds like a plan."

As they left, TJ asked, "Tell me, what do you make of all this?"

"The croc, assuming it is a croc, would have rested while it digested Judy Herzog. We know she disappeared four days ago. The remains look to be less than one day old. This leads me to two conclusions. One, the croc's probably still in the area, and two, it's done with its last meal, so it's going to be looking for a new one."

CHAPTER 18

TJ and Sam headed off to a little place he knew not far away on the intercoastal in Lake Worth. The Drunken Manatee was a classic Florida waterfront bar, open on three sides, a bar along the fourth, dark wood floor and railings, all covered by a thatched roof.

After sitting down, the waiter took their drink order. Sam asked for a Sprite and TJ ordered a Yuengling beer. "Only place in the area that has it on tap," TJ said to Sam. "Sure you wouldn't like something stronger?"

"No thanks. I don't drink."

"Oh, sorry. I didn't mean—"

"That's okay. It doesn't bother me. I gave up drinking when I moved to Florida." She touched the small silver ring in her nose. "And this little sucker is my reminder not to."

TJ laughed. "People usually start drinking when they come to Florida."

"I don't miss it. And, believe me, you can get quite a buzz from Sprite."

"What about California. Do you miss that?"

"Stanford? Academia? No . . . Maybe sometimes, but the lifestyle was destroying me. The competition. Peer pressure. Always trying to be the best. It led to too much drinking and other things." She paused again. "But I have a reminder. Sam stuck her leg out and pulled up her pants leg. On the back of her lower calf was a vertical six-inch double helix tattoo—the structure of a DNA molecule. "Seemed like a good idea at the time."

TJ rolled up his left sleeve. On his upper bicep was a discrete pair of wings with a shield in front of an anchor—navy pilot wings. He grinned. "Seemed like a good idea at the time, too."

Sam laughed. "So why does a flyboy start worrying about the Everglades? I thought you just shot at everything you saw."

"Landing jets on a carrier pitching in a rough seas is a hoot, but I put in my time. I wanted to get back to really being on the water. The peacefulness of it. Being right there among the wildlife. Joining the FWS was a different way to serve."

"And somewhere along the way you became known as the python hunter of South Florida."

"That wasn't the plan, and it's a title I really don't want. Now every time I mention pythons, I get into trouble. I wish I hadn't done that TV show."

Sam softened. "You were just doing your job. Nothing wrong about that."

"Anyway, enough about pythons. I've told you about me. How about you? Leaving Stanford. Chasing crocs on the other side of the world and writing children's books. That's a big change," TJ said.

Sam wagged a finger at him. "Well, well, Mr. Forte, you've been checking up on me."

"It's from your bio when you were on my show." He didn't add that he goggled her after they'd met in the sheriff's office.

Sam grew somber. "I was married to a Silicon Valley entrepreneur. Big deal in the tech world. Turned out, he was into his business and recreational drugs and not much else. I grew tired of trying to outdo my peers on the faculty, and as my marriage dissolved, I started drinking too much and using my husband's drugs. I had to get out."

"Oh. Sorry. But Stanford to Lake Trafford. Doesn't it get lonely at times?"

Sam gave him a knowing look. "If you're asking me if I'm seeing anyone, I'm not. You?"

TJ squirmed in his seat. He hadn't realized he was being so obvious. "No. Nothing serious since Annapolis. One time there was this one lieutenant on board and we . . ." TJ saw the look on Sam's face and stopped. "Been pretty busy. Anyway, pythons and cars aren't great conversation starters with women."

"Believe me, I know the feeling. Ever try talking to a guy about alligators being ectothermic and how they use their surroundings to regulate their body temperature?"

TJ laughed.

The waiter returned with their drinks, and he began recounting old navy stories. That round was shortly followed by a second round and their dinner order. Then the conversation shifted to more serious matters.

"Let me ask you something," TJ said as they finished their dinner. "Why didn't you tell the sheriff crocs don't vomit up remains?"

"I wanted to call a couple of people first. I don't want to speculate. It's too important because if the Animal World crocodile didn't eat Judy Herzog, what did?"

* * *

After dinner, TJ dropped Sam at The Waters Edge and drove to the Twenty Mile Boat Ramp. It was quiet except for two highway patrol cars. He presented his credentials and was waved through. He parked in front of his airboat and strapped on his Sig Sauer.

On the water, he ran at just above idle, stopping to explore a tree mound. In the fading light, he saw what appeared to be a bright yellow worm wiggling at the edge of the bank. He traced the yellow as it thickened into a reddish-brown body with irregular dark brown bands ending at a large arrow-shaped head. *Water moccasin*, he thought. *Woe be it to any bird that thinks they've found a tasty meal.* He watched the viper swim away.

Night set in, and red eyes barely above the surface of the water looked up at him, but he didn't stop to see if they belonged to the Animal World crocodile. He was more interested in the red and green running lights of boats elsewhere in the refuge and particularly boats that were running dark. There were fewer out than during the day, and he took some comfort from the thought that it was the more serious, and hopefully safer, hunters who were looking for the croc at night.

He patrolled the refuge until dawn. Neither the temperature nor the humidity ever went below eighty. Fortunately, a steady breeze helped keep the bugs at bay. The quiet was regularly broken by animal calls, the flapping of wings, and loud splashes. Over the course of the night, he heard gunshots, one distinctly sounding like a bang stick, and he thought about Sam.

* * *

Early the next morning, TJ, Sam, and Sheriff Rodriguez met on the levee at the Herzogs' house, looking out over the refuge. TJ's airboat gently bobbed in the water below them. All three had binoculars hanging around their necks and radios attached to their belts.

Sam looked at TJ. "Forget to shave this morning?"

"Forgot to go home last night."

Sam wrinkled her nose. "Yeah. I can tell. You're a little ripe."

The three scanned the refuge and saw only FWS boats.

"Maybe news of the two guys yesterday not getting the reward for finding Judy Herzog's remains will discourage people from coming out," Sam said.

"I hope so," TJ replied.

But soon afterward boats began to appear.

"There's still a $100,000 reward for the croc," the sheriff said. "And these guys probably don't even care if they get it or not. The thrill of killing a man-eating crocodile in Florida is a big enough draw."

A muffled retort, the kind of sound when the muzzle of a shotgun, or a bang stick, is pressed directly against the skin, caused TJ, Sam, and Sheriff Rodriguez to raise their binoculars and turn in the direction the shot had come from. They scanned the sloughs, hammocks, and sawgrass until they came upon a bass boat bobbing in the water. Two men, one leaning over the side, were hauling in a dead animal. "Looks like a gator to me," Sam said.

A while later, a second shot sounded very close by. "Pistol," said the sheriff.

"Another gator needlessly killed," Sam said.

"How can you tell?" TJ asked.

"If it were the croc, it would have attacked the boat. We would have heard the commotion. Hard to remain calm when a fourteen-foot croc is bearing down on you." There was a moment of silence, and then Sam wondered aloud: "Why do they have to kill these animals?"

"It's the blood- lust of the hunt," TJ said.

"They hear a gunshot and want to use theirs," Sheriff Rodriguez said.

As the sun moved high in the sky, the number of boats in the refuge increased. TJ couldn't help wondering how much damage they were doing to its fragile ecosystem. The trio watched the boats. TJ and Sheriff Rodriguez worked their radios, communicating with their teams. The official and unofficial searches settled into a rhythm, punctuated at one point by the sharp twang of two aluminum hulls colliding. Angry words were exchanged but a nearby FWS boat glided over, and peace was restored.

Later that morning, as Sheriff Rodriguez was preparing to leave, the sharp crack of multiple rifle shots caused heads to turn in unison. Everyone looked to the north. Bang sticks they could ignore but not a semiautomatic rifle. "This is about to get of out control," the sheriff said. "Governor or no, we're shutting this down now."

"Agreed," TJ said.

TJ and the sheriff jumped on their radios.

* * *

All the hunters, save one, focused on the water. Doug Kirkland knew that the killer they hunted lived on land, but at the moment, he was looking for something other than Kodra. Kirkland sat in the middle seat of a flat bottom Jon boat, working his drone's controls and guiding it over hammocks and tree islands. Wilguens Darisse sat behind him, hand on the tiller as the boat cruised slowly along. Emilio Sanchez, eyes closed and dripping sweat, was lying down on a bench in the bow.

They were well west of the other boats when the semiautomatic fired off it rounds. Sanchez moaned. "Did they kill the dragon?"

Kirkland sent the drone off in the direction of the shots. He watched the screen on the controller. After a few minutes, he said, "Dead gators, no sign of the Komodo." He directed the drone west, deeper into the refuge.

The drone had been aloft for thirty minutes and was nearly out of power. Kirkland knew he'd have to bring it in and swap out its battery for a fresh one. He'd also seen the FWS boats. At some point, one of them would spot him far away from the boats in the refuge and come to investigate. The sooner he completed what he'd set out to do, the better.

Kirkland continued watching the controller's screen until a smile crept across his face. "There you are," he said softly and issued instructions to Darisse.

Sanchez sensed the acceleration and lifted his head to look around. "Why are we going into the middle of nowhere?" he said in a weak voice. "The dragon will be near where the Herzog woman's remains were found yesterday."

Kirkland ignored the comment. They arrived at a tree island and stopped just shy of it. The boat rocked gently in the wake it'd created. He could just hear the grunting of a pack of wild boars coming from the far side of the island. He got up and stood behind the first bench. Sanchez was lying on his side and looked to have fallen asleep. *Better for him*, Kirkland thought. He landed the drone and gently secured it in its carrying case. "Time to get out," he said.

Darisse stepped forward looking at him curiously.

Motioning to Sanchez, Kirkland said, "Take his feet." Sanchez moaned but offered no resistance.

They picked up Sanchez. With Kirkland in the lead, they carried him out of the boat and laid him on the shore. Then Kirkland silently unsheathed his knife. It had a sturdy six-inch clip-point blade attached to an equally sturdy six-inch sure grip handle. He leaned and plunged the blade deeply into Sanchez's upper chest, the blade sliding between Sanchez's ribs and penetrating his heart. Sanchez's eyes flew open. His hands reflexively grabbed Kirkland's knife hand, but just as quickly, his grip relaxed. He died without making a sound.

Darisse gasped. "What the . . .?"

Kirkland spoke calmly as he plunged his knife into Sanchez's gut and slashed him open up to his sternum. "He wasn't getting any better. The Komodo poisoned him when she bit him. It was only a matter of time until he went back to the clinic. Then we'd all be behind bars."

Kirkland picked up Sanchez by his shoulders. "Take his feet," he said. "And be careful. Don't get any blood on you."

Kirkland put his hands under Sanchez's arms and lifted. Darisse took hold of Sanchez's ankles. "On three," Kirkland said as he began rocking Sanchez's body. "One, two, three!" Sanchez landed with a thump on the edge of the bushes.

They returned to the Jon boat and Kirkland backed it a few feet off the hammock. He wiped his knife with a rag and threw both into the water. "Won't take long," he predicted.

A black face, with a pig-like nose and two tusks protruding from its mouth, appeared at the top of the island. Several more faces appeared shortly afterward.

The wild boar was the first invasive animal in the Everglades. Hernando DeSoto, the Spanish explorer, brought boars with him for food when he'd explored Florida in 1539 and, of course, some escaped. Scavengers with an acute sense of smell, their diets consisted mostly of vegetation, although they much preferred meat. The pungent smell of disemboweled carrion immediately attracted them, just as Kirkland had anticipated.

The pack, the largest of which weighed almost two hundred pounds, cautiously approached the body. Then the big boar ripped into Sanchez's stomach and rooted around. Satisfied, he lifted his head. His snout and tusks were red with blood and a piece of Sanchez's intestine dangled from his mouth. That was the signal. The pack descended on Sanchez, ripping him apart.

Kirkland and Darisse silently watched the grisly scene from the safety of the Jon boat. The boars dismembered Sanchez and devoured their meal in matter of minutes. Satisfied, Kirkland swung the bow around and accelerated. "Give the boat a good washing with bleach when we get back," he said.

* * *

The sun shone brightly, and Kodra was about to leave the hammock when two humans approached in a boat. She crouched down and watched. The boat turned and motored slowly away, the men's attention focused on the shoreline and the water.

She wanted to hunt but hesitated, as the many scents of humans mixed with odors of gas and oil came to her. She retreated to the top of her hammock and saw many boats with humans moving about on the marsh. She was puzzled by the activity and unsure what to do when the sound of a bang stick firing caused her to flinch.

Her eyes flared when she caught the scent of the men from the farm and remembered the pain inflicted on her by the man with the stick. The scents faded and did not return, but she felt no relief. Humans in boats continued to pass by. Some came close to her hammock but didn't see her. There was more gun fire and, once, the sharp retorts of the semiautomatic rifle.

The wind was blowing from the east, and the island where the boars were feasting on Sanchez was to her west, so she was unaware of the boars' blood fest. But the wind carried a scent that intrigued her. She yearned to leave the hammock and investigate but was afraid to move.

CHAPTER 19

Six alligators were lined up in a row on top of the levee behind the Herzog's house as TJ, Sam, and Sheriff Rodriguez examined them. Given the number of gunshots heard throughout the day, there certainly were more floating in the refuge, TJ knew.

Three had neat bang stick holes in their heads. At least they'd died quickly. The fourth had multiple gunshots in a crude crescent shape, starting at the base of its tail and ending in its neck. It also had an exit wound in its back, indicating that it was thrashing in the water and had been shot in the stomach. The fifth gator lay there peacefully, showing no signs of trauma, but fluids leaked from its stomach, darkening the grass around it, and a yellow rope hung from its mouth. This gator had swallowed a chunk of meat attached to a grappling hook. The hunter then pulled on the rope, and the barbed prongs ripped and shredded the gator's stomach, its esophagus, and probably its lungs. The more the gator thrashed and pulled, the more its insides had been eviscerated. As it twisted and struggled, one of the barbed prongs of the hook had punctured its hide, and now blood and gastric juices drained from its side onto the grass beneath it. The final alligator was missing half its head, the result of a shotgun blast at close range. Flies swarmed the gore. Set apart from the six alligators was the body of a young panther.

TJ, Sam, and Sheriff Rodriguez walked slowly down the row of dead alligators. Sam was in tears. She pointed to the fifth gator. "Look at that. I saw him when he was brought in. Stomach ripped open by a snatch hook. I thought they were illegal. What a horrible way to die. The asshole who did this should be in jail."

"I wish I could, but I can't," TJ said. "I told these guys, and I mean that loosely because there were women out there, too, to bring in what they killed, leave, and nothing would happen to them."

"Even the guy with the semiautomatic," Sheriff Rodriguez added. "We checked his license, and the gun was properly registered."

"It was best to end this thing and get them the hell out of here before someone got hurt," TJ said. He looked into the refuge and saw only a couple of boats in the distance that didn't belong. He was both surprised and pleased that it'd taken only a few hours to clear the refuge since the decision had been made to shut it down. "Once the shooting starts, it's contagious. They just start firing at everything. Only good thing is they didn't shoot each other."

Sam sighed. "Men . . . but why the panther? You could have arrested that guy."

"Don't know who did it," TJ said. "My rangers found him lying on an island, already dead. It's a damn shame. We don't have panthers in the refuge. This one might have been staking out a new territory. There's only about two hundred left in the Everglades."

"Excuse me. Time to call the governor," the sheriff said.

After Rodriguez stepped away, TJ turned to Sam. "Shouldn't you be calling the governor?"

"I'm happy to leave that to the sheriff. I don't want anyone micromanaging my investigation."

TJ looked back at the Herzogs' house and caught a glimpse of a black Bentley turning into the driveway. *Here comes trouble,* he thought.

"Well, that ends it," the sheriff said, slipping his phone back into his pants pocket. "That was Governor Johnson. I brought her up to speed on what's been happening here, although she'd gotten the idea from the news. She's declared a state of emergency for the Arthur Marshall Wildlife Refuge, and the adjacent wetlands. She's also called in the National Guard to secure the perimeter and asked the FBI for assistance."

"That's a big area," TJ said. "Going to need a lot of Guard and a lot of boats. We haven't even begun searching the bottom two-thirds of the refuge or the Hillsboro."

"What's that?" Sam asked.

"Another major canal. It runs from Lake O to the intercoastal water-way near Boca Raton," Rodriguez said. "Also forms the border between Palm Beach and Broward counties. Croc slips through there, and it becomes the Broward County sheriff's problem. I'm sure Sheriff McDermott would love that."

"Slips past there and he's in the Everglades," TJ said. "Good luck find-ing him then."

"What will the FBI do?" Sam asked.

"Probably technical and forensics support, not that we need it," Rodri-guez said. "I suspect the governor's calling them in mostly for show."

"Speaking of forensics," Sam said, "what are you going to do with these?" She motioned toward the row of dead alligators.

"Cut 'em open, see what we find," the sheriff said.

"I'm pretty sure you won't find anything."

"I suspect not, but we have to be sure."

Their conversation was interrupted by Bennett D'Costa marching up the berm, mouth opening, chest heaving from the exertion. "Well? Do you have it? Which one is it?"

"They're gators," TJ said disdainfully.

"Then you didn't get him. Why not? I'm told it sounded like a shooting gallery out here all day."

"And that may be the reason why," TJ said.

"How dare you put the Herzogs through this and—"

"You put them through this with that stupid reward," TJ shot back.

"And what about the Powells? Don't they matter to you?" Sam asked definitively.

"I'm going to call the governor," D'Costa said.

"She already knows. I told her," Sheriff Rodriguez said.

D'Costa turned on his heels and stormed back down the berm.

Short man's complex, TJ thought. "Well, that was a pleasant interlude," he said sarcastically. "So, back to business. Now that we're going to have the refuge to ourselves, let's get back to finding this thing."

"He's probably still close by," Sam said. "Why leave his food source? Of course, he has a good homing instinct. He might just decide to return back to Animal World."

"That's an interesting thought," the sheriff said. "I'll alert our guys in the Southern Boulevard area to be on the lookout. I'll let the Guard know, too."

"I'll call Mumford," TJ said with a grin. "Tell him to leave a light on. His croc might be coming home. And no need to unlock the gate, he'll just climb over the fence."

Sam rolled her eyes. "When can we expect the Guard?" she asked Rodriguez.

"First units tomorrow, according to the governor," the sheriff replied. "Any ideas how to use them?"

"Boots and boats," TJ said. "Just like the military. Troops on the perimeter, more checking the islands and a line of boats, more than we had before. But even then . . . the refuge is over two hundred square miles."

"And the croc is fourteen feet long and blends in," Sam said. "Better odds winning the lottery than finding him."

TJ turned to her. "Does the gastric pellet still bother you?"

"Bother?" Sheriff Rodriguez said. "The ME confirmed the remains were Judy Herzog. Not that there really was any doubt."

"Sam thought it was unusual for a crocodile to regurgitate remains," TJ said.

"It's not something you'd expect from a crocodile or an alligator," Sam said to the sheriff. "They're able to digest just about anything. I made some calls last night. It's possible. Perhaps the rubber flip-flops caused it. But no one could give me a clear answer. I'd going to do some more research."

The three lapsed into silence as they watched the activity in the refuge. After a while, the sheriff said, "Looks quiet here. I'm going back to the office and see what else is happening in Palm Beach County."

"I think I'll take the airboat for a look around," TJ said. He looked at Sam. "Wanna come?"

"No thanks, airboats make me sick. I'll hitch a ride with the sheriff."

A reporter ran up to Sam and the sheriff in the Herzogs' driveway. The sheriff waved him away and kept walking, but Sam stopped and spoke with him.

* * *

As the day wore on, the gunshots stopped, the boats disappeared, and the refuge quieted. Natural scents and sounds returned, and the scent that had intrigued her some hours ago was still nearby. Kodra rose but hesitated at the foot of the water, crouching low and staying still. She took in the nearby scents. Deciding it was safe, she entered the water and swam to the next hammock, drawn by the smell of a wounded animal.

She found a young doe lying on its side, chest heaving and mouth open. The doe weakly looked up at her and waved a front hoof ever so slightly in defense. Blood oozed from a neat round hole in the doe's stomach. Kodra circled the doe. The doe turned her head, warily tracking Kodra's movements. Without warning, Kodra lunged forward and tore a chunk of flesh from the doe's stomach. The doe cried in pain, her legs thrashing spasmodically. Soon thereafter, she stopped moving. The doe could no longer lift her head, but her eyes were wide with fear and never left Kodra. Kodra approached more slowly, almost casually, and took a second bite out of the doe's stomach. The doomed animal uttered only a small sound, and her eyes closed.

The doe was more bone than meat, a meagre meal, leaving Kodra hungry. It was getting late. She would scrape out a nest here tonight. But she was learning there was not enough food in this water-based environment and no place to dig a deep nest. She remembered the areas where she'd found the boy and the woman. They were like Flores—dry land, places to nest, and find prey. When it was light out, she would go there.

CHAPTER 20

The next morning, TJ drove to his office in the pouring rain. He called Sam on his way. "Good morning, sunshine, how may I be of service today?"

"I'm in no mood for your sarcasm, TJ."

"I wasn't—"

"I'm packing up and leaving." "Why?"

"Apparently, I displeased Governor Johnson."

"Welcome to the club."

"My per diem has been ended effective this morning. I'm still on the payroll but I've been told to go home and await further instructions."

"What happened between you and Johnson?"

"See the news last night?"

"No."

"When I spoke with that reporter at the Herzogs' yesterday, I described what went on in the Arthur Marshall as *the great alligator slaughter*. The gov didn't like it. So I got the boot. At least the sheriff has offered to have one of his deputies drive me back to Lake Trafford."

He was sad that she was leaving, but maybe it was for the best, TJ thought. More animals were going to be needlessly killed, and Sam would be better off not witnessing it.

At the Arthur Marshall FWS headquarters, he received a call from Sheriff Rodriguez. "I just received the autopsy reports on the six alligators. No human remains were found in any of their stomachs."

"No surprise there."

Rodriguez continued, "In addition to the usual fish, turtles, and small wildlife there were water and soda bottles, an empty motor oil can, and cable ties. One alligator had swallowed a plastic bag that blocked her intestine."

"That animal had to have been in a great deal of pain. The hunters did her a favor by killing her."

The sheriff continued, "The blood work revealed toxins, principally chemicals found in pesticides, in all six."

TJ sighed. "Plastics and poisons in a wildlife refuge. Sometimes I wonder why I even try."

He took some satisfaction from his next call. The commander of the National Guard told him that his first troops and equipment had arrived and more were on the way. They were relieving the Highway Patrol and blocking the likely entrances to the refuge.

It rained steadily for two days, which TJ thought was more effective in calming the situation and keeping boats out of the refuge than the National Guard or the governor's widely publicized zero tolerance policy, with fines and jail time for any unauthorized person hunting the crocodile.

When the weather cleared, the guards' search for the crocodile got off to a slow start. They entered the refuge in their boats, probed along the edges of the numerous spits of land, and, as best they could, walked the larger hammocks and tree islands. The densely packed outcroppings of trees and bushes with large exposed roots weren't people-friendly, and the going was slow. A late afternoon thunderstorm brought the first day's operation to a halt.

On the second day of the search, TJ was called in. An empty boat had been found adrift in the refuge. "Where there's a boat, there's a body," he said. "Keep looking."

TJ arrived as quickly as he could. As he neared, he cut his airboat's engine to idle and let the boat's forward motion carry him in. A small boat painted in splotches of green, brown, and black was tied to a bush on a hammock with a single line. The camouflage pattern paint was worn off in some spots, revealing a dull aluminum. A guard boat floated next to it. Two other guard boats were nearby, one on each side of a body bobbing in the water. The men onboard were using paddles to hold the boats in place.

"This is where we found it," a guardsman next to the empty boat said. "It was floating free, and we thought it best to secure it in place."

"Good work. You guys tilt the motor out of the water?" TJ asked. The guardsmen said no.

TJ tied up his airboat next to the abandoned craft and carefully stepped in it. Studying the contents, the first thing that caught his eye was a length of rope with a wooden peg tied to one end. The peg had rotted meat around it that was covered with flies and insects. "Guy was drifting, hunting gators," he said to the group.

There was a thermos and a chest, which he opened, containing more meat, a sandwich, and two six packs of beer. The last item in the boat was a dirty backpack. TJ went through it, found a wallet, and pulled out a driver's license. "Virgil Polk, from Ocala, age twenty-eight," he said and noted Polk's physical description. He took a picture of the license and sent it to Sheriff Rodriquez along with a text telling him what he'd found and asking him to research Polk.

He then walked along the edge of the hammock, stepping carefully to avoid the twisted roots and short thick plants. Polk's body floated just offshore. TJ asked a guardsman for a boat hook. He nudged the body with it, and Polk rolled over. His eyes, nose, and lips were gone. "Well, we probably just found Virgil Polk. The body matches the description on his driver's license. Looks like the fish got him pretty bad, though."

"You don't think it was vultures?" a guardsman asked. "Hate 'em," he said under his breath.

"No. Body's in the water," TJ answered. "They hunt on land." He gently prodded Polk with the boat hook. "Something gave him a pretty good bite."

"Do you think it was the crocodile?"

"Could be, but I sorta doubt it. I think the croc would have eaten him or, at least, some of him. Better keep your eyes open though." TJ took more pictures and sent them to the sheriff.

FWS rangers arrived with a body bag and removed Polk's body and his boat. The guard boats left one-by-one and returned to their pre-assigned search grids. Alone, TJ sat in his airboat floating just off the hammock pondering what he could learn from Polk's death.

* * *

The two days of storms had filled her burrow with water, forcing Kodra to abandon it. The scrawny strangler fig tree beside her lair provided no protection from the weather. She could see or smell little during the storm and, water dripping off of her, she paced anxiously around the tree mound.

When the sun appeared on the third day, she was ready to leave her island and hunt. The scent of carrion reached her, and she knew it was nearby. But just as she was going to enter the marsh, the boats came. She could smell the humans and hear their voices. The carrion continued to beckon, and she yearned to eat, but more than once as she was about to leave the island a boat appeared and she was forced to retreat.

The next day the waters around her tree mound were quiet. The humans and their boats were nowhere in sight, but scent told her they were in the area of the carrion that held her attention. Ever vigilant, Kodra slipped into the water, swam to a hammock, climbed on it, and swam to the next. The scent of her target became stronger as she went. She cautiously peered over the top of the hammock and spotted Polk's body floating face down in the water. Saliva dripped from her mouth in anticipation. But there were boats with humans around it. She tracked the activity. Another boat arrived, different from the others and containing only one human. Kodra caught his scent and recognized the man. She rose and stepped forward when the man nudged her meal, his scent intermingled with the carrion. She longed to run down the hill, into the water, and take it from him, but there were too many humans around. Her eyes flared as two men reached into the water and lifted the body into their boat. Her meal disappeared as they motored away.

All the boats left except for the one that held the man whose scent she knew. A lone human was prey, but his boat floated just off the hammock, and Kodra knew it was too far for her to jump into from the shore. She watched, waiting for the boat to touch the hammock, until its motor came to life, and it went away.

CHAPTER 21

The National Guard's search for the crocodile officially ended a week after the great alligator slaughter. Even Governor Johnson was forced to agree there was nothing more for the guard to do. The men and women were told to stand down. Wet, bruised, and battered, they gratefully went back to their families and their regular jobs. There'd been multiple snake bites, fortunately only one was poisonous, and injuries from slips and falls along with a few broken bones. The insects had enjoyed the humans in the refuge and would miss them.

The guard had searched the entire refuge and surrounding canals. Finding Polk's body had created some excitement, but TJ appeared on the news, saying it was more likely a gator bit him than the escaped croc. The press was no doubt disappointed that the crocodile wasn't responsible and hadn't eaten Polk and grew bored. They speculated that even if the croc wasn't already in the Everglades, it was never going to be found. TJ knew that was a possibility and also knew his exhausted team needed a rest.

"The croc's either gone or will make its presence known when it gets hungry," he said to Sheriff Rodriguez. "I just hope its meal isn't another person, and speaking of that, the first day of school is next week."

"Yeah. We've been lucky so far. A lot of people away on vacation, but everyone will be back by then."

"Anything more on Polk?"

"No. Guy was a loaner. Kept to himself. No steady job. No close friends. That's why nobody reported him missing. We did find his truck a ways out on Southern. Sheriff up in Ocala tracked down a sister in Ohio, evidently his nearest kin. Not much more to say."

* * *

TJ was up early as always even though it was Sunday. He tossed down his polishing cloth and stepped back to admire his 1965 Corvair convertible, Madeira maroon with a red vinyl interior, that he was prepping for sale. The garage door was open, and the red-legged iguana sat just outside, watching him.

The Corvair was an acquired taste. His father considered it a marvel of GM technological prowess, Ralph Nader, the automotive activist, considered it unsafe at any speed. TJ agreed with Nader that the swing axle on the rear of the first-generation Corvair could cause a tire to pivot under the car and flip it over, but his had a redesigned independent rear suspension that solved the problem. His father railed that Nader was anti-GM for failing to point out that the Triumph Spitfire and other cars had the same rear axle design and the same problem as the original Corvair.

TJ had done some body work and replaced the oil cooler gasket. The four one-barrel carburetors on the air-cooled six-cylinder engine had been a bear to adjust and sync, but the Corvair looked good, ran good, and was priced to move. The Corvair along with a hundred or so other cars would be on display at the BB&T arena, home of the Florida Panthers ice hockey team, in Sawgrass, north of Miami. TJ was always amused by hockey rinks in Florida. *Didn't people come down here to get away from the ice?* But, then again, he had season tickets. His thoughts quickly returned to the recent events in the refuge, and the dead panther flashed though his mind. *Almost as many cars for sale at the arena as there are panthers left in Florida.* He spirits brightened when he replaced that thought with the prospect of spending the day looking at cars and talking to car people.

* * *

The crocodile sensed the current pick up and allowed the flow to carry him. South Florida Water Management was moving water out of the stormwater treatment marsh. Most of the water was pumped east along the West Palm Beach Canal, but some flowed down a smaller canal that paralleled Flying Cow Road. The canal fed many ponds and water features in Wellington, including those at the exclusive Wellington Palm Beach Golf Club.

A member hit a tee shot on the fourteenth hole that landed at the edge of a water hazard. Upon approaching, the golfer saw what he thought was an alligator some distance away in the water. The golfer decided it was safe to play his ball. The alligator turned out to be the crocodile, which raced through the water and onto land, heading for the golfer. The golfer, intent upon setting up his shot, heard his buddies yelling but thought they were only messing with him. Moments later, he felt a sharp pain and was taken to the ground. The croc dragged the man into the water. A member of his foursome grabbed his driver and came running but could only stand by helplessly as the croc rolled the golfer around in the water.

A retired army general waiting to tee off at the fifteenth heard the commotion. She pulled her service revolver out of her golf bag and ran over. She dropped to one knee and calculated how fast the croc was spinning and timed her shot. The first narrowly missed the golfer. She put the second into the croc's head.

* * *

TJ wandered over to the refreshment stand. A number of people, one or two possibly serious, had stopped to look at his Corvair. He was going to grab a coffee and check out some of the other cars for sale on his way back. The ringing of his cell phone changed his focus. The caller ID read Richard Rodriguez. *Whenever I've got a car to sell*, he thought as he hit *Accept*. "Sheriff, what can I do for you?"

"You need to get yourself up here ASAP."

"Why?"

"We've got a dead croc at the Wellington Equine Hospital. Al Mumford is on his way, and we're helicoptering in Sam Brown from Lake Trafford."

Good thing I worked on the Corvair's engine, TJ thought.

CHAPTER 22

TJ pulled up to the Wellington Equine Center, a large terra-cotta-colored Florida-style building. Sheriff Rodriguez met him at the door and told him what had happened at the golf course. The golfer was in critical condition, and it wasn't clear if he would survive.

They passed through the waiting room which was bright, modern, spotless, and as nice as any doctor's office. The wealthy residents of Wellington wanted their horses to have the best care. Down a hall was an operating room. In it, laid out on its back and instantly recognizable by its elongated snout, was a fourteen-foot-long crocodile. TJ was surprised to see that Sam was already there. He smiled and nodded to her. Sheriff Rodriguez, Al Mumford, the Palm Beach County medical examiner, a vet, and assistants were also in the room. A PBSO deputy with a video camera mounted on a tripod was off to one side.

"Okay, now that everyone's here, let's begin," Rodriguez said.

The deputy switched on the video camera and started recording. Sheriff Rodriguez began by recounting the events of the day.

After the sheriff finished, Mumford stepped forward, checked the microchip implant, and confirmed it was Animal World's missing crocodile. The vet then instructed everyone to put on the face masks she'd provided— for the stench, she said—and proceeded to make a large incision the length of the croc's belly and spread its skin. She opened the stomach and studied it. TJ, Sam, and Sheriff Rodriguez craned their necks to look in. With gloved hands, the vet began removing its contents. One by one, she placed them on an adjoining table.

She pointed with a scalpel to the first one, a crushed turtle shell. The croc's teeth marks were plainly visible on the shell. "Turtle, swallowed whole." She looked at the second set of remains. "Adult toad or frog. Given its size, most likely a Cane toad." She probed the third set of remains with her scalpel. "Dog with white fur."

"Any chance it's a bull terrier?" TJ asked.

"I don't think so," replied a vet. "But we'll run a DNA test to determine the type of dog . . . wait." The vet probed some more. "Here's a tag. "Zeus.""

"Zeus," the sheriff repeated. "That solves one of the two missing dog reports we've received."

"D'Costa's going to be disappointed," TJ added. "So much for the croc eating his dog."

The vet made another incision and continued her examination. She concluded: "No evidence of human remains in either the stomach or intestine."

"Sheriff, can we get pictures of Bobby Powell's bites sent here?" TJ asked. "I'd like the doc to compare them to the crocodile's mouth."

Sheriff Rodriguez made a call. The photos were promptly emailed over from the PBSO, and the vet looked at them. Even a layperson could tell that the large teeth and V-like snout of the crocodile would make bite marks that weren't similar to those on Bobby Powell's body.

"Well, that's not a surprise, given what we didn't find," the sheriff said, "Although it would've made things easier if they'd matched."

"We need to take another look at those bites," TJ said. "Maybe there's someone out there who can identify the animal that made them."

"Let's figure out who," Rodriguez said. "Any other thoughts?"

TJ and Sam looked at each other. After a moment, Sam said, "Anne Herzog said she saw an alligator carry off her mother. We may be back to our two-gator theory."

Sheriff Rodriguez sighed. "I hope not."

TJ's face lit up. "What if she was mistaken? What if she only thought she saw a gator?"

"Good point," the sheriff said. "We never spoke with the girl. Seeing her mother carried away in the mouth of an animal . . . Well." The sheriff paused. "I'll call Martin Herzog. Tell him we're coming by tomorrow morning to talk with his little girl. He won't like it, but it's going to happen." He concluded by saying, "I'm heading back to my office. Got the governor and the press to deal with."

"How about you?" TJ asked Sam.

"I'm hungry."

"After just seeing a crocodile get its stomach split open?"

"I've seen worse. If you're up for it, I'm buying." She paused and smiled slightly. "Or should I say the state of Florida is buying."

"Got your per diem back I assume."

"Yes, and it's going to be another working dinner. We need to figure out what ate Judy Herzog."

They walked out to TJ's Corvair. Sam said, "Different car."

"Yeah. I've got six.

Sam rolled her eyes.

"Not so fast. I restore and sell. Cars are a business as well as a hobby. Some people put their money in the bank, some in the stock market. I buy old cars, fix them up, and hope to make a profit. Now before I bore you, any thoughts on dinner?"

"Same place as last time is fine." Sam smiled. "Where else can you get an ice cold Yuengling?"

As they walked into the Drunken Manatee, TJ stopped and looked at the big screen TV over the bar. A Florida Panthers game from last season was playing.

After they'd sat down and ordered drinks Sam asked, "Hockey fan?"

"Big time. High school varsity team."

"So you're a cold weather guy. Why didn't you go back to Michigan after the navy?"

"Nothing for me there. Parents both gone. My dad was laid off from GM and just gave up. Drank too much. I've got a younger brother, but we don't talk much. He should have gotten out as well."

"I'm sorry."

"How about you?" TJ asked. "Parents?"

"Retired and living the good life in California."

"Brothers, sisters?"

"One of each. Brother's married. A lawyer. Sister a bit of a lost soul. Still trying to find herself."

The first round was followed by a second round, and the conversation shifted to more serious matters. "If not the croc, then we're back to . . . what?" Sam asked.

TJ thought for a while before responding. "Let's start with what we have—the remains—what was left of Judy Herzog. Lots of different animals could have eaten her, but what would they have left behind? The mammalian predators in the Everglades—bear, boar, panther, and so on—don't swallow their prey. They eat the flesh and leave the carcass." He hesitated a moment and then his eyes flashed. "It just dawned on me—there wasn't a carcass."

"How can you be sure?"

"Vultures. There were no vultures. If there was a carcass, there'd be vultures circling. And there were none anywhere near where the gastric pellet was found. I did see a flock farther west, but they appeared after all the bounty hunters were in the refuge, so the vultures were attracted to a recent death, not Judy's."

"Hmmm. If it's not an animal that eats its prey, it's gotta be one that swallows it whole. In the Everglades, the only animals big enough to do that are alligators and pythons."

"Let's be careful about bringing pythons into this, they get me into trouble," TJ said with a wry smile. "Anyway, none have been found in the Arthur Marshall . . . yet."

"Okay, then. We're back to our two-gator theory. To paraphrase Sherlock Holmes, when you've eliminated everything else, whatever remains, however improbable, might be the answer."

That bit of wisdom called for another round of Sprite and beer. "You sure about a python?" Sam asked.

"I've always said it's a matter of when, not if, a python kills a human, but pythons typically digest everything they eat."

"I've spoken with John Robertson. He's the chair of the herpetology department at the University of Florida. He told me that gastric pellets are generally associated with lizards. Their digestive juices are not as potent as those of other reptiles."

"Lizard? That'd be some big lizard," TJ said. He thought some more. "The biggest lizards we have down here are monitors. Invasive species. Established breeding colonies around Cape Coral and from West Palm to Miami. But they're too small, although . . ."

"Although what?"

Before TJ could answer, the waiter came around with their meals and asked them if they'd like another round.

"I'm driving, so two's my limit," TJ said.

"Hey, it's been a long day," Sam interjected. "If you're not embarrassed to share my room at The Waters Edge, you can crash there for the night."

"Embarrassed?"

She smiled. "Just don't get any ideas flyboy. I have a nice comfy couch. And I'll drive."

"Can you drive a stick?" TJ asked.

She held out her hand playfully. "Hand over your keys, sailor."

TJ accepted her offer and ordered another beer. "Want to hear more about monitor lizards?" he asked.

"I'm all ears."

"Well, most of them are small, two-three feet long, but there are some . . . Nile monitors can grow to be five feet or longer. There was a news story last year about a family in Cape Coral. A Nile monitor lizard broke through their pool screen enclosure and appeared at their back door. It was estimated to be six feet long and weigh over one hundred and twenty pounds. It came and went for two days, just staring into the house when it was around. The parents were afraid to let their children go outside. Trappers were called, but the lizard evaded them and finally disappeared to who knows where. It's believed to have been someone's escaped pet and was waiting at the door to be fed. You can see it on YouTube."

"I'm aware of monitors, of course, but I've never paid them any attention. There aren't any around Lake Trafford. Do you think there are other Niles on the loose?"

"I'm sure of it. There's been other sightings. They've been classified as a conditional species in Florida for a number of years. That means you need a license to have one, and the licenses are restricted to researchers, zoos, and the like. But the definitions are loose, and there are Niles illegally bought and kept as pets. Some are released or escape . . . you know the story."

"Yes. Well, maybe we'll learn more in the morning when we talk to Anne Herzog. Right now, it's getting late, and I promised to drive you."

On the way to the motel, the Corvair lurched and stalled, the gears grinding as Sam shifted. It was obvious she didn't know how to drive a manual transmission, TJ noted with dismay.

* * *

Kodra sensed something was different. The refuge was quiet, the scent of humans and the scents she associated with humans were gone. She cautiously approached the edge of the hammock and looked around. She saw no people, no boats. She'd wanted to leave the marsh since before the rains and the guard had come. Seizing the opportunity, she swam the marsh and crossed the canal. Sampling the air as she went, she retraced her steps to the berm behind the Herzog's house and stopped to rest among a grouping of coconut palms and ornamental shrubs.

She continued on, skirting the lawns and traveling along the edge of the berm. Keeping low, she worked her way south, drawn by the natural scents of water, birds, and other animals until she arrived at the Wellington Environmental Preserve. She spent the day exploring the preserve, skirting its marshes, stopping to drink at a natural pool, and hiding when a group of hikers passed by. As hungry as she was, there were just too many humans, and she knew there was other prey around.

As TJ and Sam drove off to dinner, Kodra was again on the move. It was getting late, but the wind from the east had brought fresh scents of dogs, horses, and cows. The ground cover ended, and she emerged from the bushes, head bobbing right and left, gathering scents. She was greeted by a hot flat surface, Flying Cow Road, and the noxious odors of gas, oil, grease, and rubber. Beyond it was a large expanse of grass, dotted with trees, the smell of fresh water, and only a weak scent of humans. She stepped on to the pavement, preparing to scamper to the other side.

A car raced down the road, radio blaring, the teenage driver more interested in the girl next to him than the speed limit. At the last moment, he swerved. The girl screamed.

"Damn dog!" he exclaimed.

"I think it might have been a gator," the girl said.

The boy looked in his rearview mirror but saw nothing.

Unphased, Kodra crossed the road and disappeared into a field which gave way to a closely cropped grass plain. The principal scents were birds and water. She looked around and saw small hills, outcroppings of trees, shrubs, and ponds. The landscape was similar to her native island, except for the swaths of short green grass.

She was on a golf course, although she didn't know what one was. It was the same course where the crocodile had been killed earlier in the day. The course had been closed after the incident and was quiet. The general who'd dispatched the croc and the other witnesses had been interviewed, and along with the PBSO investigators, had departed.

Big heavy drops of water pelted her, running down her body. Surprised, Kodra rose up on her hind legs. Then the water stopped. She dropped down, looked around, checked the air for scents, and resumed walking. Soon thereafter, a second blast of water hit her, not as hard as the first but more drenching. The rotating golf course sprinklers had come around again. To Kodra, it was rain, and with night approaching, she sought safety and shelter. The fairway she was on—a smooth savannah to her—offered no protection. She looked around. Not far ahead was a small hill, covered on three sides with grass. The fourth side was bare earth. She ambled over to the dirt and began to climb. The dirt turned out to be sand and she slipped as she clambered to the top. Sliding back down, she scooped out sand from the crook of the bunker and made a cavity large enough to curl up into. She would spend the night in a sand trap on the fifth hole of the Wellington Palm Beach Golf Club. Tomorrow she would hunt.

CHAPTER 23

TJ awoke to Sam shaking him on his shoulder. He groaned and rolled over on the couch.

"Time to get up flyboy," she said. "You need to get home, shower, and change your clothes. We're due at the sheriff's office at nine."

TJ rolled back over. "I'll just shower here."

"No you won't. Your clothes have a distinct odor of crocodile guts. You show up like this, and the rumors will fly. You need to go home and clean up."

Back at his house, showered, shaved, and fortified by strong black coffee, he opted for his '64 Thunderbird. It was bigger and faster than the Corvair and had an automatic transmission, just in case he gave the keys to Sam again. He shuddered to think how she'd react if the steering column popped out of position and decided he'd better be the T-Bird's only driver. The day was hot, muggy, and overcast, with afternoon thunderstorms expected to roll in. *Another typical August day*, he thought.

On a whim, he rooted around in his garage and found a metal cage. He set the open cage in front the garage, placed the iguana's food in it, and stepped out of sight. In a matter of moments, he heard the clicking of the iguana's claws on the cement driveway and cautiously peered out of the garage. The iguana bobbed its head looking through the metal bars that separated it from its meal. Then it walked around the cage and entered it. When it began to eat, TJ quickly moved in and closed the cage door. The iguana stopped eating and looked back at him, then it went back to its breakfast.

He hoped Miguel was out today. The boy wasn't at his usual corner, but TJ spotted him walking up the street, holding an iguana by its tail. *One iguana. Does that mean business is good or bad?* TJ wondered.

TJ stopped and powered down the window.

The boy smiled. "Hola, señor." He spied the caged iguana in the back seat. "He looks lonely." The boy held up his iguana. "Do you want another?"

"Not today. But I want to ask you if you've heard anything about other kinds of lizards being sold, or big lizards, in the area?"

"No, señor." "Well, let me know if you do. There's a twenty in it for you."

TJ called Sam on his way north and told her his idea. She was waiting when he pulled into The Waters Edge parking lot. Greeting TJ with a smile, she peered into the car. In the back seat, in a cage on an old brown blanket, the iguana blinked his eyes.

Sam and the iguana nodded approvingly to each other. On their way to the Herzogs', Sam said, "I think we should name him."

"Really?"

"Yes. Let's name him Tomàs."

"Thomas? You got to be kidding."

"Tomàs, and no I'm not kidding."

"We don't even know if it's a boy."

"His name is Tomàs. Why? Are you too good to have an iguana named after you?"

The matter settled, they arrived at the Herzogs', and were met by Sheriff Rodriguez. "I spoke with Martin Herzog last night and, again, a few minutes ago," the sheriff said. "D'Costa advised him not to let us speak with his daughter. He gave Herzog some legal mumbo jumbo. Mr. Herzog is understandably concerned that any questions will worsen the girl's trauma, but I told him we'd be careful with our questions, and his daughter's answers may help us find Judy's killer."

As the sheriff went to knock on the front door, TJ took the blanket from the back seat and set Tomàs' cage on top of it on the trunk of the T-Bird.

Martin Herzog opened the door, jaw clenched and gave the trio a hard look. Anne stood just in front of him, her father's hands resting protectively on her shoulders. They stepped outside, and Anne's eyes lit up when she saw the caged iguana. The girl broke free from her father and ran over to the car. Herzog's expression softened. "She loves animals."

"It's an iguana," TJ said.

"I know that," Anne responded.

"His name is Tomàs," Sam said.

Anne studied Tomàs. "He's different."

"Different?"

Anne's faced turned pale. "Then the one that ate my mother."

"Annie!" Herzog said. He reached his daughter and clutched her to his chest.

Tomàs sensed Martin Herzog's anger and nervously danced around in his cage.

The young girl squirmed in his father's arms and turned around to face TJ, Sam, and Sheriff Rodriguez.

"What do you mean, Anne?" Sam asked softly.

"It was a lot bigger, and its head was different."

"That's because it was an alligator," his father said gently to his daughter.

"Do you think it was an alligator, Anne?" Sam asked.

The girl looked at the ground. "No."

"She's just a child," Herzog said. "Of course it was an alligator. What else could it have been?"

Sam bent down toward the girl and asked softy, "How else was it different, Anne?"

"It was . . . I don't know . . . different colors."

"What colors was it?"

"All different colors . . . green, brown, gray . . ."

Sam continued in a soft voice, conscious of Herzog's stare. "Do you know what color an alligator is?"

"They're dark . . . brown . . . black."

"That's right," Sam said. She took out her phone, punched a few buttons, and showed the screen to Anne. "Did the animal look like this?"

Anne started to cry. "Yes."

Sam turned the screen around and showed it to the three men. On it was a picture of a Nile Monitor lizard.

"That's enough," Herzog said and marched Anne back inside.

The sheriff looked at Sam. "What was that all about?"

"I think a monitor lizard ate his sister. An alpha male Nile monitor lizard."

Rodriguez frowned. "You'd better explain."

"It's the gastric pellet. It just doesn't fit with an alligator or crocodile, and we know the crocodile didn't eat Judy Herzog. Monitor lizards are here in Florida, and lizards regurgitate gastric pellets."

"There's a breeding population along the C-51 canal just north of here," TJ said. "We sent some men in earlier this year to eliminate them. Monitors take off when they see you. They're fast and good swimmers. We didn't get many."

Sheriff Rodriguez nodded. "You better run me through your thinking, Sam."

"Okay, here goes. As TJ said, there are established breeding populations of monitor lizards in South Florida. Here, in Broward and Dade counties, and on the west coast in Lee County."

"They were first spotted in 1990," TJ added.

"Nile monitors are the biggest member of the monitor lizard family," Sam continued. "They typically grow to five feet, although there have been reported sightings of seven-foot monitors here in Florida."

"I've seen a couple myself," the sheriff said. "Small ones, though. Had reports of them eating kittens but never any problems with humans."

"A five-foot monitor is big enough to kill a child," Sam said. "A seven-footer. Who knows? Maybe an adult. Take a large enough breeding population over a long enough period of time, and you're going to get some extremes. We might be dealing with something bigger than a seven-footer. It's just basic biology. Males are bigger than females, so I think it's a male. And males are more aggressive than females, unless the female is guarding a nest. It's big and aggressive, hence, an alpha."

"Nile crocodiles, Nile monitor lizards. Why is everything named Nile so mean?" Rodriguez wondered aloud. "Any history of these lizards eating humans?"

"That's where my theory gets a little soft," Sam admitted. "The only documented case of Niles eating a human occurred in London a few years ago. Seems a guy kept four Nile monitors as pets in his apartment. Let'em roam free. One bit him, but he didn't get the bite treated. There's a lot of bacteria in a monitor's mouth, the bite became infected, then sepsis developed, and the guy lost consciousness. At least, that's the theory. He wound up on the floor leaning against the door. The monitors ripped into his stomach and ate his organs. Ate most of his face, too."

"Big lizards?" Rodriguez exclaimed. "Running free? In an apartment? The guy was a nut."

"There's a second reason to consider a Nile Monitor," TJ said. "The bite marks on Bobby Powell. They always bothered me."

"Yeah, I know they have," Rodriguez said.

"One was definitely a gator, but the others suggested a smaller and rounder snout. And, of course, we all saw the girl's reaction to the picture Sam showed him."

"You think a lizard was responsible for both attacks? Seven-year-old children aren't the most reliable of witnesses."

"No, they're not," TJ responded, "but I imagine Anne has seen a number of alligators. They've sure been on television lately. She's saying it's a lizard, not a gator, and a Nile monitor lizard fits what we know."

"Are you suggesting we abandon our search, even though there are lots of alligators out there, and they're known to attack humans, and look for an animal no one except a seven-year-old child claims to have seen and has never attacked anyone in the state of Florida?"

"Not abandon our search," TJ said, "but expand it and alert our people to be on the lookout for big monitors. Lizards live on land, not in the water like gators and crocs, so we should focus more on land."

"I agree," Sam concurred.

"Great. Now we've doubled our area to search, and we're going to need a new plan," Sheriff Rodriguez said. "I'm sure Governor Johnson will love this."

TJ looked over at his car. "One more thing." Tomàs, craned his head, watching the three as if he was following their conversation. "Like our friend Tomàs here, Nile monitors are smart animals. This one discovered that humans are easy prey. He'll remember that."

CHAPTER 24

Kodra emerged into the sunlight on the sand trap near the fifth green. She shook herself like a dog, sending a fine mist of sand into the air around her. She felt, as much as heard, the vibrations of the fairway mowers working their way through the golf course. She left the trap and walked up onto the green. Later, when the course maintenance crew arrived at the fifth hole, they cursed at the mess. Some golfer must have been drunk, they thought.

She looked around and saw the close-cropped green grass of the fairways, the bunkers, the unkept grass of the rough, and the water hazards. There was tall grass around the water but not nearly enough to hunt in. She remembered the looseness of the sand in the bunker and how the hill gave way when she'd tried to climb it. There were no suitable nesting areas there either. She saw a mower in the distance, coming down the fairway toward her. The morning breeze carried many scents; some indicated that humans were nearby. She was exposed on the green and knew she had to move.

She walked down the back of the green, and the mower disappeared from sight. She turned her snout into the breeze. The human scents had diminished and were replaced by the strong scent of horses. Hungry, she violated golf course etiquette and cut across a number of fairways heading in their direction.

She reached the rough at the edge of a fairway when she heard voices nearby. The humans had come from downwind and were almost upon of her. Darting into the undergrowth, she hunkered down. Only her eyes moved as she watched them come closer. The sun glinted off the long slim sticks the men were wielding. Kodra recoiled, then tensed, eyes flaring. Memories of being burned by the shock stick flashed through her mind.

The men wandered around, stopped, and waved their sticks again. Then they got into a cart and sped off. Kodra waited before cautiously sticking her head out of the grass into the fairway. She pulled back, lay down, and waited. A group of women drove past. Men and women, some stopping near where she hid, and some passing by, kept her in place the entire morning.

The sun was high in the sky when the human scents faded away. Kodra once more turned her attention to the horses she'd smelled earlier in the day. She moved through the tall grass, swam a canal that was little wider than she was long, and arrived at a row of neatly trimmed bushes. Pushing her way through the plants, she emerged onto a lawn in the backyard of one of the houses that ringed the golf course. The short grass, small clusters of trees and shrubs, and chemical-smelling water and houses no longer surprised her.

The scents that attracted her were stronger and coming from the front of the house. She moved toward its side, where a black aluminum fence ringed a swimming pool. A new scent, sight, and sound registered simultaneously. A black toy poodle was barking angrily and moving furiously up and down the fence. Kodra stopped and cocked her head at the sight. She knew it was a dog, and she knew she could easily climb the low flattop fence to get it. But she was puzzled. She'd never encountered an animal smaller than herself that didn't try to run away. This one was desperately trying to get through the fence and attack her.

After a brief hesitation, Kodra continued on her way. In front of her was a street, beyond which lay a ditch and a white split-rail wooden fence. This being August, the houses were almost all empty, their owners at their northern homes or vacationing in Europe. She looked both ways and, seeing no humans, crossed the street.

The wooden fence formed a border for a turnout field of Paradise Stables, one of the many equestrian facilities for which Wellington was famous. The farm boarded and trained jumping horses, polo ponies, and those who rode them. It was particularly known for instructing young riders.

The horses were stabled in large matted stalls with fly-spray systems and over-head fans. The facility was, of course, hurricane proof. Full grooming, tacking, and untacking services were provided, so those tedious tasks wouldn't inter-fere with the busy schedules of the riders or their mothers. Laundry service was provided so that dirty clothes didn't have to be transported home. Riders and trainers were pampered with air-conditioned tack rooms and a plush club house with a full bar for the adults. There was an indoor ring—lessons and revenue were not dependent upon the weather—an outdoor working area, and thirty acres of grass paddocks. The stables backed up to Flying Cow Road and the riding trails that ran through the Wellington Environmental Preserve.

Kodra slipped under the fence and lay flat, her tail touching one of the wooden posts. She was close enough now that she could see as well as smell the horses. In the field, in front of her, a groom walked to where a mare and her foal grazed. Further away near a long low wooden building were two adults and a slowly moving horse with a child seated on it.

She crept toward the groom and closed to within a few feet of the man when the mare whinnied and pinned her ears back. The groom turned to see what had upset the mare. He let out a piercing scream and fainted next to the foal. The horse in the training ring bucked, throwing its young rider. The child's mother let out an anguished cry and raced to her fallen daughter. The trainer lunged and grabbed the horse's reins, lest it kick the mother or child in its frenzy. Kodra salivated as she approached the motionless groom.

Hearing the two screams, a stable hand stopped mucking a stall and looked out a barn window. In the field, he saw the mare rearing up on her hind legs in front of her foal. He knew the groom was out there but couldn't see him. The mare drove her front legs down hard, trying to crush the animal that threatened her foal, but Kodra twisted out of the way. The mare quickly reared and struck again.

Rake in hand, the stable worker ran through the paddock and into the pasture. Snapping its jaws and lunging at the mare was an animal he assumed was an alligator. The mare held her ground, rising up on her hind legs and stomping, staying between Kodra and her foal, preventing Kodra from reaching her meal. The stable attendant looked again at the attacker and realized it was no alligator; it was the largest lizard he'd ever seen. He watched the lizard back up, then dart to her left. Teeth bared, the mare lunged at the lizard trying to bite its neck. As the horse sprang, one leg came down on the groom's back. The stable hand gasped. He knew he had to do something before the groom was trampled.

The stable worker cautiously circled behind Kodra as she battled the mare. Seeing his opportunity, he moved in and swung his rake like a baseball bat. The rake's tinges dug into her hide, and she spasmodically twisted sideways. Quickly righting herself, she whipped her tail, knocking the man off his feet. She moved to attack him when she saw the rake in her hand. She knew the stick was the source of her pain. She turned to her other side to see the mare bearing down on her. Caught between the two enemies, she fled. The mare pursued her through the field, intent upon trampling her. The rough wooden railings ripped scales off Kodra's back as she rushed under it.

Kodra ran through the ditch and looked over her shoulder to see the mare at the fence watching her. She was back on the street with the houses that bordered the golf course. The pavement was hot on her paws, and a sharp pain shot though her side as she ran. Her back stung where the railing had scraped her hide. Instinct told her that her injuries weren't serious, but her blood would attract predators. She was aware but not fearful. She'd been hurt before back on Flores, badly bitten by an overzealous suitor she'd rejected, and she'd had two ribs broken by a well-placed kick from a deer she'd been pursuing. She was strong and would heal quickly, but now she needed to find a place to hide and rest.

Retracing her steps, she arrived at the canal that ran between the houses and the golf course. She lowered her head, took a mouthful of water, then raised her head high and swallowed. Satiated, she moved behind the row of houses. There was a hitch in her walk as she went. Still hungry, the smell of chicken drew her to a sandy lot between two houses. There sat a large metal container—an open construction dumpster. The dumpster was taller than the fence, but she rose on her hind legs, put her front paws on the top of it and used her powerful rear legs to propel herself upward. She landed among pieces of cut wood and a jumble of construction debris. There were sharp objects that poked at her and the only chicken she found were bones—the remains of a construction worker's meal.

Disappointed, Kodra scrambled out of the refuse container. She saw shade and cover nearby, although it wasn't like anything she'd seen before. It was a house under construction. The outer walls and the plywood roof were up, providing protection from the sun and anyone looking for her. She entered through an open doorway, her three-inch nails making clicking sounds on the floor as she walked. The electrical and plumbing were roughed in and attached to the studs that would become rooms. Building materials were stacked at irregular intervals. She sensed this wasn't a permanent nesting site, but she was tired, and it appeared safe. She settled in to spend the night on the newly poured concrete slab for the house under construction backing on the sixteenth fairway at the Wellington Palm Beach Golf Club.

CHAPTER 25

TJ and Sam were following Sheriff Rodriguez from the Herzogs' house back to his office when he called with news of the attack at Paradise Stables. "Stay close," he warned.

The light bar on top of the sheriff's SUV came to life, and he made a quick three-point turn. The T-Bird leaned heavily, tires crunching on the gravel shoulder, as TJ did the same. Tomàs' cage slid across the rear seat as the car turned, and Sam reached back to stop it. TJ stayed on the sheriff's tail. They didn't have to go far. After a couple more quick turns, they drove up a gravel road and parked behind a single story building with clean lines and a long row of windows, each flanked by two shutters. "We're not far from the Herzogs," TJ noted.

Sheriff Rodriguez left his SUV and walked over to TJ and Sam as they got out of the T-Bird. "Welcome to Paradise Stables," he said. "Stalls better than many apartments. The horses are in paradise. Given how much the boarders pay, the owners of the stables are probably in paradise, too." His tone quickly changed to serious. "Okay, let's see what we can find out."

The stable worker was waiting for them in the paddock. He told his story rapidly in Spanish. TJ struggled to follow the conversation as Sam and the sheriff listened and asked questions. Sam saw his consternation and asked, "Do you want me to translate?"

"No thanks. I get the drift." *Am I the only person in South Florida who isn't bilingual?* he wondered.

The stable worker's eyes bulged as he spread his arms as wide as he could. It was the biggest lizard he'd ever seen, as big as a big alligator. They were surprised when the man said the beast changed colors as the sunlight washed over its body but was mostly brown and green with a black and white face.

With gestures, the stable hand described how he struck the animal with his rake. He pointed toward the fence, indicating that the animal had run away and disappeared under it.

"Muy peligroso," the man said, fear still hovering on his bronzed face. "Very dangerous," he repeated to himself in English.

"Did it try to attack you?" Sam asked.

"No, ma'am, and I don't think it was after the horses. It looked like it was trying to get the groom."

"Thank you," Sam said.

The sheriff also thanked the worker and the man disappeared into the barn.

Next they spoke with the trainer and the mother of the thrown rider. Her daughter was fine. She'd been thrown before. The trainer and mother had been focused on the girl and the horse. They saw the commotion in the field but couldn't add any details.

"What about the groom?" TJ asked the sheriff.

"In the hospital with four broken ribs and a punctured lung," Rodriguez replied. "I'll talk to him later, but from what I'm told all he saw was a big lizard bearing down on him."

"Any video?" TJ asked.

"Ah. Your favorite question, TJ," the sheriff said. "Around the rings and stable, yes, but not out in the fields,"

"Too bad."

The three headed into the pasture. The mare appeared exhausted but continued to stand guard over her foal. She whinnied nervously as they approached. Sam walked over and talked to her quietly while stroking her nose as TJ and Rodriguez looked around.

"Nothing to see here," the sheriff said.

"Well, now we know for sure what we're looking for," Sam said. "A lizard matches Anne Herzog's description of the animal that carried off her mother. And, the vomit sac is consistent with a lizard."

"That accounts for one death, but what about Bobby Powell?" the sheriff asked.

"The bite marks," TJ said. He turned to Sam. "Who can tell us if any of the marks on Bobby Powell match the bite of a big monitor lizard?"

"UF has studied monitors for over fifty years. I'll ask Professor Robinson to take a look," Sam said. "And what about DNA? The rake must have the lizard's skin and blood on it."

"It also might have left some on the rail it went under," TJ added.

"We've got the rake. We'll get the rail, too," Sheriff Rodriguez said. "Right away."

"I suggest you send the samples from both to Gainesville as well," Sam said. "UF has an excellent herpetological research facility."

"And get the governor to make herself useful." TJ snorted. "Fast track this."

Sheriff Rodriguez smiled. "With pleasure."

"I hate to raise this," Sam began. "But how do we know we aren't looking for two lizards?"

"Oh please, I hope not!" the sheriff said.

"It's certainly possible," TJ said. "But for the time being, let's assume there's only one. Afterall, a Nile monitor that big would be a rarity. And, if there's only one, it most likely would have entered the canal at or above the Powells' house. It's just like we said about the crocodile—swimming up and down the canal and getting past the pumping station twice is just too improbable. Sheriff, you might want to have your deputies canvass the area around the canal north of the Powells' house."

"Good idea," Rodriguez replied.

"We may have big problem though," TJ said.

"What?" Rodriguez asked.

"This lizard isn't afraid of humans. It's aggressive, so maybe it was kept by someone who abused it. I've seen that before. Maybe it attacked its owner and learned humans bleed just like other animals. We know it preys on people."

"And it seems comfortable in an urban environment," Sam added.

They walked back to the stables as the skies darkened. By the time they arrived at the barn, the first fat drops of rain were falling. As they sheltered from the rain, they discussed what to tell the governor. Sheriff Rodriguez called her and began the update.

They heard the angst in the governor's voice. "This is terrible," she said. "We have a monster on the loose."

"We'd like to send skin and blood samples from the lizard to UF for DNA analysis," TJ said, "we think it's a Nile monitor," he stopped and looked at Sam who nodded in agreement. "But we'd like to know exactly what kind of lizard we're dealing with."

"Of course. I'll send a helicopter for the samples and put the university on notice."

"Governor," TJ said, "the lizard could be somewhere between the stables and the Herzogs' street. There's also the golf course community where the crocodile was killed, but if it goes there, it's going to be spotted. As we've said before, if it travels farther west, it'll be in the Arthur Marshall Refuge or the Wellington Environmental Preserve, and it may disappear."

"Your job is to find it and kill it before it kills again or it gets away," the governor snapped.

"Monitor lizards live on land," Sam said, "so we know where to look. And they're only active during the day, because they have poor nighttime vision, so we know when to look."

"Here all along you've told me it's water based and likes to hunt at night."

"That's what a crocodile does but now we know we're looking for a lizard—"

The governor cut Sam off, "You've been looking in the wrong place and at the wrong time the entire time.

TJ jumped back in, "Being a daytime predator makes the lizard easier to spot, but it still won't be easy, because its coloring provides natural camouflage." He paused knowing what he was about to say would provoke the governor. "We believe the lizard is staying around because of the abundance of prey, specifically humans—"

"Oh my god!" the governor wailed. "Don't say that to anyone. We'll have a panic on our hands."

"Governor, people are more active during the day—" TJ continued.

"I'm not stupid, Forte. Just tell me what you're going to do."

"The lizard's going to look for large wooded areas near water," Sam said. "That's where it'll feel safe." She didn't see the need to add that it was also where it would look for prey.

"We'd like to put out baited traps," TJ said. "They'll be no-kill traps, and we'll watch them, but that's going to meet with a lot of resistance—"

"Just do it!" the governor angrily yelled. Without another word, she hung up.

The three headed back to the parking lot. News vans with their satellite antenna extended were being held at a distance by PBSO deputies. Cameramen and reporters were huddled under umbrellas. *How'd they get here so quickly?* TJ wondered. Waiting, just like at the Herzogs' and the Powells' before now.

* * *

Kirkland was working in the barn listening to a country and western station when Mumford walked in. "They found the Komodo, but it escaped. At least for now."

"What?"

Mumford described what he'd heard on the news. Then he looked at the cages in the barn. Two Lavender Albino Ball pythons, three yellow anacondas, and four blue tongue lizards. The albino pythons came in from West Africa and were surprisingly cheap. Mumford had a buyer for the pair, at $40,000 each. The anacondas had been prohibited from import since 2012 and didn't sell for a high price, but they came in from South America and were plentiful. About four feet long, they would grow many times that length. The blue tongued lizards were from Australia.

He'd had good luck with his shipments. They'd come in by freighter, and a crewman would smuggle them off ship after it'd docked in Miami or Fort Lauderdale. Sanchez and Darisse would drive down and bring back the animals. The damn Komodo dragon had been the exception and trouble from the beginning. A buyer wanted a breeding pair and had offered $500,000, plus expenses, for them. The Komodos were too big to hide on a ship and sneak past customs, so he'd arranged for them to be flown from Indonesia to the Bahamas. From there, a motorboat was going to bring them to a beach north of Hobe Sound. But the male Komodo had died on the flight. Sanchez and Darisse had met the boat at the beach and transferred the surviving Komodo to the back of the farm's pickup truck. The buyer was still interested in the female Komodo and willing to pay $250,000 for it. He'd still make a nice profit.

It'd been his first experience with large reptiles, and he regretted it. He'd also violated his policy about dealing in poisonous reptiles. He wouldn't make either mistake a second time. Despite requests for a cobra from a particularly insistent and well healed buyer, he knew they were skittish and aggressive, and he had no intention of bringing in an animal that could kill him. Why so many people were willing to pay so much for dumb reptiles, particularly poisonous ones, was beyond him.

If only the damn lizard hadn't escaped. Anger welled up in him at the thought of Sanchez's mistake. He almost wished the man were still alive, so Kirkland could kill him again.

Kirkland looked at him expectantly.

"Oh, hell," Mumford said. "We've got enough problems with the croc attacking the golfer. Once they figure out the lizard's an exotic . . . We'd better shut down operations for a while. Get rid of the inventory."

"We'll lose a lot of money, boss."

He gestured to the reptiles. "We can't risk getting caught with any of these. Someone might have seen something, or the law might come snooping around." Mumford thought some more. "And Sanchez . . . the state may still come looking for him."

"I've been spreading the word that he went back to Honduras."

"Good, but we still have a problem."

"Up here? When the lizard is in Wellington?"

"I always suspected she swam down the canal. Someone might figure that out and start working backward. We need to cover our tracks."

After he left, Kirkland radioed Darisse to come in from the field. He explained what he wanted done.

"Do you think she ate those two people?" Darisse asked.

Kirkland was surprised at the question, although he felt sure of the answer. Darisse was not one to follow the news; maybe Sanchez had said something to him. *Darisse might have to disappear like Sanchez,* he thought. "Don't think so. It was an alligator."

"Okay." Darisse gestured toward the reptiles. "Do you want me to release them?"

"No." He knew Darisse liked the reptiles, but they were just product to him, and too dangerous now to keep. "We can't risk someone finding them. An illegal reptile found here would draw cops quicker than shit draws flies. Run them through the woodchipper mixed in with cane pulp. Then set the chipper and the pulp on fire."

"You want me to burn the chipper, too?"

"Gotta get rid of all traces. You say the machine caught fire. I'll back you."

It was Darisse's turn to look at the cages. "This means I'll have to kill all these guys first."

"That's up to you," Kirkland said.

CHAPTER 26

TJ dropped off Sam at The Waters Edge. As much as he'd like to have dinner with her, he had to meet Billy Howard, brother of the chairman of the Seminole tribe, in Miami. He was checking to see if there were any rumors among the exotic animal dealers as to where the lizard came from. Sam was going to get a pizza delivered and research Nile monitor lizards. Sheriff Rodriguez was looking into licensed imported reptiles, and possible sightings, in the Loxahatchee area.

Rush hour traffic on I-95 was slow going. On his way south, TJ passed the Seminole Coconut Creek and Seminole Hardrock casinos and signs for the Seminole Classic. The Seminoles had lived in the Everglades long before the white man came. No air conditioning. No bug spray. They were fierce and proud, the only Indian tribe to never have signed a peace treaty with the US government. Now they operated casinos. *The most valuable properties in South Florida. They've adopted to our culture better than we could have adopted to theirs*, he thought.

Two hours after he'd dropped off Sam, TJ drove into an area of single-story industrial buildings that housed a variety of distribution and repair businesses. All the storefronts were dark, except one. Howard had stayed late to meet him. The reputable animal dealers were like that—always willing to help.

Once he'd asked Howard if he and the chairman were half-brothers, since the two men had different last names. Howard had said no; he'd changed his name to Howard for business purposes. It was an easier name for the white man to pronounce. On the reservation, he was still Billy Holata.

TJ took the cage containing Tomàs from the back seat and entered the store. He was greeted by a man of medium build with long silver hair tied back in a ponytail and a deeply weathered face from years in the South Florida sun and by the aroma of hot buttered popcorn.

"You're bringing me an iguana?" Howard asked in mock disbelief.

"He's been assisting me with my investigation."

Howard gave him as quizzical look.

"Poor guy's gone all day without water. Thought you could help."

"Of course." Howard held out a small black box. "But first would you mind putting your cell phone in this. Prevents ease dropping," he said apologetically. After TJ complied, Howard quickly rustled up bowls of water and food.

"Now that he's taken care of, that popcorn sure smells good. I've had nothing to eat since breakfast," TJ said.

"That's binturong piss you're smelling," Howard said, pointing to another cage. A large cat-like animal with thick bristly black hair was curled up in it. "From Southeast Asia. Special order for the Jacksonville zoo."

The store was quiet except for the hedgehogs in a dark corner who were trying to outdo each other on their exercise wheels. Howard saw TJ looking at them. "Nocturnal," he said. "A lot of buyers don't know that. Causes all sorts of problems. They keep prodding the animals to be active during the day, or they turn on bright lights at night that can damage the hedgehogs' eyes."

TJ knew Howard liked to talk. He wasn't running the kind of business that got a lot of foot traffic, and his animals weren't great conversationalists, but TJ wanted to keep the things moving. "I know it's late, and I don't want to keep you . . ."

"That's okay, the hedgehogs like the company," Howard said. "But I understand. You aren't here to talk about binturongs or hedgehogs. I saw the news before you called. You're after a very big lizard."

"Right. We think it maybe a Nile monitor. Maybe smuggled in. Maybe released. Escaped. You know the story. The questions are who, how, and when? Any ideas about the who?"

"Not really. You might try talking to people at one of the exotic pet amnesty days. The next one is in West Palm in a few weeks. It's amazing, the animals people bring in. There was just one held here at the Miami zoo, a man brought in a tiger cub. Where he got that, I can't imagine. But I'm glad he turned in the cub. Not many people know how to care for exotics. Too often, they get sick and die or are killed when they get too big." Howard paused for only a moment before he was on to his next thought. "And there was a piranha. We see a lot of those. This one . . . guy puts it in his koi pond and becomes upset when the piranha starts eating his fish."

TJ gave Howard a thin smile, trying to hide his impatience. "Good idea, but I can't wait weeks. Anything else?"

"Maybe, but this has to do with exports. There's a group of reptile poachers cooling their heels in the Lee County jail. Caught driving a truck with some eight hundred turtles, including box, mud, softshell, and diamond back terrapins in the back. I estimate the market value to be $250,000."

"For the Asian market no doubt."

"No doubt."

"Where?"

"Corkscrew Swamp area."

"Hadn't heard anything about it, and law enforcement is typically good about passing the news along."

"It just happened."

"How'd you find out?"

"My brothers were involved."

"Brothers? Involved?"

"Members of my tribe. We noticed a decline in the number of turtles in the area and suspected poachers. We altered the Lee County sheriff, sent watchers into the swamp, and waited. The poachers came, harvested more turtles, and we called the sheriff."

"Good for you."

"Not really. Our Environmental Resource Management Department fears that so many turtles were removed that their populations might never recover."

"That's tragic. Really tragic. Sometimes I wonder . . ."

"You might want to talk to those guys."

"Why?"

"Strictly between us . . . A guard at the jail overheard them talking. Seems two of them wanted to make a deal with a reptile smuggler who could get the turtles out of the county. Located somewhere around Lake O. The third guy nixed the deal. They think the smuggler may have ratted them out. And we're happy to let them keep thinking that."

"How'd you come by this information?" TJ asked with a knowing smile.

"The guard is Seminole. We need to protect the land from invasive species."

"Yeah. There's too many foreign animals running around here."

"I was referring to you people who came from Europe."

* * *

On his way home, TJ's first call was to the Lee County sheriff. He wasn't sure what kind of a reception he'd get at that hour of the night, but the sheriff was happy to help and confirmed what Howard had said.

His next call was to brief Sheriff Rodriguez. "I'm glad you called," the sheriff said. "Just heard from the governor's office. We should be getting the DNA results from UF in the morning. Why don't you come by here first thing?"

"Will do. Now I've got something for you. A possible reptile smuggler in the Lake O area." TJ recounted what he knew. "The L-8 canal originates there. That could be where the lizard came from. We should expand our search all the way up to the lake."

"Makes sense. But there's nothing along the canal that far north except the Pure Sugar farm and marsh land. I'll call Sheriff Civera over in Lee and see what else I can find out about the turtle men."

TJ had just hung up when Kenny Loggins broke into song. He glanced down at caller ID and groaned. He hesitated but then hit *Speaker*. The would-be Impala buyer was on the line. The man didn't apologize for calling so late but launched right into his pitch. He'd done his research, and the Chevy was only worth $20,000. TJ's phone screen lit up again. Sam was calling. He told the buyer he had an important call coming in and hung up on him.

TJ began by telling Sam about the lead he'd given to Sheriff Rodriguez and how binturong urine smelled like popcorn.

"Good to know." Sam chuckled.

"How about if I pick you up in the morning on my way to Rodriguez's office?"

"Great. Now I don't want to rain on our parade, but my research tells me the lizard we're after isn't acting like a Nile monitor."

"Why do you say that?"

"Other than that guy I told you about in London, there have been no known Nile monitor attacks on humans."

"Well, maybe this Nile's behavior was altered by human interaction. Like we've said, maybe it bit its owner. Maybe it was taunted and became aggressive."

"Has any person been reported missing in the Loxahatchee area before Bobby Powell was eaten?" Sam asked.

"Not that I've heard. Why?"

"I don't want to sound macabre, but the lizard could have acquired a taste for humans. A Nile that had fed on a human would be more likely to go after another human than a Nile that hadn't."

"I don't even want to think about that."

"I don't either."

"But you said the lizard's behavior doesn't fit a Nile?"

"Yes, and there's a second reason. Nile's live on land. Sure, they're good swimmers but they'd rather walk. We think our predator used the canal to get around."

"So if it's not a Nile monitor, what do you think it is?"

"A Crocodile monitor."

"Crocodile monitor?"

"Yeah. Found in New Guinea and Indonesia. They grow big, bigger than Niles. Ten-twelve feet isn't uncommon. They're very aggressive and attack humans. Unlike other monitors, they spend large amounts of time in the water, even sleep there. They'd be very comfortable in a marshy environment like the Everglades."

"Wonderful. A lizard that thinks it's a crocodile."

"You got it."

"That'd put us back looking on the water."

"True but there are no confirmed sightings of any in the wild in Florida, although people have them legally, and, I have to assume, illegally. Too bad we don't have a picture from the stable. Crocodile monitors have distinctive yellow spots on their back."

"Neither Anne nor the stable hand said anything about spots."

"I know. Maybe the sheriff can follow up with both and ask them. When his people checked licensed owners, did they check for all monitors or just Niles?"

"Don't know. I'll call him back when we're done. Hopefully, the DNA results will tell us exactly what kind of a lizard we're looking for. Then we can tailor our hunt to the type of lizard. Land or water. A Nile is bad enough. I don't want to be back in the refuge looking for a Crocodile monitor. Like you've said, maybe it bit its owner. Any other lizard we should be worried about?"

"Don't think so. The only other monitor that fits the description is the Komodo dragon. But you can't import them, and there are only a few remaining in the wild. All on remote islands in Indonesia, and the Indonesian government watches over them carefully."

"Good. That's one less lizard to worry about."

CHAPTER 27

TJ, as usual, was up before the sun and sitting at his kitchen counter, both hands around a mug of strong black coffee. *How do you catch a giant lizard, especially if you don't know what kind it is?* The answer wasn't going to be found in the US Fish & Wildlife handbook.

He finished his coffee, rinsed the mug, and left the house. In his garage, he looked over his cars, deciding which one to take. There was the green Impala. He didn't want to run up the miles on it. His eyes ran over the little manual transmission Corvair that Sam had struggled to drive and the Thunderbird with the tilt-away steering wheel that sometimes tilted away when it shouldn't. There was the light metallic gold Camaro that barely ran and was waiting for an engine and transmission upgrade. Next to the Camaro a large canvas tarp was draped over a major restoration project. It had sat there for quite a while, and TJ didn't know when he'd have time to begin it. It didn't run, so it was out of the question.

He settled on the remaining car in the garage, a 1966 Oldsmobile Toronado, burgundy mist with a black interior. The length of a present-day pickup truck, the Toronado was a revolutionary automobile. A two-door hardtop, its doors were so long that they had a second handle located near the rear, so the backseat passengers could open them. The most unique feature of the door was a single-piece curved glass window that went its entire length, the largest side window in automotive history. But that wasn't the biggest engineering feat of the Toronado. It was a front-wheel drive car, the first produced in the

United States since the Cord in the 1930s and technologically years ahead of the Europeans and the Japanese. A personal luxury car with a big V8 and a good air conditioner, it would be a sweet ride. TJ fired up the big car, and the engine rumbled to life. He pulled a knob, the retractable head lights popped up like eyes opening, and set off north. The boy selling the iguanas wasn't there on the corner. *Maybe too early or maybe the iguanas got a reprieve.*

On his way to pick up Sam, he listened to the radio. Callers to the local talk shows had only one thing on their minds—the giant lizard. Some expressed fear about leaving their homes. Others made wild suggestions for finding it, including starting brush fires to smoke it out. *Wouldn't that be ironic,* he thought. Still others said the authorities weren't doing enough, and they'd form their own search parties. *Vigilantes. Just what we need!* Many of the callers said they had guns and were carrying them. More said they were buying them. TJ hoped that was just chest pounding. Groups of people running around with guns wouldn't end well. He thought back to the *Great Alligator Slaughter.*

Sam was standing in the lobby of The Waters Edge when he arrived. "Another car?" she said as she got in. "Could you find one with a bigger door?"

TJ just laughed.

They arrived at the PBSO compound and felt the tension in the air as soon as they entered the sheriff's office. There were coffee cups but no fast-food wrappers on his desk. Rodriguez greeted them with: "The governor is not a happy camper. Her chief of staff called and asked us to stand by. UF is double checking the results of their DNA tests. We should have the findings shortly."

"Good," TJ said.

"Any leads?" Sam asked.

"We've been flooded with calls of possible sightings since the news broke of the Paradise Stables attack," Sheriff Rodriguez replied. "Followed up on a number of them but no, nothing. I did speak with Sheriff Civera in Lee County. The thieves confessed to capturing and selling more than four thousand turtles over the past six months. They sold them to reptile traffickers in the Miami area."

"Howard was right," TJ said. "They were stripping the swamp of its turtles."

"They expected to be paid $25,000 for their load, with payment coming in the form of cash and drugs."

"I suppose they had no idea their haul would bring ten times as much in Asia."

"I suspect not," the sheriff responded. "Here's where it gets interesting. On their last delivery, a stevedore told them there was a big-time animal trafficker based around Lake O. He gave them a cell phone number. They called and spoke with a Hispanic sounding man who didn't give his name."

"That'd be too much to hope for," TJ said.

"The man didn't want the turtles, but they were convinced the guy was part of a reptile smuggling ring."

"Is there a record of the call?"

"The number they called is still on their cell, but it belongs to a burner phone."

"Burner phone?" Sam asked.

"Dead end. Can't be traced," the sheriff replied.

The few minutes wait for the DNA results turned into two hours. When Sheriff Rodriguez's phone finally rang, he hit speaker. On the line were Governor Johnson, some of her minions, and Professor Robinson. Sheriff Rodriguez flipped open a pocket-size notepad and placed it on his desk. He clicked his ballpoint pen, ready to write.

Professor Robinson cleared his throat and began. "I know Sam, but for those of you who don't know me, I am the chairman of the herpetology department here at the University of Florida. With the help of the university medical center, we were able to extract and sequence DNA from the skin and blood taken from the rake and wood rail we received. We found a match in our data base, but, given the unusual result, we consulted with the AZA, the

Association of Zoos and Aquariums. They have one of the best animal data-bases in the world." He cleared his throat a second time. "I find this hard to believe, because I know the DNA sample came from Palm Beach County, but the DNA is that of a Varanus Komodoensis—a Komodo dragon. Yours is a female Komodo dragon to be exact."

"It can't be!" Sam said, astonished. "How sure are you?"

"As I said, I was surprised but I'm completely sure. We ran multiple sequencings. When I saw the initial results, I made my staff go back and recheck their work. And, we are something of an authority on Komodo dragons."

"What do you mean?" asked the governor.

"One of our faculty members, Walter Auffenberg, took his family to Indonesia in the early sixties and lived among Komodos, studying them. He published the first scholarly book about them. It's become something of a bible on Komodos. Still referred to today. UF has been studying Komodos ever since."

"What can you tell us about them?" TJ asked.

"The average adult is eight to ten feet long and weighs between 150 and 200 pounds, but they can be bigger. From the description, I'd say yours is on the larger end of the scale. Komodo's are highly intelligent and quick learners. It's not unusual for Komodos in captivity to recognize their handlers by sight and the sound of their voice and to respond to verbal and hand commands. In experiments, they'd learned how to open boxes to get food, and when presented with the same puzzle two years later, they remember how to solve it."

"Wow. That's smart," Sam said.

Not what I wanted to hear, TJ thought.

"And Komodos like to play," Robinson continued. "The London zoo taught one to catch a Frisbee."

A picture of a giant lizard running in a yard, leaping and catching a Frisbee like a dog went through TJ's mind.

"They aren't predicable like, say, alligators, and they're a perfect fighting machine. Big, fast, sharp claws and teeth, powerful tail like an alligator, thick skin, strong sense of smell, good eyesight and hearing, good swimmers, and they have a poisonous bite. They regularly take down animals bigger than they are."

"Does Godzilla have any weakness?" TJ asked.

"They don't see well in the dark. That's their biggest weakness. They bed down at night and stay put."

"I have a question about their coloring," Sam said. "In the pictures I've seen, Komodos appear to be many different colors—green, brown gray, with some black, some white, and even some turquoise."

"You're right," Robinson replied. "Komodos are not a uniform color. Their colors and patterns vary. It helps them blend in really well with their surroundings. Older Komodos tend to be darker than younger ones, and females tend to have a red or brown band around their lower back. The turquoise you saw probably was new skin. Like other reptiles, Komodos shed their skin as they grow. Snakes, for example, can shed their skin in one piece."

"Yes, I've come across many," Sam said.

"But Komodos shed in patches, rubbing against a tree trunk or branch to scrape off a section of old skin. The new skin is lighter in color than the old."

"What can you tell us specifically about Komodos eating people?" TJ asked.

"Sadly Komodos have done just that. They're opportunistic feeders, meaning they eat what's available. A few years ago, a man fell out of an apple tree. There were two Komodos below it. They attacked and ate him. More recently, an eight-year-old boy was attacked. The villagers drove off the Ora, but it likely would have eaten him, too, if they hadn't. Unfortunately, the boy died."

"Ora?"

"It means land crocodile in their language."

"Land crocodile," Sam repeated. "Sounds appropriate from what we know."

"One of Governor Johnson's aides sent me a file describing what's happened," the professor said. "I think your Komodo definitely ate the woman. She also killed the boy and started to eat him but for some reason didn't."

"Has this Komodo developed a taste for humans?" TJ asked.

"Yours has learned that humans are prey, perhaps, they've even become her preferred prey," Robinson replied. "So, yes, I think she has."

"Meaning when she gets hungry, she'll look for another person," the sheriff said. "We better be prepared but we need to keep that to ourselves for now. The last thing we need is people panicking because they think a lizard is stalking them."

"You're being very helpful, Professor," TJ said.

"I'm glad," Robinson said. "There's not a lot of material available on Komodos, and you have to be careful because a lot of it is inaccurate." The professor continued, "I'm surprised there's one on the loose. They're found on just five islands in Indonesia and there's maybe only about three thousand left. The Indonesian government allows just a few to be exported every year and only to zoos that have been thoroughly vetted."

"Could this Komodo have come from a zoo?" Sam asked.

"No, although since the early 1990s, some zoos have had success with breeding Komodos in captivity. According to the AZA data base, your Komodo isn't closely related to any current or past Komodo in a US zoo."

"What about the private market?" Sam asked.

"There is none," the professor replied. "This one must have came directly from Indonesia."

"Animal traffickers. Smuggled in," TJ said softly.

"The Indonesian government might be of some assistance," Professor Robinson said. "And you might want to send them a DNA sample. They tag many of their Komodos."

"We will," Governor Johnson said.

"Anything else we should know?" TJ asked.

"Mating season in Indonesia began in May, at the beginning of their dry season. Pregnant females are laying their eggs about this time. But you haven't found any nests, and your Komodo isn't exhibiting any signs of being pregnant. If she was on the black market, it's likely she hasn't been around any males, anyway. Although, and this is an interesting curiosity, female Komodos can reproduce without having sex."

"I've heard about that in some reptiles but never looked into it," Sam said.

"It's called facultative parthenogenesis. Asexual reproduction. If no males are around, an unfertilized egg can develop to maturity. Happened a couple of times at the Memphis and London zoos. A female Komodo laid a clutch of eggs that hatched. Some other reptiles also can reproduce in this way. Don't need any men."

"Well, now I know what an endangered species feels like," TJ said.

Sam shot him a look.

"Someone must have paid a lot of money for it," the governor said. "I could see an Arab prince or a Russian oligarch buying one but not someone in Palm Beach. Where would they hide it?"

"I have to agree," TJ said. "There's a possibility it came from the Lake Okeechobee area, but perhaps that was a transit point, not its final destination."

"Then tell me how that thing got here and got loose in the first place."

"Pets are the source of eight-five percent of all invasive species in the Everglades," TJ said. "But we suspect an animal trafficker brought it in, and it got loose."

"Do you have a suspect?" Johnson asked.

"We have a lead," the sheriff said. "We have reports of illegal reptile importing in the Lake O area."

"I want a full briefing on your efforts prior to the press conference, and Professor Robinson, you and everyone involved aren't to breathe a word of this to anyone until we announce it. Whoever does, loses their job, and your department loses all its state funding. I will hold a press conference tomorrow morning at nine. I expect of all of you to be there and to show support. Even you, Officer Forte." The disdain in the governor's voice was clear.

"I have to tell you finding a Komodo dragon in Florida is really exciting," Professor Robinson said. "To observe a Komodo in a non-native environment and see how it has adapted. This is a once-in-a-lifetime opportunity."

"Our mission is not to observe," TJ said.

CHAPTER 28

In the morning, TJ drove up to The Waters Edge in his T-Bird. He looked at its weather-beaten façade. *I wonder who the state puts up at The Breakers?* he asked himself.

Sam was waiting in the lobby. "Do you ever drive the same car two days in a row?" she asked as she got in.

He was embarrassed to admit that he'd planned to drive the Toronado, but he couldn't get it started.

Without waiting for a reply, Sam continued. "I researched Komodo dragons last night."

"Oh. What did you find?"

"Professor Robinson was right. Not a lot is really known about them. If you trace back the material, much of it comes from the same sources, and a lot is contradictory. I did learn the name Komodo comes from the island where they were first discovered by Dutch traders in the early twentieth century. And, an interesting factoid, King Kong is supposedly based upon the exploits of an expedition to a mysterious island to capture a mysterious creature."

"Let me guess. Komodo and Komodo?"

"You got it."

"By the way, you know Robinson. Is he any good?"

"One of the best. You never met him?"

"No. UF is a big place. I was in a different school, and even after that, our paths never crossed."

"Okay. So what's our plan for today?"

"We brief the governor, then face the press. Afterward we . . . well . . . we come up with some brilliant idea for finding the Komodo."

Arriving at the sheriff's office, Rodriquez said, "The governor will be joining us in a few minutes, and we've got a lot to cover before then. First, I have results from the state forensics lab. The DNA taken from the skin on the rake and rail matches the DNA taken from the saliva on Bobby Powell's shoe. It also matches the DNA taken from the gastric pellet. So, we know the Komodo dragon killed both people.

He paused and looked at TJ. "Professor Robinson's team reviewed the autopsy pictures of the marks on Bobby Powell. The three bites up and down his body are consistent with a Komodo dragon's bite. The Komodo killed him. The alligator took a fourth bite out of his side after he was dead. TJ, you were right about the bites."

"I don't take any satisfaction from that, but the DNA from the shoe, pellet, and rail all being the same tells us we're only looking for one animal and that's good."

"Robinson told me the bite pattern suggests Bobby Powell was swallowed headfirst." The sheriff hesitated and grimaced. "He probably was alive at the time of the first bite. We can only pray that he blacked out beforehand. Robinson went on to say that something must have spooked the Komodo right after she ate the boy, and she regurgitated the body."

"I hope we don't have to get into all that at the press conference," Sam said.

"I think we can keep the details of the boy's death to ourselves," Sheriff Rodriguez said. "No need to sensationalize this anymore than it is or cause the Powell family any more grief."

"What's the second thing? TJ asked.

"I got a call from a doctor at MediRedi. That's an urgent care clinic in Belle Glade. A guy came in two days after Bobby Powell was eaten with an odd bite that wasn't healing. The patient said he was bitten by a small gator, but something seemed off to the doc. He reported the bite to the state public health department but didn't hear anything back. After he heard about what was going on in Wellington, he looked up the symptoms of a Komodo bite. The symptom's matched his patient's."

"Belle Glade," TJ said. "North of the Powells' and not too far from the canal. If the guy really was bitten by the Komodo, we may be zeroing in on where she came from and the trafficking operation."

"Maybe," Rodriguez replied. "I followed up with the health department. The patient's name is Emilio Sanchez. Works at Pure Sugar. The health department has called but hasn't been able to reach him. I'm meeting the doc after the press conference if you care to come along."

"Sure do," TJ said. "And maybe go see Sanchez afterward? He might lead us to the smugglers. They may have more Komodos or God knows what else. We have to stop them from bringing in any more exotics."

"I couldn't agree more," Sheriff Rodriguez said. "We'll catch them, but the Komodo is our immediate concern. We have to find her before she kills again."

As if on cue, Governor Johnson, aides in tow, breezed into the room. The first words out of her mouth were: "Tell me about kimonos."

Sam rolled her eyes.

Not a good move, TJ thought.

"It's pronounced K*e*-mo-do, governor," Sam said. "Kimonos are traditional Japanese robes worn by women."

The governor ignored the correction and began firing questions. In response to one, the sheriff said they were going to Belle Glade after the press conference to follow-up on a lead about animal traffickers.

"Why?" the governor asked.

"A Komodo dragon is worth hundreds of thousands on the black market. She must have been smuggled in and escaped."

When it was time for the briefing, the governor said: "I'll open with an update and that we've identified the killer as a Komodo dragon. You'll provide details on the animal and how you're going to find it. And just to be clear. You guys own this. You screwed up. We aren't looking for an alligator or a crocodile. We've been looking for a lizard all along. Some animal experts you are."

* * *

Mumford groaned when Governor Johnson announced to the world that a Komodo dragon had killed Bobby Powell and Judy Herzog. He was sitting in his office with Kirkland, watching the press conference. "I had a feeling that's what was going to happen," he said.

They listened as Sam described Komodo dragons and their habits. Then TJ spoke. "Komodo dragons are found only in Indonesia, so this one must have been illegally brought into the United States and escaped, most likely from somewhere north of the Powells' house."

"That's us," Kirkland said.

Mumford shushed him with a waive of his hand and leaned toward the TV as Sheriff Rodriguez stepped up to the microphones. "As Dr. Brown said, Komodos are territorial, and as long as there's a food supply, they'll remain in a one-to-three-mile area." A deputy set up an easel holding a map of Wellington with a circle drawn in yellow and red Xs with labels at each of the locations where the Komodo was known to have been. "This is our search area," Rodriguez said as he made a sweeping motion. "As you can see, the borders are Southern Boulevard to the north, the Paradise Stables area to the east, the Arthur Marshall Wildlife Refuge to the west, and the Wellington Environmental Preserve to the south. Our search will be concentrated in this area."

Mumford sat back. "Good. Stay down there."

The briefing moved on to questions. A correspondent from *Le Monde* asked if the release of the lizard could be an act of terrorism by foreign radicals or a domestic environmental group. Governor Johnson stepped up to the microphones. "Absolutely not. There's no evidence of either."

Mumford smiled. "That'd send them off in a different direction!"

Another reporter asked if animal smuggling was a big business. TJ answered, "Very big. Last year the illegal animal trade in the US was estimated to be $6 billion. That's billion, with a capital B. Only the drug trade is bigger, and the drug dealers are moving into the smuggling business. Same profit margins and a lot less law enforcement. If you're caught with cocaine, you go to prison for a long time. If you're caught with a hundred lizards . . . well, what kind are they, do you have the paperwork, and so on."

"And reptiles?" the reporter followed-up.

"The biggest part of the illegal trade."

Mumford laughed. "I could have told him that."

"Who smuggled the Komodo dragon into the US?" a TV news anchor asked.

Governor Johnson fielded the question. "We don't know who yet, but we have reason to believe the Komodo was brought in by a smuggling operation based in the Lake Okeechobee area. I can assure everyone that we will find the Komodo and the person, or persons responsible, for bringing it into Florida." Then she ended the news conference.

"Oh hell," Mumford said. *I wonder how they know my business is based here,* he asked himself. But that wasn't his primary concern. This wasn't the average animal trafficking investigation. This was international news. The Komodo had killed and eaten two humans. The investigation would be relentless and thorough.

"Pure Sugar's the obvious place to look," Kirkland said. "We're the only thing up here, and we border the canal. What are going to do?"

"Animals all gone?"

"Yes."

"Cages, too?"

"Yes."

"Then there's nothing the police can find when they come looking," Mumford said.

"Dariasse knows."

"Then get rid of him."

CHAPTER 29

"Why do you guys look so angry?" Sam asked TJ and Sheriff Rodriguez as they headed to their vehicles.

TJ answered, mimicking the governor's voice. "*We have reason to believe* . . . She just alerted the smugglers that we're looking for them and we have a good idea where they are."

"Oh."

"It's a lot easier to catch someone if they don't think you're coming for them," the sheriff added.

Sam opened the T-Bird's door and got in. "Does the top go down on this jalopy?"

TJ looked up at the sky. Cloudy and bright. "You want the top down? In August?"

"Sure. It'll brighten your spirits."

"Fine. I've got some sun block in the glove box."

The T-Bird's top disappeared into its trunk, and they followed Sheriff Rodriguez to Belle Glade. At MediRedi, they waited for Dr. Dudnick to finish up with a patient.

"We know the worker's name, Emilio Sanchez, but can the doctor disclose his case history?" TJ asked.

"I've already sent him a court order," Sheriff Rodriguez said just as Dr. Dudnick, in his white physician's coat, appeared.

"Sorry to keep you," Dudnick said. "I was treating a farm hand who was bitten by a water moccasin. Second one this month. I'm told it has to do with all the rain."

"That's okay," the sheriff said. "We're here to talk to you about another farm worker—Emilio Sanchez."

"Yes, I know. He works at Pure Sugar as does the fellow I just treated," Dudnick began. "A guy named Kirkland brought Sanchez in. He's the foreman or something. I know that because he's brought guys in before."

"Yeah. We know Kirkland," the sheriff said. Turning to TJ and Sam, he continued, "Leader of the ATV pack at the Powells."

"Sanchez first came in two weeks ago, saying he'd been bitten on the arm by a small alligator." Dr. Dudnick went on to describe the inflamed nature of the bite, how he'd cleaned and debrided it and started Sanchez on an IV antibiotic.

"Was that unusual?" TJ asked.

"Not really. We get a lot of animal bites in here. Raccoons and rats, surprised or protecting their young, are a major source of bites. Rabies is always a concern. Poisonous snakes like the one I just told you about—water moccasins near the canal and in the ponds, and rattlesnakes inland. Coral snakes don't like the muck, so they aren't a problem. Alligator bites are rare, but they happen. Sometimes we even get human bites, particularly on weekends."

"Remind me not to hit the bars on Saturday night," Sam said.

"Sanchez—what happened next?" Sheriff Rodriguez asked.

"I was surprised when he returned the next day and still had a fever. I thought sepsis was a possible diagnosis, gave him the second IV, and directed him to go to the Lakeland emergency room."

"But something made you wonder," TJ said.

"Sanchez's symptoms were unusual, so the first time he came in, I drew an extra vial of blood. It's a habit I got into during my army days. Always draw an extra vial of blood. It solved more than one mystery when I was in the Middle East. I was going to look at it myself but never got around to it."

TJ took out his phone and pulled up the picture from Bobby Powell's autopsy. He showed the photo of the bite marks on the boy to the doctor. "Does this look like the bite on Sanchez's arm?"

Dr. Dudnick shook his head. "Hard to tell."

"What did his blood work show?" Sheriff Rodriguez asked.

"Nothing very helpful. Infection, bacteria, markers consistent with diminished clotting ability. That's all we could tell here, but it continued to nag at me, so I sent the extra vial of blood to the CDC in Atlanta. Haven't heard back. It's probably somewhere in their queue. Could be weeks before they get to it."

"When did you send it?" TJ asked.

"Right after his second visit."

TJ cocked an eye at Rodriguez. "Sheriff?"

"I'll get the governor to speed that up," Rodriguez said.

"Not sure how useful it will be anyway," Dr. Dudnick continued. "Sanchez had all sorts of junk in him including a self-prescribed antibiotic, marijuana, opiates."

They thanked the doctor and left.

"Now let's pay a visit to Mr. Sanchez," Sheriff Rodriguez said.

* * *

Florida Pure Sugar was just a short drive from MediRedi. They turned off the main road and crossed the West Palm Beach Canal, arriving at the main entrance gate. A guard called Royce Mumford, alerting him that the sheriff and his party were coming. After the two vehicles passed, the guard also called Doug Kirkland.

Mumford was standing at the office doors when they arrived. He greeted Sheriff Rodriguez reservedly. It was clear they'd had dealings before. The four went into a small conference room and sat on metal folding chairs around a rectangular table.

"Has anything unusual happened recently at the farm?" Rodriguez began.

"Nope," Mumford said.

"What about Emilio Sanchez?"

"He quit a week ago and left."

"Anything unusual about it?" the sheriff asked.

"Nope. Happens all the time."

"How long was he with Pure Sugar?"

"About three years."

"What kind of an employee was he?" "Okay, I guess."

"You don't know?"

"We have a lot of workers here; I don't know everyone," Mumford replied.

"Did he give a reason for quitting?

"Nope."

"Leave a forwarding address?"

"No."

"He didn't tell you anything?" the Sheriff pressed.

"No. I never spoke with him. Doug Kirkland, the foreman of his crew, told me."

"What about his final pay?"

"Kirkland collected it for him," Mumford said.

"Don't you find that surprising?"

"I'm sure he had his reasons." Mumford gave the sheriff a dark look.

Rodriquez became exasperated. "Mumford, you have enough problems with Animal World right now. You don't want me breathing down your neck as well."

"Look it, I'm answering all your questions. What more do you want?"

"I'd like to have a word with Mr. Kirkland," Sheriff Rodriguez said.

Mumford grumbled, but the sheriff just folded his hands in front of him and waited. Mumford sighed, resignedly pulled out his cell, and made a call. "He appears to be out in the fields, and his radio isn't on."

"Send someone to get him," the sheriff said. "We'll wait."

Kirkland arrived a short time later, and Rodriguez immediately began questioning him. "Sanchez came to me after he'd been bitten," Kirkland responded. "He said he'd been eating lunch at the edge of the canal when a gator came out and tried to take it from him."

"Where?" TJ asked.

"Never asked him."

"Where was he working on the day he was bitten?"

"Not far from here."

"Alright," the sheriff said. "Then you took him to MediRedi?"

"Yes."

"What about the second time?"

"He went there on his own."

"And the doctor told him to go to the ER, but he never went. Doesn't that strike you as odd?"

"He never mentioned anything about the ER to me. Maybe he was feeling better," Kirkland said.

"Was he a good worker?"

"He was okay."

"Just okay? He was here for three years according to your boss. It seem funny to you that he would just up and disappear?"

"He didn't disappear," Kirkland responded. "He said he was going back to Honduras."

"After he'd been bitten?" TJ questioned. "At work? I'd think he'd want to stay on the payroll or go on disability. Get a free ride until he's better."

Kirkland shrugged. "I don't know. Maybe he overstayed his papers."

Sheriff Rodriguez turned to Mumford. "Did he?"

Mumford shook his head decisively. "No illegals here. We check all our workers."

Rodriguez knew that wasn't true, but it was a matter for another time. "I'd like to see Sanchez's work area."

When no one responded, Rodriguez gave Kirkland a hard look. "You're going to take me there right now." He turned to Mumford. "And you're going to get me a copy of his file, or I'll be on the five o'clock news saying that Pure Sugar refuses to cooperate with investigators regarding the deaths of Bobby Powell and Judy Herzog. By the way, I learned on my way out here that the golfer your croc attacked has died. Do you think your in-laws will like more bad publicity?"

Mumford frowned but didn't say anything.

With the issue quickly settled, they were about to head off to Kirkland's barn when Sheriff Rodriguez received a call on his radio. The Komodo had been spotted in Wellington. She'd entered a home not far from Paradise Stables with a woman and a baby inside.

"Change of plans," Rodriguez said. To Kirkland, he added: "We'll get back to you. Don't even think about going anywhere."

Kirkland followed them outside, hoping to hear something of interest. He spied TJ's metallic blue Thunderbird parked next to the sheriff's SUV. He looked at TJ. "That yours?"

"Yeah."

"I like old cars. Maybe you'll take me for a spin some time?" Kirkland laughed derisively.

TJ didn't respond as he and Sam got into the car and left.

CHAPTER 30

As TJ was leaving his house that morning to pick up Sam at The Waters Edge, the rising sun cast an irregular pattern of light and shadows in the house under construction at the edge of the Wellington Palm Beach Golf Club. One shaft of light fell on the bathtub that the delivery crew had left sitting in the middle of what would be the living room.

Kodra's head popped up and over the side of the tub where she became the first Komodo dragon to ever spend a night in a Kohler freestanding bath. She smelled concrete dust, fresh wood, dirt, and, further away, small animals. She had rested, feeling safe in the tub, letting her back and ribs heal. Her side still hurt, but she was hungry and thirsty. She rose up to leave the bathtub, but her claws just slid back down, leaving deep scratch marks in the acrylic side. Placing her front feet on top of the tub she boosted herself out and crossed the future living room, passed boxes containing kitchen cabinets, before exiting the house through the opening where there would be floor-to-ceiling sliding glass doors.

She walked past a large hole in the ground that would become the swimming pool and continued on to the narrow canal that marked the edge of the golf course. She lowered her head and drank. Satiated, she turned her attention to the dumpster in the side yard where she'd found the chicken bones. There were some rats near it, and she lunged at one, sending a sharp pain shooting through her side. The rat escaped, disappearing under the metal container.

Kodra smelled the rats she couldn't get and, in the distance, humans and other animals. She walked through the front yard, out into the road and started down the street. A woman with children were in a yard a few of houses away, and she picked up her pace but they disappeared into a car. The sun was hot on her back, and the pavement stung the pads of her feet, so she retreated to a lawn. The grass felt cool on her feet. Then she retreated farther, moving between two houses, one painted a bright white, the other a cool gray, to get out of the sun. There was a black four-foot aluminum fence on either side of her. She saw a dog two yards down, sitting in the shade, panting. She debated climbing over the fences that separated her from the dog but decided against it. Instead, she went back to the shadows between the houses, found some shrubbery, and settled in to wait for an animal to come by.

The sun was high in the sky when she sensed an ever-so-slight vibration. Kodra's eyes opened wide. Carried on the breeze was the scent of an unfamiliar animal. She tracked the animal as it unhurriedly moved along the side of the white house. It had a light brown color, with mouse-like ears, and a long mouse-like tail. The animal was about the size of a young pig, which was a frequent meal of hers back on Flores. But it wasn't a pig or a giant mouse, it was a nine-banded armadillo, a Florida resident since its ancestors were released into the wild by a traveling circus in the 1930s.

The armadillo had a strong sense of smell attuned to finding insects, its principal diet, but had weak eyesight and little awareness. It never saw Kodra coming up from behind, and it first realized it was in trouble when it felt the pressure of jaws closing around its shell. Fortunately for the armadillo, it wore natural body armor. Its shell was a series of overlapping bony plates that allowed movement but couldn't be penetrated even by Kodra's strong bite.

Kodra's teeth left jagged marks on the armadillo's shell as the animal squirmed out of her grasp. Free, the armadillo spun around and leapt three feet into the air. Kodra recoiled and froze. She'd never seen anything like that before. The armadillo landed on its feet and ran for its nearby den. Kodra quickly overcame her surprise and pursued. They crossed the small side yard to the gray house, and then to a landscaped bed of croton plants with fountain grass along its edges. Kodra nipped at the armadillo's leg as the animal dove into its den—a hole in the ground between the plants not much larger than the armadillo itself.

Kodra cocked her head and looked into the hole. The armadillo looked back, just out of reach. Kodra began scooping out dirt using her front legs and claws. The sandy soil offered little resistance. Kodra thrust her head down the enlarged hole. The armadillo responded by curling into a ball, its armored shell entirely surrounding and protecting the animal. Kodra poked at the armored ball, but it didn't open. However, blood was seeping from it. Her teeth had sliced into the armadillo's leg as they had slid off its shell. She smelled the blood and settled back to wait as her bite and her venom did their work.

After some minutes, the shell began to quiver. Kodra repeatedly scratched at it. Eventually, the shell opened slightly, and the armadillo's two front legs appeared. Kodra seized them in her mouth and dragged the animal out of its hole. The armadillo began spasming and flipped open on its back. Kodra pounced, sinking her teeth into the armadillo's soft stomach. She gorged on the armadillo's flesh and organs, although the small animal did little to satisfy her hunger. Finished, Kodra raised her bloody snout. Thin tendrils of flesh hung from her mouth. She shook her head, sending drops of the armadillo's blood flying in all directions.

The next scents registered at the same time as she heard the sounds. A human, and a very young human and a young dog were nearby. All easy prey. She rose on her four legs and quickly high-walked along the side of the gray house toward the back. Drops of the armadillo's blood left a trail as she went. The gray stucco wall of the house gave way to a thin metallic material that was waving in the breeze. Cautiously, Kodra probed the fabric with her nose. It offered no resistance. She pushed her head through the broken screen. It made a ripping sound as she pushed through and entered a caged enclosure. Her claws sharply clicked on the stone pavement as she walked.

In front of her was a partially open sliding glass door. Cold air escaped and carried stronger scents to her. It was dark beyond the door, but Kodra could make out the shapes of objects. Tongue active, she entered and wound her way through a maze of family room furniture, unfamiliar things to her, infused with the smell of humans and a dog, toward a waist high wooden wall.

The wall was the back of the kitchen island. On the other side of the island Margaret Pfister had finally corralled her squirming puppy. The six-month-old chocolate Lab was a handful. She'd picked him up and opened the sliding glass door to take him out when the dog had wiggled out of her grasp and scampered away. Pfister had chased him back to the kitchen, leaving the slider open.

Kodra paused at the side of the island. She shot out her long yellow tongue. It curved around the island, almost touching the woman's leg, and then quickly disappeared back into her mouth.

Struggling to hold the puppy, Pfister paused, unsure if she'd just seen a flash of yellow. Then Kodra stuck her head around the corner and looked up at the woman. Pfister screamed at the sight of the giant lizard with shreds of bloody flesh hanging from its mouth. She dropped the Lab and threw up her hands. The puppy splayed on the kitchen's marble floor.

Kodra stepped toward the woman. Pfister thought of her baby in the nearby bedroom and frantically looked around for a weapon. She stepped back and pressed up against the stove. On it, onions sizzled in a cast iron skillet. She groped behind her for the handle of the frying pan. Finding it, she threw the heavy pan at Kodra.

The skillet bounced off Kodra's head, covering her with hot oil and onions. She felt only the sensation of heat where her osteoderms covered her skin, but the oil penetrated the areas where the stable hands' rake had scraped her back, and she felt searing pain. Kodra wheeled around, claws furiously trying to gain traction as she went tumbling into a bar stool. She whipped her powerful tail, and the stool went flying. Legs pumping furiously, nails clacking on the marble floor, she skidded and slid back out the patio glass door and crashed through the screen panel next to the one where she'd entered. She ran across the side yard to the white house. There she made herself as small as possible in a grouping of ornamental bushes. Breathing quickly, her senses told her that she wasn't being chased.

The sheltering foliage, the smell of plants and dirt, gradually calmed her. After a while, Kodra retraced her steps across the lawns and driveways, past the dumpster, and disappeared into the partially built house. She lay down on the dusty concrete surface. The human she'd encountered had inflicted pain and was surrounded by strange things. Her sharp claws couldn't gain traction or penetrate the hard surfaces, making it impossible to run. And even though she found food here, there were no large forested areas where she could safely nest. This environment was too foreign for her. She would have to move.

*　*　*

PBSO deputies arrived quickly in response to Pfister's frantic 911 call and cordoned off the area. Once again, the press beat TJ, Sam, and Sheriff Rodriguez to the scene of the event. *They must be sold out of police scanners in Palm Beach County,* TJ thought. He and Sam drove past the white TV vans with their satellite antennas extended into the sky. A reporter was speaking into a camera, while a third crew member stood nearby, holding an umbrella at the ready. Evidently, rain was expected. The whole scene had become so commonplace to TJ that it almost didn't register as he pulled into the driveway of the gray house.

Everyone assembled in the kitchen where Pfister, along with her husband, James, who'd been her second call, described what had happened and how Kodra escaped. A kitchen stool lay askew on top of a side table, where it had landed after being sent airborne by Kodra's tail. A scattering of cold oily onions coated the floor nearby. The base of a broken lamp sat on a second table, with pieces of it scattered on the floor around it. The woman's chocolate Lab puppy slept peacefully in his basket in the family room, unfazed by the reptilian visitor or his fall.

Pfister pointed out the screen through which Kodra had entered. They'd cut some screens to save the cage in anticipation of Hurricane Chris and were on the repairman's list to have them replaced. Next to the cut screen was one with a jagged rip in it, that Kodra had escaped through.

"Any chance you have surveillance cameras?" TJ asked.

"Cover all four sides of the house, front door, pool, and we have monitors in the baby's room," James Pfister replied.

TJ clapped his hands with delight. "Finally!"

The husband booted the system and fast forwarded to when Kodra appeared outside the screen. There was a collective gasp.

"Wow, she's big," Sam said. "At least eight feet, maybe two hundred pounds."

"Back the tape up," TJ said.

The side yard camera had recorded Kodra's movements as she dashed through a shaft of bright sunlight and into the shadows under the eaves of the gray house, chasing the armadillo.

"Look how her colors appear to change from a dirty green to brown to gray," Sam said.

They watched transfixed as Kodra scooped dirt out of the armadillo's den, then dragged the struggling animal out by one of its front legs. They all looked away at various times as she bit into the still-living armadillo's stomach and ate. TJ thought about Bobby Powell and Judy Herzog and how they'd died. *This family was lucky.* Nothing had happened to them except some broken furniture. Not to mention that they now possessed the first footage of the Komodo dragon, which would be worth a lot of money.

Leaving the Pfisters behind, TJ, Sam, and Sheriff Rodriguez explored the side yard. From there, they walked to the back of the property. They took in the aluminum fence at the end of the back yard, the tall grass, the canal, and the golf course beyond.

"Another canal," Sam said. "This might be how the Komodo is getting around. It's not usual Komodo behavior, but it's possible."

"What do you make of her going into a house?" TJ asked.

"She's adapting to an urban environment."

"Don't you think that's a stretch?" TJ responded.

"Not at all. She has everything she needs here—food, water, shelter, no predators . . . except us. There's nothing unusual about it. Animals everywhere are adapting to an urban environment. There are falcons living amid the skyscrapers in New York City. How often do you see a coyote? Raccoons, deer, bear, all moving in. We bulldoze their existing home, and they have to find a new one."

"If she adapts to being here, she'll be harder to find," TJ said.

He called in FWS teams from the refuge to assist the PBSO in the search. The officers and rangers walked the streets and yards, along the small canals and probed clumps of foliage. The fairways of the adjoining golf course were searched. But no one thought to check a house under construction.

CHAPTER 31

TJ dashed into the coffee shop at The Waters Edge.

"You're late," Sam teased.

"Sorry," he said as he sat down at the table. "I was coordinating today's search with Sheriff Rodriguez."

"I guess that's an acceptable excuse."

The waitress brought coffee and menus. TJ waved his away. "Three pancakes, four strips of bacon, and two scrambled eggs."

"Sounds good," Sam said. "I'll have the same."

The waitress gave Sam a look but said nothing and left. TJ took a mouthful of coffee. He made a sour face. "I hope our breakfast isn't as burnt as this."

"We'll see. What did you and Sheriff Rodriguez decide?"

"The sheriff is in Wellington, prepping his deputies. They'll patrol by foot and car. Florida Fish and Wildlife will be checking the local canals and the surrounds. My officers and rangers will be on the banks of the L-40 and in the Arthur Marshall. PBSO will put their drones in the air. Western Wellington has been declared a no-fly zone, and that includes civilian operated drones, so the sheriff's people will have the sky to themselves. After breakfast, we'll meet Rodriguez at Pure Sugar and talk to Kirkland."

"The sheriff asked about using infrared," TJ continued. "That's how they look for people in the Everglades. I told him that Komodos, like all reptiles, are cold blooded and their body temperature would be about the same as their surroundings, so there'd be no contrasting heat bloom."

"That's right," Sam agreed.

"Good. So let's see if we can figure out where Kodra came from—"

"Kodra?" Sam's voice rose, and the couple sitting at the next table looked over at them. "You've named her?"

"Sure. Why not? Kodra. Komodo dragon. Get it?"

Sam made a face.

TJ feigned annoyance. "May I continue? The first location we have for Kodra is where Sanchez was bitten. We don't know exactly where that was but if Kirkland is to be believed, it was somewhere along canal. I estimate the site to be about ten miles north of the Powell house. The canal was flowing south at a pretty good clip, so it's unlikely she entered it downstream and swam north. Also, there's nothing around there except Pure Sugar to the west and the JW Corbett Wildlife Area to the east. No houses, no boat launches, rec facilities. Nothing."

Their breakfasts arrived, and TJ immediately dug in. "So she must have come from somewhere inside Pure Sugar. What better place to hide an animal smuggling operation than on a big farm with tall leafy plants."

Sam nibbled on a piece of bacon. "I'm betting you think Mumford is involved."

"And Kirkland."

"Yeah. I never trusted guys with crosses tattooed on their chests."

"I'm sure there were a lot of those at Stanford," TJ said with a smirk.

Sam made a face but didn't respond.

Kenny Loggins singing caused the couple at the next table to glare at TJ again. "Gotta remember to put that on mute," he said. He glanced down at the caller ID and answered the call. "Rodriguez is on his way to Pure

Sugar right now. The CDC found Dudnick's vial of Sanchez's blood and spun it overnight."

"What'd they find?" Sam asked.

"Anti-bodies that would be produced to fight a Komodo dragon's venom."

"Wow. The governor really came through."

"I suspect the international coverage of a Komodo running amok in Florida may have had more to do with it. The press helped us for once. Let's go"

Sam signed the chit to her room, and TJ longingly eyed his partially eaten pancakes as they rose to leave. Retrieving the T-Bird, they drove west, leaving behind the congestion and expensive cars of Palm Beach, and turned north on Conners Road toward Lake O, driving through tall rows of sugarcane plants as the West Palm Beach Canal flowed alongside. They passed a sign on their left that read: Muck City Road.

"Muck City Road. Flying Cow Road. What is it with road names in this part of Florida?" Sam asked.

"Don't know, but this one has a story too. Named after Fingy Conners. Got his nickname, or so the story goes, after he lost his thumb as a child."

Soon after, they turned off Conners Road at the entrance to Florida Pure Sugar Incorporated and crossed the canal. A guard opened the gates, without asking them for ID, and waved them through. Apparently, he recognized the T-Bird. TJ pulled up next to the sheriff's SUV, and the pair went into the administration office. The guard at the front gate was the same as the day before, and, like the day before, he alerted Kirkland.

* * *

Darisse walked into the barn dripping sweat, machete in hand, in response to Kirkland's radio call.

"They're on their way," Kirkland said. "Everything done?"

"All done, and the chipper's been fired."

Kirkland retrieved a burner phone and handed it to Darisse. "Take the farm truck. Drive to Wellington, call 911 using this phone, and tell them you've spotted the Komodo. The dispatcher will ask you some questions. Don't give your name but give them a location. Make sure it's believable. Somewhere around Flying Cow Road will do. Then come back and meet me at the number four equipment barn. Understood?"

Darisse nodded. The cages had been emptied, and the chipper had been burned after sugarcane stalks had been run through it, just as Kirkland had directed, but Darisse hadn't had the heart to butcher the animals. He'd set them free.

* * *

Sheriff Rodriguez was speaking with Royce Mumford when TJ and Sam arrived. A warrant sat on Mumford's desk. "There's a Komodo loose that's already eaten two people." Then added sarcastically: "I'm sure you've heard."

Mumford glared at him.

"Your employee was bitten by her, and he's disappeared," Rodriguez continued. "I issued a missing persons alert for him yesterday."

"Do you have any proof?"

"Of the bite? Yes," Rodriguez said. "Forensic evidence. We also believe there may be an animal trafficking ring operating on Pure Sugar land."

"We know nothing about that," Mumford insisted, but his face betrayed concern.

"You better start cooperating, Mumford."

"I'm calling our lawyers."

"Go right ahead."

Mumford picked up his phone and hit a button on his speed dial. A short time later, he said, "Okay, I understand," and hung up.

"Now take us to where Sanchez worked and make sure Kirkland's there," the sheriff said.

The four got into an open-sided jeep with deep treaded tires. The jeep churned through the muck that comprised the path through the sugarcane fields and headed to the barn that doubled as Kirkland's office. They pulled up, and they got out. Kirkland emerged from the building, feigning surprise. "Back again? What's going on?"

"Our lawyers are on the way here," Mumford told Kirkland. "You don't have to answer any questions."

"I don't have anything to hide," Kirkland said.

"Sanchez was bitten by a Komodo dragon," Rodriguez said. "The blood drawn at the MediRedi clinic proves it."

"He told me and the doc he was bitten by a gator," Kirkland said.

"Do you expect us to believe he wouldn't know the difference between a gator and an eight-foot lizard?" TJ said. "Where'd it come from?"

"How should I know?"

"Do you have exotic animals on the farm?" Rodriguez asked.

"Same answer as before. How should I know?"

"Because you're the foreman and you know everything that happens around here," TJ fired back.

Kirkland glared at TJ. "How do you know it even came from here? Sanchez said he was eating lunch along the canal when the thing came out of the water and bit him. It could have come from Lake O and been carried down the canal, just like the papers said happened in Wellington."

TJ pressed, "I doubt it. It came from here. Are there other animals? Other Komodos?"

Sheriff Rodriguez jumped in. "Where's Sanchez?" he demanded.

"Honduras? How should I know?"

Sheriff Rodriguez looked at Mumford. "I want to speak with every member of Sanchez's crew. Have them come up to your office. Now."

* * *

As Sheriff Rodriguez continued interrogating Kirkland, TJ and Sam looked around. TJ spied the drone sitting on a work bench. He asked Kirkland, "Business or pleasure?"

"Business," Kirkland said. "Helps me watch over the cane and keep tabs on my crew." He was so used to the drone that he'd left it in plain sight. There was nothing incriminating about a drone, but he kicked himself. He'd never thought to check the drone's app on his laptop to see if it'd recorded his trip with Sanchez and Darisse in the refuge.

The drone was forgotten when Sheriff Rodriguez received a call on his radio. He listened intently and said, "I'll be right there."

"There's been another sighting," he said to TJ and Sam. "A motorist saw the Komodo enter a culvert running beneath Flying Cow Road. We're moving search teams into the area. I need to get down there."

"I'll go with you," Sam said.

"I think I'll stay and look around Pure Sugar some more," TJ said.

Mumford took Sam and Rodriguez back to the sheriff's SUV. Kirkland stayed close to TJ as he continued to study the barn's contents. Stepping outside, TJ walked around the building. He stopped, looked down, and nudged something with his shoe. Before Kirkland could see what it was, TJ quickly set off down a row of cane toward the canal. Kirkland sensed a change in him and hurried to catch up. On their way, they came to the burned-out cane pulp shredder.

"What happened?" TJ asked.

"Caught fire," Kirkland replied. "Happens all the time. Overheats and dried pulp is like kindling."

They walked to the canal and back in silence. TJ headed to the spot outside the barn where he'd stopped before. Both men looked down. On the ground was what looked like a thick cellophane tube with a crescent shaped pattern on one side. He poked at it again. "Interesting," he said.

"It's a snakeskin," Kirkland said. "What's so unusual about that?"

"Have you ever seen any pythons around here?"

"Never. Why?"

"The skin is too wide for a native snake. Only pythons and boas have bodies this thick. That's what this skin is from."

Kirkland didn't respond, but he knew that the shedded skin was the size of a boa constrictor that he'd told Darisse to kill. *This damn fish and wildlife officer is going to figure it out,* he thought. *Change of plans. It was going to be a twofer today.*

TJ looked around some more. When he said he was done, Kirkland offered him a ride back to his car. The farm truck Kirkland used was parked beside the barn and the two men got in. Just as soon as they did, Kirkland jumped out. "Be right back," he said. "Forgot my radio." Kirkland went into the barn. He grabbed his radio off a workbench and put it in his left pants pocket. Working quickly, he pulled a stepladder up to a row of shelves and retrieved a metal box with a combination lock from the top shelf. He thumbed the digits on the lock and removed his Smith & Wesson. It was a small, easily concealed, but powerful pistol. He put the gun in his right pocket, descended the ladder, and left the barn.

As Kirkland drove TJ back to the administration building, he said: "I'd like to help you find this Komodo. It's a horrible thing it did to that woman and child. I didn't want to say this to Mumford or the sheriff, but I did see some empty cages a few days ago."

"What kind of cages?"

"Don't know but big enough to hold a big lizard or an alligator."

"Where are they now?"

"Probably same place I saw them, near a maintenance building a little ways south of here."

"Can you take me there?"

"Sure, but we'll need to take your car. The truck's scheduled out."

"Okay."

"Looks like I be getting that ride in your car I asked for," Kirkland said with a grin.

* * *

Kodra's eyes popped open. She raised her head and looked left and right, her tongue investigating the morning air. She'd slept on the living room floor next to the bathtub the previous night. The tub was just the right size for her to curl up in, but she disliked the tall smooth sides. As TJ and Sam were having breakfast, she rose on her thick powerful legs and ambled out of the partially constructed house for the last time. For days, she'd roamed around in populated areas, walked across yards, past houses and down streets without being spotted.

She was continents away from her home on Flores. Food was plentiful, some prey were familiar, and some were new to her. The large open spaces of the fairways, lawns, and paddocks made her feel uncomfortably exposed. Groupings of plants and trees were too small to provide safe cover, and the house she'd just left was a very foreign environment. There was more water than on Flores, but some of it was tainted with chemicals. And there were just too many humans around. Secure nesting sites were impossible to find, and she was driven by her need to nest.

Memory and scent induced Kodra to head west. She crossed Flying Cow Road, not far from where Darisse had falsely reported sighting her, and walked over an equestrian trail that ringed the Wellington Environmental Preserve. She was greeted with the sights, sounds, and smells of nature.

Kodra entered the three-hundred-sixty-acre nature and wildlife sanctuary which was comprised of dry ground snaking around wetlands. There were five large marshes in the western half of the preserve. The largest, located to the south, was shaped like a number seven. Two smaller marshes were in the northeast and southeast corners of the preserve. She passed bulrush grasses, bald cypresses, and cabbage palms. She heard the sharp cry of an osprey and took in the varied scents of small animals. The scent of humans was faint and behind her. As natural as it looked to her, the preserve was man-made, and its primary purpose was to cleanse phosphorus from rain-water before it entered the Everglades.

The subdivision the Herzog's house was in lay to the preserve's north. The Cracker Ranch, home to horses and cows, ran along its southern border. The preserve's eastern border was Flying Cow Road, beyond which was the Wellington Palm Beach Golf Cub and Paradise Stables. To its west was the L-40 canal and the Arthur Marshal Wildlife Refuge.

Not many people visited the preserve in August. The days were steamy, and the afternoons brought thunderstorms. There were even fewer visitors than usual this August. Everyone preferred to stay inside when a Komodo dragon was on the loose.

Kodra immediately began exploring, driven by a desire to find a suitable nesting site. Head turning, sampling the air, she walked along a path eventually arriving at a six-story tower, almost at the western edge of the preserve. The steel and concrete structure was of no interest to her, but had she climbed it, which she could have done, she would have looked out over the Arthur Marshall. She could have seen the hammock where she'd rested after eating Judy Herzog and the hammock where she'd later regurgitated the woman's remains.

There was the smell of human offal around the tower, and it grew stronger as she went. Passing a chemical restroom, the smell became so overpowering that Kodra kept her tongue in her mouth and crossed to the far side of the path.

She turned around and walked back along the path moving into the heart of the preserve. Ever alert, the wind carried the unmistakable scent of two adult humans, horses, and leather. In short order, she heard two women's voices. They were coming toward her, out of sight just beyond a bend in the path. Kodra looked around and chose her spot. She slipped into a thick patch of three-foot-tall fakahatchee grass at the edge of the path and made herself small. A boat-tailed grackle looked down from a bald cypress tree, head swiveling back and forth between Kodra and the approaching women.

The fakahatchee grass didn't completely hide Kodra, but the browns and greens of her hide blended in with the foliage. She tensed to strike. The women came into view riding two large horses. Kodra looked up. The women were an easy target, but she remembered the kick from the mare in the field. She lay motionless as the riders receded into the distance.

Kodra didn't return to the path but followed an equestrian trail deeper into the preserve. Not far from a small marsh was a small rise covered with a copse of thick green three-foot tall evergreen-like Jamaican capers and surrounded by shorter leafy St. John's wort plants. In the center stood a twenty-foot tall red maple tree. She plowed into the St. John's wort and began to dig. The intertwined roots of the dense foliage made digging difficult even with her sharp claws. As she enlarged the hole, a black snake tumbled into it. Without hesitation, she lunged and snapped. Most of the snake disappeared into her mouth. The snake's bloody, still-twitching, tail was kicked out of the pit along with the dirt as she resumed digging. She managed to scoop out a small burrow. Exhausted, she settled in for the night.

CHAPTER 32

TJ found himself alone with Kirkland outside the Pure Sugar offices. Sam had driven off with Sheriff Rodriguez. Mumford had gone back into the building. TJ had an uneasy feeling about Kirkland. *Why is he offering to help?* He must have known that anything he said would be passed on to the sheriff. But TJ was certain the smugglers were operating out of the farm, and the more time he spent here the more likely he was to learn something. And if he could get Kirkland talking, so much the better. "Okay. Let's go see this equipment shed you told me about," he said to Kirkland as he climbed into his T-Bird.

Kirkland got in and slid his hand across the top of the dash. "Just love these old cars." He rested his arm on the top of the door.

TJ didn't buckle his seat belt. *Just in case.* He noticed Kirkland didn't buckle his either.

As they passed through the main gate, Kirkland gave a small wave to the guard. The guard nodded back. They drove down Connors Road, with the seemingly endless tall stalks of sugarcane on its right and more on its left beyond the West Palm Beach Canal. As they drove, TJ asked Kirkland about working on the farm. Kirkland gave noncommittal answers. After a couple of miles, Kirkland said, "There's a service road coming up on your left. Take it."

TJ slowed and turned. They crossed over the canal onto a dirt track that disappeared into the fields. The cane hung over the left side of the roadway, and the long green leaves brushed against the T-Bird as it passed. On the right, the first few rows of cane had been cut down. TJ felt like they were in the middle of nowhere. They came to a clearing with a large corrugated metal building with the number four on a sign centered over its sliding doors. The area was pockmarked with pools of stagnant water of all sizes. *Like craters on the moon* flashed through TJ's mind. To the right of the building, TJ saw a flatbed truck. Next to it was a backhoe with its claw-like bucket resting on the ground. The construction equipment was sitting in muck at the edge of a partially dug ditch some twelve-feet wide. The ditch ran through the clearing and stopped just short of the freshly cut rows of cane. A large blue hose, with a brass fitting on one end, sat on top of a pile of dirt. The hose gurgled and spit out some water, adding to the already sizable puddle in front of it. TJ heard the sound of a gasoline engine coming from down in the ditch. After a moment, the hose coughed up more brown water.

"Digging a new drainage canal," Kirkland said. "As you can see, we have flooding issues here."

TJ pulled up near the truck and stopped, holding his foot on the brake. "Car'll get stuck if we go any farther."

"This is fine." Kirkland's voice tailed away. He was looking in the distance.

"Something wrong?"

"Just expected one of my workers to be here, that's all."

"Where are the cages—" TJ stopped speaking when a rustling sound caused him to turn. Kirkland was pointing his Smith & Wesson at him.

"Get out and start walking," Kirkland said, motioning with his gun toward the ditch.

"You don't want to do this," TJ said. "You won't get away with killing a federal officer."

"Two people eaten. I'm an accessory. Ex-con. That's life in a real bad prison. No way. I'll take my chances."

With a sudden movement, TJ stomped on the gas pedal. The T-Bird lurched forward and fishtailed right. Kirkland slid left on the vinyl seat. TJ violently shoved the steering wheel. The steering column made a grinding noise as the broken lockout mechanism released and the tilt-away steering wheel swung right. Kirkland's eyes went wide at the sight of the steering wheel coming at him, and he reflexively grabbed it, his gun becoming caught between his hand and the wheel.

TJ lunged for the pistol. The mens' hands wrapped around one another, the barrel of the gun waved back and forth as they struggled. The car continued forward, its tires churning through the muck, not stopping until it bumped into one of the backhoe's large rubber tires.

TJ planted his feet and drove himself into Kirkland. Kirkland slammed into the passenger's door. TJ bent Kirkland's arms back and banged the gun hand against the top of the door until Kirkland's hand opened and the Smith & Wesson clattered down the side of the T-Bird. With a splash, it disappeared into a pool of water.

Kirkland broke free of TJ's grip and threw open the door. He twisted out of the car and lurched through water, running around the door. Putting a hand on the front fender, he jumped up and slid over the hood. Stumbling to his feet, he ran to the truck next to the backhoe.

TJ flung open his door and followed. With each step, he sank up to his ankles into the mud. The ground reluctantly gave up each boot with a sucking sound. As he reached the truck, his mind registered the image of a thick dark brown body with black crossbands lying in the shadow of the flatbed. He veered right at the last moment. His years in the Everglades had honed his senses. A large water moccasin with a broad arrow-shaped head and cat-like eyes was watching him.

Jumping in the cab, Kirkland pulled down the passengers' side sun visor, and a key fob dropped on the seat. He grabbed it and was about to insert the key in the ignition when TJ seized him by the shoulders and yanked him out of the cab. The two men tumbled backward. TJ landed hard with Kirkland on top of him. Kirkland flipped over and drove a knee into TJ's stomach driving the air out of his lungs. He felt Kirkland's powerful hands close around his throat. His legs flailed as he grabbed Kirkland's arms trying to break his grip.

As his vision began to swim, TJ caught movement out of the corner of his eye. The water moccasin. He took a hand off of Kirkland's arm, reached over, grabbed the snake by its tail and swung it at Kirkland. The viper planted it fangs in Kirkland's leg. Kirkland screamed at the searing pain and rolled on his back; the snake held on. He struggled to his feet, and gripping the snake with both hands, he pulled it off his leg and threw it into the ditch.

TJ jumped up and moved away. Breathing heavily, back pressed against the truck, he watched Kirkland limp into the sugar cane and disappear. *The moccasin will take care of him.*

Exhausted, covered in mud, TJ walked unsteadily back to the Thunderbird, reached in, and turned off the engine. Then he slumped down with his back against the side of the car. *That was damn close*, he thought, his body shivering as the adrenaline wore off. He pulled out his cell phone and punched in 911. Somewhat surprisingly the call went through. Pure Sugar had invested in a signal booster network throughout the farm.

Deputies from the Belle Glades PBSO substation, with lights and sirens on, arrived minutes later. After checking on TJ, they went into the cane looking for Kirkland. EMTs came soon afterward. TJ asked one of the first responders for a blanket. The woman immediately pulled a large blue blanket out of the ambulance and draped it on his shoulders. He removed the blanket and placed it on the seat and floor of the T-Bird. He didn't want his car's interior to get muddy when he drove home.

* * *

Sheriff Rodriguez arrived a short time later, but before he could say anything, TJ asked, "Did you find anything in Wellington?"

"No. Nothing. Now you. You okay?"

"Yeah." TJ related what had happened. "I just hope the steering column stays in place on the drive home."

"Sorry, TJ, but your car isn't going anywhere. It's evidence."

TJ groaned.

"But I'll give you a lift. And Sam called. She's worried sick about you. She asked that I bring you by her hotel."

* * *

Sam looked him over when he arrived. "God, you're a mess. Are you okay?"

"Fine. Just a little worn out. That's all."

"Why don't you shower, although I have no idea what we're going to do about your clothes. Meet me downstairs when you're ready."

They sat at a picnic table overlooking the parking lot. TJ had scraped most of the dried mud off his clothes. "What's in the bag?" he asked.

"Dinner. Tacos, chips, and a large sprite." She nodded at a six pack of Sam Adams. "They didn't have Yingling."

"Anything named Sam is good in my book."

"That's right. And there'll be no shop talk tonight. You deserve the night off."

"I'm on board with that."

It was dark out when TJ finished his third beer. "One work question before I go. What happened at the culvert today?"

"The sheriff and I were met there by a SWAT team. They were some serious-looking people dressed in black, I can tell you. They were standing at both ends of a culvert that went under Flying Cow Road. One of your guys was there, too. He had a snare pole. I took it, waded into the canal, and poked it around."

"Brave woman."

"There was a commotion, and a rather annoyed six-foot alligator appeared. We let him go about his business. No Komodo. False alarm."

TJ laughed. "Better for the gator than being made into a handbag. At least Kirkland won't be importing any more reptiles." He balled up the taco wrappers, gathered up the beer bottles, stood, and yawned. "I'm beat. Time to call it a day and get some rest." He pulled his phone. "I'll get an Uber to take me home."

Sam laid her hand on the phone. "Why don't you come upstairs instead?"

"Your couch was pretty lumpy, and I'm beat."

"I have a nice comfy bed."

"Thanks, but I don't want you sleeping on the couch either."

"Boy, TJ, you really have been spending too much time with your cars."

CHAPTER 33

Kodra awoke to a hot, muggy morning, but she didn't mind. She looked around and took in the scents. The scrapes on her back from the stable hand's rake were crusted over, and the pain from the oil the woman threw on her was gone. Nearby was a raccoon, but she paid it no attention. She walked to the top of the marsh shaped like a seven. The Jamaican swamp sawgrass that bordered it yielded as she brushed past. A human trying to walk through would suffer numerous cuts and scratches because the serrated spear-shaped stalks, which gave the grass its name, were made of silica but the strong grass slid harmlessly off of her thick skin. Two ducks noisily took to flight when she emerged from the sawgrass onto a sandy plain. She smelled a rabbit not far away. There were gaps in the sawgrass where animals would come to drink. They'd feel safe, with the thick grasses providing protection. The grasses would also provide a good place for her to hide.

Nearby were some swamp bay evergreens surrounded by thick floppy firebushes intertwined with purple-flowered pickerelweed plants. A hole dug in the thicket would make an ideal nest. She pushed her way through the underbrush until she found a suitable spot and dug. The roots were close together and hard to break, but she worked determinedly, flinging dirt over the sides of the increasing depression. When she finished, the cavity was three feet deep and only slightly bigger than her body, but she'd selected the location and dug it out with care. Close to water and prey, this was a better place than where she'd spent the previous night, and she would make it her home.

She left her newly dug nest, skirted the big marsh, and passed through tall grasses and scrub pines before arriving at the ring road that doubled as the equestrian trail around the edge of the preserve. Across the trail was a drainage ditch and a strip of grass that ended at a tall chain-link fence. Beyond the fence were the large open fields of the Cracker Ranch. Kodra saw horses and cows. She remembered the pain from the mare's kick at Paradise Stables and would be careful, but it wouldn't stop her from preying on these animals. Then she caught the unmistakable scent of a human.

* * *

A mug of coffee gone cold sat on a work bench as TJ tinkered with his Toronado to get it running. It turned out to be a simple fix. An alternator wire had come lose, draining the battery. He tightened the nut and hooked up his battery charger. *Off to a good start,* he thought.

His second project was more involved, the gold '68 Camaro. He put the car on his scissors lift and disconnected the drive shaft from the transmission. He lowered the car, then made quick work of the motor mounts. With one hand, he slowly pumped the cylinder on his engine hoist, while his other hand steadied the engine. The old inline six-cylinder motor, a grimy black, with the transmission attached, rose out of the Camaro's engine bay. A bright red rebuilt Chevrolet 327 V-8 mated to a four-speed manual sat on the floor nearby. He rolled the hoist next to the shiny new V-8 and lowered the old motor and tranny to the floor. All the while he thought about finding Kodra. Wiping his hands, he called the sheriff.

"How'd you sleep last night?" Rodriquez asked.

TJ smiled to himself. "Like a baby. Nothing like a good fight in the mud to tire one out." He didn't tell the sheriff he'd spent the night with Sam—that was their secret—or that he'd Ubered home in the morning. "By the way," TJ continued. "You didn't have to impound my car."

"Yes, we did. It's evidence and you're lucky I don't issue you a ticket for having a defective steering column," the sheriff said. "But don't worry, you'll get it back in the few days. Meantime, we'll take good care of it. What are your plans for today?"

"FWS told me to take the day off. Get some rest. I'm working on my cars, but I'll be in contact with my team."

"You're lucky. The press is going crazy over what happened. It's not every day a water moccasin is used as a weapon."

"It was self-defense."

"That's what they all say." Rodriquez chuckled.

"What are your plans?"

"On my way to Pure Sugar. I've had teams there all night looking for Kirkland, but there's been no sign of him."

"The farm's a big place. He could be anywhere."

"Do you think the snake killed him?"

"I don't know," TJ said. "The moccasin didn't bite him in a vulnerable area like his chest or neck. I think the snake got him with both fangs, but it happened so quickly I can't be sure. How much poison was in its sacks or how hard did it bite down? I don't know. Kirkland could just have a swollen leg or be lying dead in a cane field. If he's alive, he'll probably seek treatment."

"We've put out an alert to all the docs, including veterinarians, in the area to call us immediately if a man comes in with a poisonous snake bite."

"Good. Any news on the Komodo?"

"You might want to give Sam a call, she has a lead."

TJ wished the sheriff good hunting and called Sam. "Good morning again."

"Where are you?"

"Still at home."

"Working on your cars, I bet."

"Yes. Rodriquez said I should call you. What're you up to?"

"I'm following up on shit," she said.

"Huh?"

"It's Komodo shit. Poop. Droppings. A state wildlife officer found it."

"Where?"

"Along a canal that runs along the edge of the Wellington Palm Beach Golf Club. The PBSO is closing the course now, and they're calling in all available officers. We're going to search the course and the surrounding homes."

TJ took the keys for his Chevy Trailblazer off the peg. "I'm on my way."

* * *

Kirkland watched the Pure Sugar offices emptying out for the evening. He ignored his labored breathing and forced himself to stay calm. Pulling up his pant leg, he saw a single angry red puncture wound. The area around it was swollen and bruised. He also saw the hole on his work boot from the water moccasin's other fang. He'd felt the venom run harmlessly run down his ankle. The sturdy boot had kept the viper's fang from reaching him.

After the last office light went out, he used his master key to enter the infirmary and found the vial of antivenom the farm kept for just such emergencies. He injected himself, then picked up the landline, and called Mumford. The call would go through Pure Sugar's main telephone switch and could have come from anywhere within the farm, should the sheriff try to trace the call from Mumford's phone.

Kirkland grabbed some pain pills, filled a jug with water, and left the treatment room. He stayed in the shadows, being careful not to be seen as he made his way to one of the smaller service roads. He unlocked the gate and crossed the canal and Conners Road. Then he headed into the rows of sugar cane in the western fields. He was sitting against a work shed when Mumford arrived a short time later.

"You've looked better," Mumford said.

Kirkland struggled to his feet. "I'll be fine. It was only a one fanger."

"Assault and attempt to kill a federal officer . . . It's all over the news. What the hell were you thinking?"

"He knew."

"He knew? How?"

"Saw a shedded boa skin."

"What? How could that be? Darisse was supposed to get rid of everything."

"Evidently he didn't. My guess is he let the animals go. He always had a soft spot for them."

"Great. Now I've got a bunch of exotics slithering around the farm."

"Don't worry, nobody will ever find them."

"And what about Darisse, did you get rid of him?"

"Not yet, but I will, then I'm gone. Got friends in Miami. They'll get me on a freighter to New Orleans or Houston."

"Not so fast. We have to catch the Komodo before the law does."

"Why? They can't trace her to us."

"Yes they can. I got a call from our supplier in Jakarta. Seems news of a Komodo on the loose in Florida is a big story over there. And now the government's involved. Komodos are something of a national treasure, and they've been told it's one of theirs."

"So?"

"So, our friend tells us our Komodo is microchipped. So was the male that died."

"Oh, that's just great," Kirkland said with disgust.

"Yeah. The chip will tell them the lizard came from Flores. If they're smart, they'll find out a male is missing, too. Then they'll start asking questions, like why wasn't the missing Komodo reported? One can be explained—dies, disappears, chip stops working. But two at the same time? There'll be an investigation, and someone will talk."

"Okay. Darisse first, then we find the Komodo, then I go."

* * *

Wilguens Darisse did not have much of a formal education, but he was street smart. Word of Kirkland trying to kill the US Fish & Wildlife officer had spread quickly through the farm community. He'd thought it over and decided that running would be a sure sign of guilt. It was best to show up for work. His apprehension rose when he saw there was a new guard on duty at the gate. He asked among the workers and was told Kirkland's friend hadn't reported for his shift. Then Sheriff Rodriguez and his deputies, warrants in hand, arrived and began questioning the farmhands who worked under Kirkland.

As Darisse milled around the barn, a call came summoning him to the main office. Reluctantly, he went. Entering the building he heard indistinct conversations in English, Spanish, and Haitian Creole which only heightened his fear. But instead of meeting with the sheriff or one of his deputies, he found Mumford waiting for him. Mumford thrust a small package at him. "Take this to Kirkland. He's where the harvesters are kept in the west fields. Don't let anyone see you. I'll cover for you here."

Darisse found Kirkland sitting in the cab of a sugar cane harvester. The fields were empty. He quickly crossed himself as he always did when he first saw the half-million-dollar machine. More than twice his height and almost three times as long, the harvester had a seventeen-foot-long boom with two rotating blades that seared off the top of the cane plants. It reminded Darisse of an elephant's trunk. Near ground level at its front were two thick blades, like an open scissors, which spread apart the rows of cane. Attached to the scissors were angled six-foot-tall vertical rollers that drew the cane stalks into the machine. There the base cutters, two twenty-four-inch circular blades, sheared off the stalks. Next, the buttlifter pulled the cane into the overlapping ten-inch blades that chopped it. Finally, the pieces of cane were propelled up an enclosed conveyor belt attached to the side of the harvester and dumped into the tall-sided bed of a waiting truck. When the harvester was running the many large blades, some rotating vertically, some diagonally, and some horizontality, all at thousands of RPMs, made Darisse think it was the devil.

Kirkland got out of the cab and climbed down the harvester. Darisse handed him the package. Kirkland opened it and pulled out a syringe and a small vial. "Antivenom," he said. "By the way, why didn't you show up at the equipment barn yesterday, like I asked you?" He paused for only a moment. "Never mind. It's not important." He plunged the needle into the bottle. The syringe full, Kirkland held it up as if admiring it. Then he extended his hand holding the vial to Dariasse. Puzzled, Darisse stepped forward to take it. Kirkland dropped the vial, grabbed Darisse's arm, and plunged the needle into it.

Darisse clutched Kirkland around the shoulders, but his hands quickly fell away and he slid to the ground. Darisse tried to move but couldn't. He looked up and saw Kirkland looking down at him.

"Oops," Kirkland. "Guess that wasn't antivenom. We have to be quick now because your lung muscles aren't working, and I don't want you to pass out." Kirkland disappeared from view, and the harvester roared to life.

Kirkland loomed over him again. "You're going to get what you should have done to the snakes," Kirkland said. Darisse felt two hands around his ankles. He slid easily over the thick moist earth. The sound of the spinning blades grew louder, and he saw the topper boom pass by overhead.

"This is so going to give buttlifter a whole new meaning," Kirkland said as he dragged Darisse.

The shadow of the harvester washed over Darisse, and he saw the bottom of the cab. He closed his eyes and prayed. He felt the wind made by the rollers, then felt an odd sensation as the base cutters sliced his calves in half, and the chopping blades severed his feet.

The pieces of Darisse were carried up the harvester's conveyor belt and dumped into the truck parked next to it. There they would remain undisturbed until the truck unloaded it contents at the processing plant where the cane would be washed, cut into small pieces, and crushed to extract the sugar juice. An attentive worker would spot the remnants of Darisse's body during the washing. It would be superficially investigated and quickly forgotten as just another farm accident.

CHAPTER 34

As TJ drove closer to the Wellington Palm Beach Golf Club, the more he noticed the change. Neighborhoods appeared deserted and fear was in the air. Doors and windows were securely closed and locked, and garage doors were open just long enough for cars to enter and leave. Residents exited their cars inside their garages and only after the outside door was securely shut.

Some pool and lawn services wouldn't enter the area, he'd heard. Those companies that continued to provide service came with armed guards or additional crew to stand watch. A few homeowners refused to pay the surcharges for the extra personnel, saying a contract was a contract, and the companies stopped coming. The result was overgrown yards and green pools, a reminder to all that the Everglades wanted to return to its natural state.

The most noticeable difference were the children and dogs. There weren't any outside even though families were returning from vacation for the start of the school year. Almost immediately, kids began driving their parents crazy because they couldn't go outside. Chauffeuring their children to play dates and outdoor activities well beyond where parents thought the Komodo could appear provided some relief, but the adults remained anxious and vigilant.

He arrived at the golf club and found Sam walking in the high grass bordering the canal. She was swinging a three iron in front of her. "Didn't know you played," he said.

"Better this than my leg getting bitten off." She continued spreading the grass in front of her with the club.

"Find anything?"

"Other than the spoor, no, and it wasn't fresh. I don't think Kodra is around here. The teams will continue looking, but I'm going to head back to the sheriff's office, the governor wants an update."

"And after that?" he asked with anticipation.

Sam playfully put her index finger on his nose. "Not so fast, flyboy. It's not a good idea to mix business and pleasure."

TJ laughed. "Oh. You mean I have to almost get killed before you break your vow?"

Sam smiled. "This will be over soon enough. Then we'll see."

* * *

Sheriff Rodriguez was staring at his speaker phone as if willing it to ring when TJ and Sam walked into his office.

The call finally came. Governor Johnson and her aides were on the line. "I'm told you found Komodo droppings," Johnson began.

"Yes," Sam said. "But they aren't fresh."

"Then I take it you're no closer to finding the thing?"

"No we aren't but—"

"And your principal suspect in the animal smuggling is still on the loose?"

"That's correct," the sheriff responded. "But we'll find him. He was bitten by a cottonmouth. He can't get far."

"Do you have any other suspects?" the governor asked.

"Not at this time, but Kirkland couldn't have acted alone."

"Any evidence of where the operation's based?"

"We believe it's in Pure Sugar, but we have nothing concrete yet. My deputies are searching the farm and talking to the employees."

"So you've got nothing, either. I'm glad to see you guys are doing your usual good job," Johnson said with contempt. Without waiting for a response, she moved on. "We've got a bigger problem to deal with right now—school starts tomorrow—and you better not fuck this one up." The governor took a breath. "There's been a great deal of discussion, and it's been decided that since no one knows where the Komodo is or when she'll be killed, school should open as usual. We saw the results of closed schools and home schooling during the coronavirus pandemic, and it wasn't good. Schools will open on time, and all of you will make damn sure the Komodo does not get anywhere near a child. Understood?"

Young children walking to and from school would be tempting targets for a hungry Komodo. TJ shuddered at the thought.

"We'll be ready," Rodriguez said. "The media and the schools have blasted out the info. Any child walking to school must be accompanied by an adult. Bicycle riding to and from school is prohibited. Parents are being urged to drive their children to school or to a designated bus stop. The number of bus stops have been reduced, and a PBSO deputy, armed with an assault rifle or tactical shotgun, will be stationed at each stop during pick-up and drop-off times."

"It's not just the children we have to worry about," TJ added. "Their parents are back, too. That means a lot more people walking around, and a lot more prey for the Komodo."

"I know that," the governor said. "I expect you to protect them, too. What about the traps?"

"They'll be set out but nowhere near schools or bus stops. Their locations will be publicized, and the public will be warned to stay away. There'll be two armed officers concealed downwind of each trap, and we'll have live video feeds from each location."

"Okay," the governor said. "Doctor Brown, you say the Komodo is no longer around the golf course. Where do you plan to search next?"

"The Wellington Aero Club community," Sam said. "It's adjacent to the golf course and not far from the locus of the Komodo's recent activity."

"What makes you believe the lizard is still in the area?"

"Komodos typically stay within a two-mile radius of their nest if food is plentiful."

"Two miles isn't a big an area."

"It is when you're looking for an eight-foot animal that can smell you and see you before you see her and who I suspect is adapting to an urban environment," Sam replied.

* * *

Kodra headed east toward Flying Cow Road sampling the air as she went. The human scent grew stronger. Along the way she nudged the fence with her snout. It was shiny and firm and didn't give in, even when she tried to wedge her nose between the bottom of it and the ground.

She came to a two-story beige building with a green metal hip roof that sat at the southeast corner of the Wellington Environmental Preserve. It was a pumping station, one of hundreds, that regulated the flow and level of water among the many canals, lakes, and ponds, in South Florida. Residents joked that if all the pumps went quiet for a week, they'd be back living in the Everglades. It was truer than they realized.

Parked on the ring road in front of the substation was a white pickup truck with a red and green South Florida Water Management logo on its side. The driver was sitting sideways in the cab with his feet dangling out of the open door. A feral cat and her kittens cautiously circled around the truck, looking up at the man. He peeled back the aluminum foil holding his lunch and tossed bits of ham to them.

Kodra emerged from the grasses and ran across the parking lot to the back of the pumping station. She peered around the building and saw the man seated in the truck, the mother cat, and her kittens. Remembering her experiences with the man with the stick at the sugar cane farm and the man with the rake at Paradise Stables, she'd strike quickly.

The water worker registered a greenish streak a moment before he felt a searing pain in his lower leg. He screamed as Kodra's one-inch-long teeth penetrated his leather work boot. The man's ham sandwich and the aluminum foil it was wrapped in tumbled to the ground. His eyes went wide with fear when he saw the eight-foot lizard with her teeth in him. Kodra yanked his leg, like a dog playing tug-of-war, and the man grabbed the steering wheel to keep from being pulled out of the truck. She shook, and he desperately kicked at her with his other leg. Then she released her bite but only for a moment. Before the man could react, she bit down harder, severing the water worker's leg below the knee. She swallowed it whole.

The man quickly pulled himself into the truck and slammed the cab's door shut. It was not until he looked down at the jagged stump and the blood pooling on the floor below it did he realize that his leg was gone. Then, with a loud bang on the driver's door, the truck tilted sideways. His attention snapped back to the threat outside. Kodra launched herself at the door a second time, her face and the man's separated only by the window glass. She snapped her jaws and shook her head sending ropes of thick silva flying. She disappeared from sight for a moment then leaped onto the hood of the truck. One front foot rested on a windshield wiper while she scratched at the windshield with the sharp claws.

The worker started the truck and pushed the gas pedal to the floor with his remaining foot. The truck fishtailed wildly, and Kodra slid off, her claws gouging silver streaks in the hood's white paint. The truck's tires peppered her with gravel as the water worker sped away.

On the ground, she turned and faced the mother cat. The cat arched her back and hissed. The kittens stayed close to their mother, too young to know that they should flee. Kodra rose up and walked past them into the preserve, her hunger not satiated.

* * *

"C'mon, I want to show you something," Sheriff Rodriguez said.

TJ and Sam followed the sheriff to a field behind his office. They stopped next to a van, and the sheriff pointed skyward. The trio looked up at two drones dancing in the air. "The PBSO has the first FAA certified law enforcement drone fleet in the state," Rodriguez said with pride. "At fifty feet off the ground, they can see a fifty-foot square area."

"Nice," said TJ. "How long can they stay aloft?"

"About an hour. Then we bring 'em back, slap in a new battery, and off they go."

"How are you going to use them?" Sam asked.

"As soon as we have a sighting of the Komodo, they'll be on their way. They'll be able to follow her unless the shrubbery is too thick or she disappears into a culvert."

A call to the sheriff interrupted the demonstration. The group learned about the South Florida Water Management worker who'd had his leg bitten off. "He used his belt as a tourniquet and drove himself to the Wellington Regional Medical Center," Rodriquez said. "Unlike Sanchez, he said that he'd been bitten by a Komodo dragon. The hospital staff would have thought him crazy a week ago, but since then, they'd rehearsed for just such an event. South Florida Water Management has downloaded the surveillance camera footage from the pumping station, and it confirmed that the worker was attacked by the Komodo."

TJ pulled out his cell. "I wonder . . ." He pressed the keys and moved his index finger around the face of the phone. Satisfied, he turned the screen so Sam and the sheriff could see it. Google Earth showed the area around the Wellington Environmental Preserve with four dots around it with an equal line drawn from each one. "The points are the Herzogs' house to the north, Paradise Stables to the south, the east is the Pfister's house near the golf course, and the west is where the water management worker was attacked."

"All around the preserve and the lines come together in it," Rodriguez said.

"X marks the spot," Sam said. "And the preserve would be to Kodra's liking."

"What happened to all the talk about her adapting to urban living?" TJ asked.

"I have no doubt that she is, but, all things being equal, she'd still prefer a natural environment. She'll like the preserve and probably stay there. I don't think she'll swim the canal or go back into the Arthur Marshall unless we force her to. Same with crossing Flying Cow Road. She's crossed it before, but it's still something foreign to her. And maybe she went into the preserve because she didn't like all the houses and strange stuff."

"The Herzogs' neighborhood borders on the preserve. There's no water barrier, and she's had success hunting there before," TJ said. "We need to watch it."

"What's to the south?" Sam asked.

"The Cracker Ranch," The sheriff answered.

Sam laughed. "Run by a bunch of crackers?"

"Not really," TJ said. "Cracker is the state horse of Florida. They were brought here by the Spanish in the fifteen hundreds. The name is believed to have come from the crack of the riders' whips as they herded cattle. Crackers aren't very big, but they're well adapted to the Florida climate, and they're great trail horses."

"I never knew that. I thought maybe the guy's first name was Graham?"

TJ's snorted. "You just won't let this go, will you?"

"Nope."

"Okay, back to business you two," Rodriguez said. "We'll check out the ranch, but I'm pulling my people from the Aero Club. The Wellington Environmental Preserve is our new ground zero." He looked up at the darkening sky. The afternoon thunderstorms were moving in. "We plan tonight. Tomorrow morning we go in, find her, and kill her."

"That poor man . . ." Sam mused. "But that's not the worst of it."

"What could be worse?" TJ asked.

"Half a leg isn't much of a meal. Kodra is still hungry."

CHAPTER 35

TJ left his house in the darkness and climbed into an oxford white FWS Ford F-150 pickup. On each door was a large gold shield with the words: National Wildlife Refuge System, Law Enforcement. Above the rear wheel wells, Federal Wildlife Officer was printed in large gold letters. He wore a long-sleeved shirt and long pants to protect him from the brush and insects. Eight-inch-tall lace-up waterproof boots would keep his feet dry in the preserve and be a safeguard against snake bites. Over his uniform shirt, TJ wore a brown vest with US Fish & Wildlife Federal Officer emblazoned on the back. His Sig Sauer was strapped on. No classic car or being mistaken for a civilian today.

The only person he encountered on his way to the Wellington Environmental Preserve was a man walking a rottweiler. *Brave man,* he thought. The big brown dog was straining at its leash, but what held TJ's attention was the large pistol the man carried on his hip. People running around with guns made law enforcement nervous, but there was nothing they could do. Florida was a right-to-carry state, and it seemed like every adult was armed. There already had been one accidental shooting. A man mistook a neighbor's dog for Kodra and killed it in its own backyard.

The preserve was closed to the public. PBSO cars patrolled the streets. Their red and blue flashing lights coming alive with the all-too-frequent reported sightings that proved to be false. TJ's rangers and the sheriff's deputies patrolled the perimeter of the preserve to keep the thrill seekers and the just plain curious out. *You'd have to be crazy to go in there with a Komodo dragon on the loose,* TJ thought.

It was still black out, with only the glow of lights from downtown West Palm Beach on the horizon, when TJ turned off Flying Cow Road and drove past heavily armed deputies. The preserve was to his south, and the last row of houses in the Herzogs' subdivision passed to his right. At the staging area, the air was so thick even the bugs were still. The skies were quiet, except for the occasional bird in flight. He'd gotten there early, so he could be alone with his thoughts. He exited the truck and let the stillness wash over him. He thought about Kodra and was surprised to feel sadness, not anger, even though she'd killed a mother and a little boy and would keep killing until she was killed. She was just trying to survive, and it wasn't her fault she was here. It was due to human greed.

Streaks of sunlight appeared, illuminating fluffy white clouds and another picturesque South Florida sunrise. An hour later, the first car appeared. It was followed by three more with children inside. The vehicles idled with their windows up as they waited for the school bus. Even more cars would be coming soon, he knew. It was near the time for the school bus to arrive. TJ got ready.

Sheriff Rodriguez drove up with Sam shortly thereafter. They found TJ standing by his truck, pump action shot gun in hand, and the folding Ka-Bar knife he'd carried since his navy days, and a canteen on his belt.

Sam smiled and saluted him. "Dragon hunter reporting for duty, sir."

"Something's different . . ." He cocked his head and looked at her. "You've removed your nose ring."

"Yeah. Don't want the sun glinting off of it and attracting attention. Anyway, I don't need the reminder anymore."

"Good for you," TJ said.

"Okay, down to business," the sheriff said. "Let's review our plan."

"Sam and I will enter the preserve from here," TJ began. "We'll proceed southeast, which will keep the wind in our faces as much as possible."

"No need to give the Komodo a heads-up that we're coming her way," Sam added.

"We'll concentrate on areas around water and . . . well . . . we'll see what happens."

"I know we agreed to this last night," Sheriff Rodriguez said, "but I still don't like it. Only two of you looking, the preserve is a big place. I'd still prefer to send in a line of deputies."

"The more people in the preserve, the more likely she'll scare and flee," Sam said. "Two won't alarm her." Sam hesitated. "She might even attack."

"Great. Now you're telling me that you're bait," the sheriff said.

"Speaking of bait," TJ said, "are the traps out?"

"One's near the pumping station where the South Florida Water Management employee was attacked," Rodriguez said. "It's already been set out. The other's up here, to our east. It'll be set out until after the school bus leaves."

"Makes sense."

"I've got deputies watching the school bus loading zones. Two more are in the observation tower armed with high-power binoculars and sniper rifles."

TJ looked around and saw the white PBSO drone van parked nearby. He didn't have high hopes. He knew that Kodra's osteoderm covered skin would blend in with her surroundings and would render her invisible unless she moved in an open area. Overhead the sheriff's helicopter was flying a lawnmower pattern over the preserve. *Too high, too fast.* He didn't have much hope for the copter, either, but everything was in place. "Let's go."

Sam picked up a backpack that was at her feet, unzipped it, and pulled out an electric cattle prod. Looking up, she said, "In my experience, you often don't see the animal until you're right on top of it." She held up the shock stick. "This has saved me on more than one occasion."

"We're going to kill this animal, not tickle it," Sheriff Rodriguez said.

Sam nodded at TJ, her eyes briefly resting on the shotgun he was holding. "Takes a long time to swing that thing around, aim, and fire. Stun the animal, and you've got time for this." She put down the shock stick, reached into her backpack once more, and removed a holster holding a large Glock. She pulled out the pistol, ejected the clip, inspected it, checked the chamber, slapped the clip back in the butt of the gun, and fingered the safety. "I'm ready."

"A woman after my own heart," the sheriff said, touching the Glock holstered on his service belt.

"Impressive," TJ said. He didn't ask her about her ammunition. The clip in his Sig held lacquer-sealed bullets. Guns where he worked often got wet.

"Keeps me safe from gators but attracts men," Sam replied.

"That's a good reason to carry a shock stick," TJ said. He then watched Sam pull out a pair of leather gloves. "How do you use your pistol with those on?"

"I don't expect to be in a quick draw contest, and I can manage the shock stick just fine. Easier to handle the brush wearing these."

"Okay," the sheriff said, looking up at the bright sky. "Weather's good for now, but there's a storm moving in later today. As soon as the kids are loaded on the school bus, you two go in."

* * *

"You sure about this?" Mumford asked.

"Of course, I'm sure," Kirkland replied. "Nobody will pay attention to a truck parked here. They'll think we've gone fishing." He pointed at a narrow path. "We follow this old horse trial past the Cracker Ranch, and we'll be in the preserve." He paused. "Are *you* sure about the chip?"

"My contact told me they're always put in the same place—upper left front leg, just below the shoulder."

"Well, we can't just dig it out; it'll be too obvious what we were after and we just can't cut the leg off, either. That'll raise too many questions."

"So what do we do?"

"Cut off all four legs and the head. Make it look like a trophy killing. That's why I brought this with me." Kirkland removed an eight-inch butcher hunting knife. The sun glinted off the blade as he turned the knife over in his hands. Then he lovingly retuned it to its sheath.

"Get the bag and let's go."

Kirkland took a garbage bag containing three freshly killed chickens from the pickup. "I don't see why we need these."

"Komodos have a great sense of smell and love carrion. If we don't find her on the way in, we'll make a hunter's blind—climb up some sturdy trees near water, put the chickens out upwind and wait." Mumford pulled a small map out of his pocket and stabbed the paper with his index finger. "We try this marsh first. It's the nearest to the pumping station that's big enough for a lot of animals to be around it. The Komodo will like that."

"You sure about all this?"

"I am. Did you get the silencers?"

"Yeah. No problem." Kirkland laughed. "They're legal in Florida."

"Good. No sense shooting the thing only to attract every lawman from miles around. And the radio?"

Kirkland switched on the police radio clipped to his belt. "Got that, too."

"Then let's go hunting."

* * *

Kodra rose with the sun and left her nest among the evergreens, pickerelweeds, and firebushes in the middle of the preserve and headed back to Cracker Ranch. Head turning, tongue gathering scents, she confirmed the horses and cows were still there. Humans were in the area, too. Many more humans than the day before and all around her, but in the distance. She stopped and looked up when a flock of boat-trailed grackles took to flight, their wings nosily flapping. Then a new scent reached her . . . carrion . . . deer. In the same direction as the ranch.

The bloody hind quarter of a deer was thick with flies as it sat in the long metal box near the pumping station. Downwind of it, two FWS officers, armed with high-powered rifles, sat in a pickup, watching the live camera feed.

Kodra walked quickly, navigating around the bushes, lest another predator beat her to the easy meal. Before she could reach it, a coyote popped up in front of her. The coyote danced but didn't flee as Kodra approached. With the wind at her back, Kodra couldn't smell the animal, but it looked like a dog. She decided this creature would be her first meal of the day. She came closer, and the coyote skittishly moved backward.

Kodra sprang.

The coyote jumped back just as Kodra's jaws snapped shut. It danced away but didn't run off. Kodra lunged a second time. Again, the coyote evaded her. The coyote ran a short distance, stopped, and looked back. Kodra hesitated, and then gave chase. The coyote proved to be too quick, running and stopping, taunting her, until Kodra gave up.

The mother coyote had done her job and led the big predator well away from her den. Kodra found herself far from the Cracker Ranch and almost back at the first nest she'd dug at the base of the red maple. She heard the rhythmic thumping of a helicopter's rotors and felt the change in air pressure as it came near. The chopper's shadow fell upon her, and her pineal eye warned of the large predator passing overhead. She dove into the thick vegetation. She lay motionless, heart beating rapidly from the exertion of the chase and stress.

The shadow passed, and she briefly rested then sampled the air. The scents of cows, horses, and rotting deer meat were now distant, but the wind brought new scents—humans, young and old. She followed the scents, stopping at the edge of the preserve to peer through the ground cover. She saw a large yellow object that smelled of metal and oil. But what caught her attention was the people and the high-pitched children's voices that triggered memories of Bobby Powell.

A shallow drainage ditch and a strip of dirt stood between Kodra and the street, the yellow school bus, and the vehicles with parents and children inside. Her long tongue was active as she watched a child emerge from a minivan and walk to the school bus, his mother hovering anxiously next to him. Kodra took a step forward, half in, half out of the bushes, about to attack. Then a more attractive target caught her attention. Only a few feet away, a man was standing next to a large BMW, talking on his cell phone, while distractedly watching the children board the bus.

Kodra charged. The man screamed, and the phone flew from his hands as she bit into his hip, driving him to the ground. She released him. He got to his knees when she distended her jaw and grabbed him firmly by the waist. She rose and leaving a trail of saliva drove the man into a palm tree. With the sound of his back cracking, the man's arms and legs bent around it. Kodra pushed harder. As she'd done with other prey in the past, she was trying to force this animal down her throat whole.

She heard a sharp crack and felt a wood chip bounce off of her. She looked to one side. She didn't see a PBSO deputy raise his assault rifle and take aim or a terrified mother throwing her child up into the school bus and jumping in behind him, with the bus door immediately hissing shut. But she did see a SUV hurtling toward her, the driver intent upon running her over. Instead, the driver saved her life because the deputy had to hold his fire to avoid hitting him.

Kodra dropped her meal and ran. The SUV crossed the dirt shoulder. Its front end dipped into the drainage ditch, and its rear wheels rose into the air. The vehicle came to a stop in front of her. She scrambled back into the scrub brush.

The deputy raised his rifle again. He held his fire until he was sure the man was staying in his SUV, and then sprayed the moving bushes with bullets.

* * *

Heads jerked up. "Shots," TJ said.

"My deputies," Sheriff Rodriguez said. He jumped on his radio. Then he told the others: "Man in an SUV tried to run over the Komodo. My officer saw her but had to hold off firing until he was sure that the guy was going to stay in his car. He and another officer are searching the bushes, but there's no sign of blood so we think she got away clean. The chopper moved in, but it was too late. I'm calling in everyone we've got." Rodriguez turned to TJ. "Your guys, backup from Broward. We'll form a human chain, each six feet part, and we'll search till we flush her out."

"That won't work," Sam said. "She'll know we're coming long before we see her, and she'll disappear. We now know for sure she's in the preserve, but if we scare her, who knows where she'll go?"

"And if she gets into the Arthur Marshall, she may be gone for good," TJ added.

"Then what do you suggest?" the sheriff asked.

"No change in plans," Sam said. "Two people only. We go in. Quietly."

"And call off that helicopter," TJ added. "All it does is stir up the brush and make noise."

The sheriff got on his radio, and the chopper moved away. "Okay. Your way but I won't say for how long."

TJ and Sam headed into the preserve.

CHAPTER 36

Parents frantically whisked away their children. There'd be no ride on the school bus today. The SUV running into the ditch and the PBSO deputy shooting into the brush was caught on the smartphone of more than one parent. Clips immediately went viral. Texts were sent, phone calls were made, and local TV stations interrupted their programming as newsreaders announced in breathless tones that the Komodo had almost eaten another person.

Sam and the sheriff watched one of the videos on TJ's phone. "Sam, where do you think she's gone?" he asked.

"The car and the shots scared her. She's probably fled a good ways back into the preserve. She'll follow her instincts. Probably lead her to a cluster of trees or bushes on dry ground that's big enough to conceal her and near water and what she'd think is a game trial."

"Understood," TJ said.

The sheriff handed each of them a radio. "The men in the tower have these as do the men watching the traps. But don't use them unless you have to. Too many people are listening in on the multiagency radio frequency. We'll communicate through our phones."

"How's the cell service in the preserve?" TJ asked.

"Not the best in spots but good. There's a cell tower not too far. Set your Find My Friends app. Delete everyone else. We can track each other's progress."

TJ, Sheriff Rodriquez, and Sam busied themselves with their phones until they each saw three dots.

Then the sheriff seemed to think of something. He walked to his SUV and rooted around in the back. He returned holding four thin orange cylinders, each about a foot long and handed two to each of them. "Flares may be a bit old fashioned, but if you get into real trouble, send up a signal."

TJ pocketed his, then checked his shotgun and made sure the safety was on. He'd keep it at the ready, although he was mindful of Sam's warning that it could take too long to swing it toward his target. Sam had her shock stick and her Glock.

Almost simultaneously, TJ and Sam took a deep breath and steeled themselves. The bright sun cast long shadows on the ground in front of them as they entered the preserve.

"Be alert," Sam said. "She's still hungry, and now she's frustrated and angry."

* * *

Kodra fled deep into the preserve, scared by the large object that hurtled toward her and the deputy's shots. She knew both had meant her harm. She crossed the walking paths and skirted smaller bodies of water, the sawgrass swaying as she passed. She didn't stop until she'd reached a mass of pickerel-weeds and firebushes at the top of the big marsh. Here the scents she knew prevailed and those of humans and their machines were distant. She found comfort in the thick undergrowth and being near natural water, but her nesting instinct emerged once more. This time with urgency.

She knew her time was at hand and she had to find a safe place to lay her eggs. Since escaping from the sugarcane farm, she'd encountered humans everywhere except on the small spits of land in the marshes. Across the water, on a hammock, she saw a cluster of tall satinleaf trees, their leaves were dark green on top and brown on the bottom almost matching the coloring of their trunks. They would provide excellent cover for young Komodos. She entered the water and swam to the island.

* * *

TJ and Sam crossed an equestrian trail and moved into the preserve. The soil was hard and dry, and the brush was small and far enough apart that they could walk between the plants. They crossed the inner trail near where Kodra had hid from the two riders. As they got deeper into the preserve, the foliage became denser, slowing their progress.

Sam slapped at a bug on her neck. "We could walk right past Kodra and never see her. Her coloring matches the greens and browns of the preserve."

"If you can find alligators and crocodiles on two continents, I'm sure you can spot a giant lizard," TJ replied.

They moved cautiously, eyes sweeping the area as they went. Sam probed the denser clumps of bushes with her shock stick. TJ was just as alert, registering each squawk of a bird and rustle of an animal in the undergrowth and keeping his shotgun at the ready.

Arriving at a small marsh, Sam's eyes opened wide. "There!"

"There, what?" TJ looked to where she was pointing and a trail of flattened grasses.

She touched his arm and took the lead. "I'm the tracker."

They followed the trail, and Sam stopped at each large tree and good-sized cluster of shrubbery, examining the ground for signs of digging. Her perseverance paid off. She spotted the broken branches of St. John's wort and Jamaican capers. She stepped in and spread some branches apart revealing a scooped out depression. "It's her nest."

"How do you know some other animal didn't make it?"

Sam got down on one knee and studied the hollow. "See the inter-twined roots along the sides. It took a lot of work to dig this hole. And the claw marks. Only a Komodo could make those."

"It's very recent," TJ said. "No debris, nothing growing in it, and things grow quickly here."

He texted the news and the coordinates to Sheriff Rodriguez as Sam took pictures of the nest.

"You think this is where she stays?" He looked around warily.

"I'm not sure, but it doesn't feel quite right. It looks a little small, almost like she gave up digging. Ideally, she'd pick a place where prey would pass by. Sure there's water close by, but I don't see any sort of trial, and we haven't come across any animals. I think she's moved on. We need to find a good place for her to hide with lots of wildlife and water."

TJ pulled up a map on his phone and showed it to Sam. "The biggest body of water in the preserve is this marsh shaped like a number seven."

"Let's go."

* * *

Royce Mumford was neither graceful nor quiet, despite having grown up in South Florida. He took wide steps and used the butt of his rifle as a walking stick, studying the ground in front of him as he went. Even with that, there was the occasional lurch and hard footfall as he stepped in a depression. A flock of purple gallinules burst into flight at the sound of his latest stumble. Kirkland picked his spots as he walked, moving easily and quietly. Both men's heads jerked up in unison at the sounds of shots.

"Oh hell. They got her," Mumford said.

Kirkland held up a hand. "Just wait a second." He turned up the volume on the police radio.

The two men waited in silence until one very agitated deputy described a man almost being bitten in half and being rammed into a tree, a SUV trying to runover the Komodo and her disappearance into the preserve.

"We're good," Mumford said relieved.

"Even better. We know where she was and that she's most likely heading in our direction."

"Where should we go?"

Kirkland pointed. "This way, and be careful. The cops didn't mention it, but they may be sending people in after her."

They crossed the main walking trial. Further on they came to the top of the marsh that was shaped like the number seven. It was separated by a sandy plain from a dense thicket of pickerelweeds and firebushes surrounding a cluster of evergreens.

"This is a good place to look," Kirkland said. They walked slowly along the shoreline, avoiding the sawgrass but occasionally stepping into the plants and bushes to look around. "Quiet now," he said. "She could be near. I'll walk along the shore. You circle around the thicket."

Mumford headed inland and disappeared from view.

Kirkland took a step and stopped, taking in the sights and sounds before he took another. It was a feeling at first, and then conscious awareness. The faint sound of cracking branches and something hard scraping against the earth caused him to look out over the water.

About ten feet into the marsh was a hammock covered with heavy foliage. The noise was coming from there. The wind was gusting, and the grasses and plants swayed with it. Pulling out a small pair of binoculars, he scanned the islet. A few bushes were shaking, but not with the wind. Something else was moving them. He looked up at the sky. Clear and bright to the west but dark and cloudy to the east. The rains were moving in. He didn't want to get caught on the marsh in a storm. He debated his next move, then he took a cautious step into the water. It washed over his ankles. He slowly moved forward trying to make as little noise as possible. The water gradually rose and was almost up to his waist by the time he reached the hammock. He stepped onto the shore and moved toward the activity, holding his rifle at the ready.

He reached the moving plants and peered over them. Kodra was busily scooping dirt and broken foliage into an oblong hole. His eyes grew wide when he saw a partially covered clutch of eggs, each the size of a softball. *Fifty, maybe one hundred thousand dollars each,* flashed through his mind. He dumped the dead chickens he'd been carrying in the black trash bag on the ground. He'd found the Komodo, and he needed the bag to carry his valuable prize.

The smell of the carrion caused Kodra to stop digging. She looked up as Kirkland was taking aim at her with his rifle. Kodra burst out of the hole.

CHAPTER 37

Kirkland pulled the trigger, but it was a moment too late. Kodra slammed into him, knocking the rifle barrel up toward the sky, and his shot went wild. He let out a piercing scream as she bit hard into his thigh and he landed on his back. Blood spurted out of his wound, hitting her above her eye and ran down the side of her face.

He swung the rifle hard and hit her in the head. Kodra released her grip on his leg and staggered backwards. He readied the rifle for another shot, but Kodra recovered and charged again. She grabbed the rifle in her mouth and shook it out of Kirkland's hands. He struggled to his feet, one hand trying to stench the flow of blood from his wound, the other brandishing his hunting knife, and backed away. He hoped Kodra had attacked to protect her eggs and wouldn't pursue him. Rifle in mouth, she watched as he limped off and waded into the marsh.

Kirkland staggered a few steps onto the mainland before his maimed leg buckled under him. When he looked up, Kodra was right in front of him. His eyes grew wide. He smelled her putrid breath and felt the hot puffs of air as she exhaled. He raised his knife, then his hand flew open, and it fell harmlessly to the ground. Kodra has his head in her mouth. She reared back and her one-inch-long serrated teeth ripped off Kirkland's face.

He collapsed aware that something horrific had happened but not sure what. With the one eye that still worked, he looked up at the blue sky.

Kodra leisurely moved in, and the last thing he felt before he died was flesh and muscle being ripped from his wounded leg.

Kodra took another bite when the screech of a red-tail hawk interrupted her meal and diverted her attention to the hammock. She left Kirkland and swam back to her eggs.

* * *

Mumford didn't like being alone in the preserve. He was a big picture guy who sat behind a desk and told others what to do. Hot and sweaty, he'd normally be longing for a cold beer, but he was too nervous to be thinking about one. The Komodo could be hiding anywhere, ready to spring. He scanned the ground around him looking for snakes as he moved. Then his head jerked up at the sound of Kirkland's cry. Cursing, he retraced his steps as quickly as he could to where he'd left Kirkland.

Rounding the trees, he saw the faceless body already covered with flies. The clothes told him it was Kirkland. Mumford fell to his knees and threw up.

Recovering, he gripped his rifle and nervously looked around. Satisfied all was quiet, he got up, wiped his mouth, and took a swig of water from his canteen. There was no sign of the Komodo, but she must have been Kirkland's killer.

This could be the answer, he thought. He'd pin it all on Kirkland. Kirkland ran the reptile smuggling business. Even though it operated out of the farm, Mumford knew nothing about it. The farm was a big place, and he was a desk guy. He'd leave the preserve and no one would be the wiser. Then he heard thrashing in the undergrowth and ran.

* * *

"What was that?" Sam said.

"We've got company, and he's in trouble," TJ said. He radioed the sheriff, and the two headed off in the direction of the scream.

Moving as rapidly as they could, stepping on small plants and around bushes and trees, they arrived at the top of the large marsh and slowed to a walk. "Seems like it came from around here," TJ said.

Sam stopped. "It did."

TJ looked at her, then at where she was looking. A body with a bloody pulp of flesh where its face should have been and a leg bone exposed with jagged flesh around it lay on the ground. "You okay?" he asked.

"I've seen worse. Any idea who he is?"

"None. Not dressed like law enforcement. But I don't think he just wandered in here." TJ stepped closer and looked at the body when Sheriff Rodriguez's voice came though his radio and the radio on the dead man's belt. "Interesting," TJ said. "He's got a police radio."

The sheriff wanted details, and TJ told him what they'd found.

"I've got your location on my phone but send up a flare," Rodriguez said. "I want a visual everyone can key in on."

TJ lit a flare and waved it above him. The officers in the observation tower, sniper rifles at the ready, snapped around and searched the area through their binoculars. The men in the PBSO van launched their drone."

"I'm coming to you," Rodriguez said as Sam looked around.

"Look at the bent and broken branches," she said as she pointed into the tall grass and pickerelweeds. "Something big just went through here in a hurry."

"You think it's Kodra?"

"There's only one way to find out."

They set off through the undergrowth and reached the top edge of the marsh. In front of them was a thicket of bushes. Running along the edge of the marsh, the landscape changed to hard soil that was barren, except for a few spotty grasses.

"Follow the marsh south or head inland?" Sam asked.

"Listen," TJ said. The sound of grasses rustling and plants breaking under foot came from the south.

"Sounds like she's injured," Sam said.

They set off in the direction of the noise veering toward Flying Cow Road as they ran along a creek that flowed from the marsh.

Just beyond a thick growth of dahoon hollies, the noise stopped. TJ and Sam halted. "Be ready. She's just on the other side of these trees," TJ whispered. He took the safety off his shotgun and pushed through the bushes stepping onto a horse trial. He scanned the area, with his finger on the gun's trigger. Then he exhaled and lowered the gun, sliding the safety back on.

"What? What is it?" Sam asked as she pushed the hollies aside.

TJ nodded with his chin. In the middle of the trail, Royce Mumford, the sides of his shirt stained with sweat, was on his hands on his knees gasping for breath.

"Mumford!" TJ exclaimed.

Mumford looked up at them. "I'm having a heart attack!"

TJ kicked away the rifle that lay alongside Mumford, took him by the collar, and dragged him into the shade. "Sit down. Drink some water."

Mumford did as he was told and his breathing gradually calmed down.

"Let me guess," TJ said. "The guy without the face back there is Kirkland."

"Yes."

"And you guys were in here hunting the Komodo?"

Mumford stared at the ground and didn't answer.

"You smuggled her in. Didn't you?"

Again Mumford didn't answer.

"Fine." TJ retrieved Mumford's rifle, pulled out the clip, and checked the chamber for a round. "Kirkland have one of these I suppose?"

"Yes."

TJ made a mental note to look for it when they returned, relieved that they didn't have to watch out for Kirkland with a loaded weapon.

"Okay then. On your feet." TJ put an arm on Mumford and pulled him up. "Let's go."

"Go where?"

"Back to where we found Kirkland. The sheriff is coming, and I'm sure he'll want to speak with you."

* * *

Kodra swam back to the hammock. On the islet, she flicked her tail as she passed Kirkland's rifle. The gun landed in the water with a splash. Examining her nest, she satisfied herself that her eggs were undisturbed, and she returned to her task. She ripped away loose brush from the surrounding plants and dropped in on top of her eggs. Over that, she kicked the dirt she'd dug out to make the hole. Her work completed, she walked around the top of the nest, dragging her tail and tamping down the soil. Satisfied, she moved away. The daily rains told her instinctively that she didn't need to guard the nest, just as her mother had left her nest when the rains had come to Flores.

The scent of three humans carried on the breeze to her. She recognized all of them. One was from a time ago when she'd been held captive in the cage, and the other two from her time in the marshes. The scents became stronger. Then she heard their voices and knew they were coming closer. She moved to the edge of the hammock ready to defend her nest.

The humans were across the water gathered around the one she'd killed.

"Why were you looking here?" TJ asked.

"Seemed like a good place. The biggest body of water in the preserve. That'd mean other animals to eat."

TJ kept Mumford close to him as he looked for Kirkland's rifle. *It has to be around here somewhere,* he thought.

Sam moved away and poked at the bushes with her stun stick. She was knee deep in some firebushes with her back to the men when she called. "TJ, I think I've found something."

He came to look with Mumford in tow. At the base of a swamp bay evergreen was a large hole. "Another nest?"

"And bigger than the other we found," Sam said. "I just remembered something Professor Robinson said. If she's digging multiple nests, it may mean that she's preparing to lay eggs."

"Kodra is pregnant?" TJ asked in dismay.

"That's one possible explanation. She'd dig false nests to throw off predators."

"Or maybe she dug this nest because this is a better location than where we found the first one. You said so yourself—it wasn't the best place for a nest."

"That's true, but we need to be extra careful. If she has laid eggs, she'll defend them to her death."

"Okay. We'll keep looking as soon as the sheriff arrives and takes Mumford off our hands."

Sam continued searching past the trees. TJ looked into the marsh when an object bobbing in the water caught his attention. To a less experience eye, it might look like a piece of wood, but TJ knew it was something else. He yelled for Sam to come and watch Mumford. He snapped off a long branch and waded into the marsh.

Kodra rose with alarm when she saw the man enter the water and come toward the hammock. She continued watching as he used a stick to pull something toward him.

The rifle floated butt up, barrel down. TJ grabbed it and headed back to shore.

"I didn't think guns floated," Sam said.

"Most don't." TJ turned over the rifle in his hands. "Lightweight, hallow carbon fiber stock. Kirkland must have been at the shoreline when he was attacked."

TJ was about to pull out the clip when Sam screamed. He looked around to see Kodra rising out of the water, charging him. In a single motion, he wielded Kirkland's rifle, thumbed off the safety, and pulled the trigger. It made a clicking sound.

Kodra sprang, leaving him no time to wonder if the gun was water-logged or there was no bullet in the chamber. Her throat caught the silencer, and it snapped off the barrel. She fell to one side as the rifle flew out of his hands, and he fell to the other. Man and beast scrambled to their feet. TJ drew his Sig Sauer and fired. Kodra spasmodically twisted and rolled onto her side. He was about to fire again when Mumford picked up Sam and threw her into him. TJ and Sam fell, arms and legs entangled. Kodra disappeared into the bushes as Mumford ran off in the opposite direction.

"Stay here. I'll go get him," TJ said with disgust as he got up.

He returned a short time later frog-marching Mumford.

Sam was focused on the bushes. "There's blood on the plants. I think you wounded her."

CHAPTER 38

Kodra knew her blood would attract predators. She would lead them away from her eggs. She hugged the long side of the marsh, staying on the bare soil or in the low grass whenever she could. Her side hurt with every step, and she leaked blood. In places where she had to move though the undergrowth, the sharp grasses and stiff branches yielded to her solid body but chaffed her wound, ensuring the blood trail she was leaving would continue. She crossed a stream and neared the bottom of the marsh. Beyond it was a gathering of plump coontie ferns, as wide as they were tall, a dense cluster of muhly grass, and thick-trunked cabbage palms. Breathing hard, she stopped to rest at the base of the large trees.

* * *

Sheriff Rodriguez arrived on an ATV with two deputies following on one of the preserve's small utility vehicles. The first thing he did was snap hand-cuffs on Mumford.

"I need my hands," Mumford whined. "What if the Komodo comes back? How will I be able to protect myself?"

"Guess you'll just be her lunch," Rodriguez said.

"Any sightings?" TJ asked.

"Nothing from the drone or the tower. She must be staying in the undergrowth," the sheriff answered.

"What about the BMW driver?"

The sheriff looked at Kirkland's body while one of the deputies took pictures and shook his head. "He didn't make it."

"We're going after her," TJ said.

"Then go. I've got things under control here, and I look forward to having a nice conversation with Mr. Mumford."

Sam was standing at the edge of the firebushes. "There's blood on the leaves. She's hurt, and she's leaving us a trail to follow."

They stepped carefully into the brush. Sam probed the bushes in front of her with her stun stick. TJ kept his shotgun at the ready. They waded through the undergrowth, following the streaks and smears until they rounded the corner of the marsh arriving back at the marl plain dotted with short grasses and the thick vegetation where they'd pursued Mumford. They looked around until Sam found blood, now dried brown, on the ground. The spots appeared less frequently than in the bushes, but they led down the side of the marsh. The pair quickened their pace.

They splashed across the shallow stream they'd run along before, the water almost up to their knees, and stopped on the far shore. In front of them was a mass of intertwined coontie ferns and muhly grass. The plants were only three-feet tall but so dense as to be impenetrable in places. Behind the thicket was a stand of cabbage palms.

TJ touched one of the plants and rubbed together a red stained thumb and index finger. "Still tacky. She's close."

Sam moved aside a coontie frond with her shock stick and took a step into the thicket.

TJ put his hand on her shoulder. "Stop."

"What's wrong?"

"It's too quiet. The Seminoles once told me that if you're looking for something in the Everglades, look for the hole in the noise."

Sam thought for a moment. "You know, you're right. Even the birds are silent. There should be birds in these trees."

Kodra lay motionless in the dense muhly grass behind the ferns. Her yellow tongue sprang halfway out and then retreated into her mouth. The same humans as before. They were chasing her. A moment later, her eyes flared when she saw Sam's shock stick swing through the grass near her. Memories of being trapped in the cage as Sanchez taunted and tortured her flashed through her mind. She arched her back and took a step forward, but a sharp pain went through her side. She dropped down and retreated deeper into the grasses.

"There!" Sam waved her shock stick. A line of grass swayed, while the grass on either side remained still. She waded deeper into the plants prodding them with the stick. She gasped when she pushed aside some stalks and saw Kodra's green and brown body. Kodra looked up at her. Sam was used to the eyes of an alligator, a dull green, with a thin vertical slit in the middle, but Kodra's eyes—fiery red with a yellow corona surrounding a round black pupil—were alive and calculating.

Kodra lunged, knocking Sam backward. She bit down on Sam's hand, snapping the shock stick in two. Sam screamed and kicked as she tried to wrestle her hand free from Kodra's mouth.

TJ pumped his shotgun, but immediately realized he couldn't get a clean shot as Sam and Kodra thrashed. He had to get them separated. He reached into his pants pocket and pulled out his remaining flare. He ripped the cap off the top igniting it and waved it in Kodra's face. At the sight of the flame and orange smoke, Kodra released Sam, reared back and fled.

Dropping the flare, he grabbed his radio. "Sam's been bitten! I need medics here right now!" He knelt down next to Sam. "Help's coming. We'll get you out of here and patched up." Then he gently asked. "How bad is it?"

Sam held up her bloody hand. "Lucky it's still attached." She laughed weakly.

TJ took off his shirt and used his knife to cut off a sleeve. He wrapped it around Sam's hand. "I'll stay—"

"No you won't. You go after her before she gets away." Sam took a breath and gave a small smile. "And as much as I may like seeing you bare chested, put your shirt back on. The plants in here will cut you up."

TJ handed her his shotgun. "Keep this in case she comes back. It's ready to fire."

He drew his SIG and warily moved into the ferns and grasses, looking for any sign of movement. He passed through the cabbage palms and found himself back on open ground. He saw Kodra heading toward the Cracker Ranch. She turned and seeing him, broke into a run.

TJ's pilot training kicked in, registering everything around him: Kodra running on a white surface of hard marl dotted with grassy plants, the marsh off to the right, the equestrian path in front of them, and beyond that, a drainage ditch and a strip of mowed grass ending at the tall chain-link fence that separated the preserve from the Cracker Ranch. He estimated it was about three hundred yards—the length of three football fields—from where he was to the fence. Not a long distance for a guy in good shape like him, but he was wearing boots that were designed for protection from snakes and sprained ankles but not for running and no amount of training made running in ninety-degree temperatures with ninety percent humidity easy.

He holstered his gun and gave chase. Glancing down, he saw blood. Kodra was bleeding freely now. As he crossed the marl plain, Kodra splashed into the drainage ditch, swam to the other side, and clawed her way onto the grass. TJ charged into the ditch, then slipped, and with a splash, he went under and swallowed a mouth full of water. Staggering to his feet, his right side was coated in mud; he slogged through water above his knees.

Kodra sprinted to the tall chain-link fence and ran back and forth, franticly looking for an opening. Finding none, she flung herself against it, but it held firm.

TJ emerged from the ditch. He saw Kodra at the fence and pulled out his Sig. He pointed the barrel at the ground and shook the pistol. Water dribbled out of it. He racked the slide and heard a grinding noise as it moved. He had to push it back into place. He knew his gun wasn't right but hoped the lacquered coated bullets would fire.

Kodra was intent upon finding a way through the fence when he took aim and fired. The gun recoiled sharply in his hand, and the slide failed to eject the spent cartridge. His shot missed. He knew he'd have to get a lot closer if he wanted to hit a moving lizard, but his malfunctioning gun was an even bigger problem.

Kodra darted to her right at the sound of the shot and disappeared into a clump of scraggly bushes surrounding a single pine tree. TJ could see her crouched low among the bushes, her sides heaving with rapid breaths. He worked the slide on the gun back and forth until the spent cartridge sprung from it and a new bullet slid into the chamber. Firmly gripping his Sig, he approached slowly not wanting to spook her. He knew he'd have only one shot. At the edge of the bushes, he stopped and aimed.

Kodra remained still until suddenly her tail lashed out. TJ realized he'd gotten too close, but it was too late. He was knocked off his feet. His Sig discharged sending a shot into the air as he fell. Kodra reared up. TJ rolled to see a two-hundred-pound Komodo dragon leaping at him. He racked the slide and fired again. The bullet went cleanly through Kodra's lower jaw and exited the top of her head. She fell hard and landed next to him, her front paw on his shoulder, their faces almost touching. Kodra weakly raised her chin and looked at him. First her red irises, and then the yellow coronas surrounding them, faded away. Her eyes went black.

TJ studied her warily. Her chest was still, and there were no signs of life. He got to his feet and checked her once more before heading back to Sam as quickly as he could. As he rounded the cabbage palms, he heard the woosh of helicopter blades. There was Sam sitting on the ground, his shirt sleeve still wrapped around her hand.

Sam looked up. "Did you get her?"

"Yes. It's over."

Sheriff Rodriguez was standing off to one side with Mumford next to him. "Medivac copter will be here in a moment."

TJ sat down beside Sam. His body sagged, and he felt his remaining energy drain out of him. "You're going to be fine."

Sam rested her head on his shoulder. "I know."

EPILOGUE

Eight months had gone by. TJ was up early as always and working on his latest purchase, a 1971 Chevrolet Monte Carlo, antique green with a green interior and dark green vinyl top when he felt a pair of sharp claws on his back. He turned to look, and Tomàs, resting comfortably on his shoulder, looked back at him.

The T-Bird, tilt-away steering wheel fixed, had been sold. He didn't need to be reminded of Kirkland or the water moccasin. The Impala he'd been trying to sell the day Sheriff Rodriguez had first called him was sitting in his garage. He knew from the car's VIN number and Chevrolet's classic car data base that its hydro-matic transmission had come from the plant in Saginaw where his father had worked. It was just possible that, over fifty years ago, his father's hands had touched that transmission. He'd decided to keep the car and stopped returning the indecisive buyer's calls.

Royce Mumford was unsuccessful in convincing anyone that he wasn't behind the reptile smuggling business. TJ and the sheriff suspected he was involved in the disappearance of Sanchez and Darisse and the escape of the Animal World crocodile, but what they believed and what they could prove were two different things. Mumford was held responsible for the deaths of the people Kodra killed and was sent off to prison. His wife divorced him.

Sheriff Rodriguez's job was safe, his pension secure, and his wife didn't have to worry. Martin Herzog lost the suit brought against him and had to pay the reward for finding his wife's remains. Bennet D'Costa had wrongly advised him not to pay and then to go to trial. D'Costa also lost his lawsuit over the death of his dog. No one believed the Animal World croc had killed his bull terrier.

The man whose cell phone TJ threw in the water dropped his charges after receiving his share of the reward for finding Judy Herzog's remains and seeing the many social media posts that were critical of him for going after the man who'd risked his life to kill the Komodo. TJ had apologized and bought the man a new phone.

Life had returned to normal in Palm Beach County with the story of the child-eating Komodo dragon rapidly becoming a tale that grandparents told their grandchildren when they came down to visit. The story grew bigger and bigger with each retelling.

The days were turning hot, and the snowbirds were leaving South Florida, a sure sign the rainy season was coming. Kenny Loggins broke into song, announcing the call TJ had been waiting for.

"Good evening or should I say good morning," Sam said. She'd returned to Australia and rejoined the Queensland saltwater crocodile project shortly after Kodra was killed. Her reputation embellished by hunting down a Komodo dragon; the university had asked her to stay on a while longer.

"G'day mate," TJ said.

"Give it up, TJ. You don't sound Australian at all."

"Can't blame a guy for trying . . . Anyway, how's your hand?"

"Pretty good. I'm doing my exercises every day, and other than some scars, it's going to be fine. Good thing I was wearing those gloves you teased me about, otherwise the docs said the damage would've been much worse."

"Yeah. I guess I was wrong about the gloves." TJ turned somber. "You know, it was eight months ago today."

The call went silent for a moment. "I know, but let's talk about good things. I'm wrapping up here, and I'll be home in a week."

"Can't wait. Your place or mine?"

* * *

Kodra was autopsied by the same vets who'd examined the Animal World croc. There were no unaccounted-for human remains in her stomach. At Sam's request, a dissection revealed that she was not carrying any eggs. The examination was cursory because the vets took their orders from the governor. The microchip was found in her front left shoulder, confirming that she'd come from Flores. The governor didn't care about that, either. It was the Indonesians problem. She wanted the ordeal to be over and the tourists to return. Kodra was cremated, and the matter was quickly closed. No one objected.

Meanwhile, in the warm sandy soil of the Wellington Environmental Preserve, eggs wiggled, then shook. Whether Kodra had been pregnant when she was captured or through parthenogenesis would never be known, but tiny lizards with light yellow-green heads and black chevrons on their bodies emerged. Bits of shell clung to their bodies. Guided by instinct, they dug up through the soil and reached the sunlight. Each hatching was less than a foot long and weighed less than a pound. They hesitated for only a moment, then dashed for the nearby trees. An alert hawk picked off one, and a large black snake got another, but thirteen newborn Komodo dragons made it safely into the satinleaf trees, already hungry and seeking prey.

ACKNOWLEDGEMENTS

As with most things in life, you need the help of others to succeed, and writing a novel is no exception, particularly when the author wants to get the facts right. I was very fortunate to have an outstanding Komodo dragon support group, starting with Sara Hasenstab and Matt Neff at the Smithsonian's National Zoo and especially Murphy, the zoo's resident Komodo dragon, who graciously posed for pictures. I especially want to thank Dr. Joseph Mendelson, director of research at Zoo Atlanta, who was unceasingly gracious with his time on the phone and in answering my many emails. For all things medical, I pestered my good friend Dr. Michael Dudnick. With the information he provided, I could have written a medical thriller, but I'll leave that to him.

Chauncey Goss was kind enough to introduce me to Randy Smith and Paul Linton at South Florida Water Management. They gave me a graduate-school-level education in the flow of water through the canals from Lake Okeechobee through the Arthur Marshall. I also got to see their control room which may be second only to the something at the Pentagon. Sergeant Brian Sawyer of the Collier County Sheriff's Office provided an overview of search and rescue procedures and firearms. Christina Meister at the US Fish & Wildlife Service described to me the law enforcement role of her agency. The staff and volunteers at the Arthur R. Marshall National Wildlife Refuge, who I visited with on multiple occasions, were most helpful.

Thanks to Paul Witcover for his thoughtful editing and always responding to my questions. Thanks also to Adam Chromy for his many helpful observations which made for a better story and to Jack Adler and Mary Kale for their help. Last, but not least, my wife, Lisa, provided many helpful comments and read my drafts enough times that she probably could recite them word for word. Many others provided help and information, and I thank them all as well.

I tied to be as accurate as possible in all things, but to keep the story moving, I did pick and choose from the information my many helpers provided and, thus, inaccuracies are solely my responsibility. Those of you familiar with South Florida will note that I took some liberties with the topography, primarily moving the Herzogs' housing development and the environmental preserve to abut the L-40 canal. With no pun intended, this was done to help the story's flow.

I was surprised, although perhaps I shouldn't have been, by how little information is available on Komodo dragons. Much of the information comes from the same few principal sources, and much of the information found on the internet is contradictory or inaccurate. I found a couple of good scholarly texts (which I didn't list below), but they made even my eyes glaze over. Sadly, the bible on Komodo dragons: *The Behavioral Ecology of the Komodo Monitor* by Walter Auffenberg is out of print, although I was able to find a copy. Some of his findings are incorporated in *Komodo Dragons*, referenced below.

SUGGESTED NONFICTION READING

Komodo, the Living Dragon by Dick Lutz and Marie Lutz

Komodo Dragons: Biology and Conservation edited by James B. Murphy, Claudio Ciofi, Colomba de La Panouse and Trooper Walsh.

The Lizard King: The True Crimes and Passions of the World's Greatest Reptile Smugglers by Bryan Christy

The Swamp by Michael Grunwald

ABOUT THE AUTHOR

Bill Byrnes is a former investment banker, college professor and self-proclaimed pragmatic environmentalist who lives with his wife in Naples, Florida. Fortunately, he's yet to encounter a python on his Sunday morning bike rides. He's seen plenty of iguanas and cane toads and wonders what other exotic animals are yet to make their presence known.

ALSO BY BILL BYRNES

The Banker Spy